SOUL STRUCK

Also by Natasha Sinel

The Fix

SOUL STRUCK

NATASHA SINEL

Sky Pony Press
New York

Sky Pony Press books may be purchased in bulk at special discounts for sales promotion, corporate gifts, fund-raising, or educational purposes. Special editions can also be created to specifications. For details, contact the Special Sales Department, Sky Pony Press, 307 West 36th Street, 11th Floor, New York, NY 10018 or info@skyhorsepublishing.com.

Sky Pony® is a registered trademark of Skyhorse Publishing, Inc.®, a Delaware corporation.

Visit our website at www.skyponypress.com.

10 9 8 7 6 5 4 3 2 1

Library of Congress Cataloging-in-Publication Data is available on file.

Cover design by Kate Gartner

Print ISBN: 978-1-5107-3118-9
Ebook ISBN: 978-1-5107-3120-2

Printed in the United States of America

For Andy,
who has enough
determination and strength
to light up the sky

ONE

Thunder is good, thunder is impressive;
but it is lightning that does the work.
–Mark Twain (writer)

My trusted local storm channels, sites, and blogs all lied. Even the big ones like weather.com, and Weather Underground. They all said overcast with a slight chance of showers, which is typical for early April on the Cape. Nothing about a storm.

But they were wrong. The sky suddenly turns dark gray, almost purple, and I can smell the moisture in the air, not just from the bay but also from the soaked heaviness of the thunderstorm on its way.

Even though I should know better now—that it won't change anything, that it's probably hopeless, that none of it makes sense anymore—my body feels the familiar rush anyway.

I try to ignore it by focusing on the sealed cardboard box I lugged out to the deck. I wipe a spiderweb off the label that reads FOR NAOMI FERGUSON'S EYES ONLY. Although I am not Naomi Ferguson, everyone tells me I have my mother's eyes, so I figure it's within my rights to open the box. On the other hand, according to mythical wisdom, nothing good ever comes from opening a box not meant for you. That's why I'm hesitating.

I sit on the edge of the lone lounge chair, its faded fabric worn and ripped down the center, and look out at the bay. In this light, the water is a soft gray with touches of white where the breeze makes a spray. A few cormorants swoop down to catch their late afternoon snack. A salty-sweet mist settles gently over my skin. Mom and I have been living in Wellfleet for almost three years already, but I'm still in awe every time I look outside—the wide yawn of the bay, smooth tan sand, clumps of tall green grasses swaying. The breeze blows the low-tide marshy stink over from the other side of the road, but even the smell feels new and promising. Like nature—mud and grass and life.

I assess the small side deck for anything that needs to be repaired. I'll have to pull the thorny vines that grow through the cracks of the planks and replace a few rusty nails that poke up but nothing major. The garage itself, though, is a dusty, smelly wreck; the concrete floor is an obstacle course of rusted garden equipment and mildewed boxes that have never been cleared out after my grandfather, whom I never met, died and left the beach house to Mom and me. It's going to take even longer than I thought to clean it out and make it into my bedroom. And the sliding door to the deck is off its track and warped so badly, I'll probably have to replace it entirely, and that will cost big bucks.

The separate entrance is one of the reasons I want to move into the garage. I can come home without having to talk to anyone. Day or night, I'm never sure who will be in the house at any given moment: no one, just Mom, or any number of the members from her lightning-strike survivors support group. Before we lived here, I used to love when it was time for meetings, when everyone would be at our place. We moved around so much, but the survivors came no matter where we were. When they were all with us, I'd imagine this was what it was like for normal kids who had families. I'd imagine the meetings were like other people's Thanksgivings—big gatherings with aunts and uncles, cousins and grandparents.

But now, the days when people are around seem to far outnumber the days it's just Mom and me. Since we live on the beach now, the survivors are willing to travel farther to get to us and stay longer.

"Oh, I decided to make it a vacation," they say. "I'll just find a hotel—oh, no, I don't want to impose. Really, I can't accept. Oh, well that's so sweet. Maybe just for a night or two." But it's never just a night or two.

Right now, though, the house is unusually quiet. Mom's at work and the others are wherever they are when they're not at our house.

I try gently lifting one of the flaps on the top of the box. If it comes up without the need for a knife or a pair of scissors to slice through the packing tape, then I will consider that to be a sign to look inside.

A sudden flash out of the corner of my eye makes me freeze.

I want so badly to resist, but the compulsion to go after it is still too powerful.

I grab the box, put it back in the corner of the garage where I found it, then go down the hall to my room. I knock over the pile of renovation books for dummies and idiots. FLASH. One-one thousand, two-one thousand, three-one thous—CRASH. Less than a mile. I'm breathing fast, panicking that I'll miss it. I pull a pair of steel-toed boots on over my bare feet and yellow and pink–flowered pajama bottoms and stomp around until I finally find the golf umbrella I'd shoved in the back of my closet. I haven't done this since before Reed came to town.

As I limp down the front steps, nearly tripping over the pointy toes of my boots, my mind is spinning, unable to land on a decision. Should I go to the tall pine on the MacPhersons' hill? Or should I go down to the bay? I remember that a few of the beach steps are missing after a couple of brutal high tides, and the last thing I need is to fall down another set of stairs. I run as fast as my sore legs will take me down the crushed-shell driveway, thankful that Mom's out. She'd want to lock me in my room if she knew I was leaving the house in a thunderstorm.

The rain hasn't started yet, but the sky is even darker than it was a few minutes earlier. Ominous and overbearing. Exhilarating. I run on the dirt road in my clunky boots to the MacPhersons' side yard and then up the hill to the small grassy area with a lone tall pine tree. I've been in this exact spot so many times these past three years, sometimes I wonder if the tree recognizes me. Just as I get to it, I see another flash of light.

One-one thousand, two-one thousand—CRASH. I haven't been this close in so long. Before Reed came, the storms were infrequent and short-lived, and nothing ever seemed to come close enough for me to have a real chance. When I was with Reed, I didn't pay much attention to the weather. I thought I'd never need to again.

The rain starts. A few big fat drops first, and then all at once. Another flash. One-one thousand, two—CRASH. Yes! I open the umbrella and stand under the tree. Waiting. Now the rain comes down in sheets. The gutters at the house a few yards away spill over like a faucet. I stand still and close my eyes, trying to calm myself, to become the perfect conduit, to will it to me.

The healed wounds on the backs of my thighs itch and tingle as I wait, reminding me that I've been so stupid, so naive. I picture Reed's contrite expression just before I fell. I imagine the conversation he must have had with Mom while I was in the hospital, right before he left town more than a month ago.

"You should go," Mom would have said. "You and Rachel aren't meant for each other."

"Tell me who is *meant for me," Reed might have said.*

And then maybe Mom did. Even though she swears she won't tell people who their soul mates are anymore, maybe she did just this once. Or maybe she told him who mine is—maybe someone, maybe no one, but not him. Definitely not him.

Mom can't help knowing what she knows about soul mates. But she says the information she carries is a double-edged sword. It has the power to ruin lives, and she never wants to be in a position to ruin my life. So, she's trained herself not to see who my soul mate is. I've never understood how she can do that. If the information appears to her, how can she control whether she sees it? I used to wonder if closing her eyes to it made her blind to other things about me, too.

A flash lights up the entire sky. A millisecond later, the crash of thunder, deafening, earth-shaking. I watch the afterglow of the lightning slice through the sky to the bay, spreading, stretching its fingers out to as many places as possible. As the thunder moves away, its rumblings a little quieter, farther apart, I drop the umbrella, collapse on the ground, and put my head between my knees. I chose the wrong spot.

I have no idea how long I've been sitting there when a car pulls up. It could've been a minute or an hour.

"Hey!" I barely hear the shout over the pounding rain.

TWO

A friend is someone who gives you
total freedom to be yourself.
—Jim Morrison (musician)

For a second, I hate Jay for finding me like this, like an addict caught in a relapse. But when I fold up my umbrella and get in the car, my clothes and hair dripping as though I've been for a swim, he doesn't say anything.

The rain rat-tat-tats its drumbeat on the roof.

"Nice outfit," he says, gesturing toward my pajama pants tucked into my boots.

"How'd you know I was here?" I ask.

"I didn't. I was on my way to Comma."

Jay, Serena, and I started calling the unnamed little curve of sand at the end of my road Comma Beach a few months after I moved here. It became our place. Serena and I snuck out and had our first beer there, and our first cigarette (and for sure, our last, based on the amount of coughing and spitting we did). The three of us made it a tradition to go to Comma loaded up with blankets, snacks, and drinks to watch meteor showers in the summer. On a clear day, you could see all the way to Provincetown. And on a day like this, you couldn't see anything but water and sky. No houses, nothing man-made. For a few minutes, you could imagine you were the only people on earth.

Jay puts the car in gear and drives to Comma Beach. The rain has let up, the sky is a shade lighter, and thunder rumbles in the distance.

When he turns the ignition off, everything is silent other than the soft pitter-patter of the subsiding rain. Jay never plays music in the car—he says it's too distracting, that he pictures each instrument playing its part, and it feels like there's a band performing live right in front of his eyes.

Even though Serena's my best friend, I met Jay first.

When Mom and I moved to Wellfleet just before the start of ninth grade, I was so excited to explore my new and hopefully permanent town. We'd been moving around for years—never in one place for more than nine months—but when my grandfather died and left the beach house to us, Mom decided it was time to settle down so I could stay in one place for high school. I suspected that Mom had "settled down" not just for me, but for her lightning-strike survivors group so there would be more room for them to stay.

I'd found Mom's old bike in the garage, and our neighbor tuned it up for me. As I rode down the curvy roads sprinkled with sand, I saw the summer people packing up their cars and locking up their houses. I'd never been a townie in a seasonal place before, but I was getting a sense of how it felt. Half relief that things would quiet down and half melancholy at being left behind. Abandoned for a different life, like we were just a quick treat. A once-in-a-while kind of thing, but not enough to keep on permanently. I'd been the equivalent of summer people in the places we'd lived before. Everyone had their lives and their history, but I was just coming through, never staying long enough to settle in. But now, I was the townie, and I was staying.

It was just a week before Labor Day, and the days were getting shorter and cooler. I'd gotten jelly donuts and decided to ride to the ocean side of town. I only had a few more days to be spontaneous and do whatever I was in the mood for at any moment. After that, I'd have schedules, homework, and new weather patterns to learn. As I rode, I smelled the ocean air and wondered if it would smell different in the winter.

I didn't bother locking my bike when I got to White Crest Beach. The parking lot was practically empty. The view from the top of the huge dune was amazing—the gray-green ocean stretched all the way to meet the gray-blue sky, and the waves crashed noisily and repetitively on the shore. I took my sneakers and socks off and went down the dune with my paper bag full of jelly donuts. The sun hadn't had a chance to warm the sand yet, so it was still cool from the night.

I sat near the water, the breeze pulling strands of hair out of my ponytail.

A few people on the beach sat looking at the water or walking. It wasn't time for sunning and swimming. I'd never realized how perfect the beach was when it was empty. Quiet, peaceful, smooth.

A lone figure walked along the water. As he got closer, I saw how big he was, almost like a giant, but I could tell by his face that he was about my age.

His lips were moving, but he didn't seem to have a phone or anything. He was talking to himself. As he got closer, I heard him.

"Sacrotuberous," he said. "Sacrospinous."

He was directly in front of me at the water's edge now.

"Hi," I said.

He held up one finger.

"Inferior pubic, superior pubic, suspensory ligament of the penis."

He let out a satisfied breath.

I stared at him.

"Did you just say penis?" I asked. This guy, tall and big with messy brown hair and deep brown eyes was cute, but he'd just said the word *penis* to himself.

"The pelvic ligaments," he said, like it was obvious.

"Okaaaay . . ." I said, drawing out the word.

He smiled and it lit up his face, a small barely there dimple on the right side of his mouth, but he didn't look into my eyes. It was like a shy, flirty smile, but I didn't get the sense that he was flirting with me at all.

"You're the girl who moved into the Ferguson house."

I nodded. I noticed the way his eyes flicked at me and then away quickly every couple of seconds.

"How'd you know that?" I asked.

"We saw you and your mom driving through town the other day. My mom recognized her."

"Our moms know each other?" I asked. I wondered whether they knew each other from when Mom lived here. She never talked about anyone from those days. I knew next to nothing about my grandfather, and even less about Carson—her soul mate, my father—who died before I was born.

"I guess they met at the high school orientation thing for parents, or whatever."

"Oh, okay. So you go to Nauset?" I asked.

"Yeah. Yay." Sarcasm.

"Not a fan of school?" I asked.

"Nope. And school is not a fan of me."

"I have a feeling I'm in the same boat," I said. "I'm Rachel, by the way. You'll be a freshman, too?"

He nodded, but he didn't offer up his name. He stood still for what seemed like forever without saying anything. The silence didn't seem to bother him at all. But I was getting uncomfortable.

"Want some jelly donut?" I asked.

"Sure."

I handed him the bag of what was left of the donuts.

"I guess I'll see you in school next week," I said as I started toward the dune.

He was digging into the bag at that point, so he nodded his head as if to say, "Yeah, okay, see ya."

I didn't find out his name—Jay Harwell—until school started, when the teacher called attendance in World History—the one class we shared.

We stay in the car, parked in front of Comma, and stare straight ahead at the gray water and the grayer sky. I wait for Jay to say something. It's a game I like to play with myself, like chicken. Loser breaks first.

I always lose chicken.

"Are you going to tell Serena about this?" I ask, gesturing in the general direction of the MacPhersons' tree where he found me.

He doesn't look at me, but his grip on the steering wheel tightens.

"Not if you don't want me to," he says finally.

"Thanks," I say. "I just—I'm just trying to figure things out."

He looks at me and I hold eye contact with him for as long as he'll let me, his pupils getting bigger and then smaller again like they're breathing. Then he flicks his gaze to my ear where he's more comfortable.

"How are your legs?" he asks.

"Good."

"That's good," he says. "They healed well."

And they did. When I looked at them this morning, twisting my head as far as I could to get a look in the mirror, I could see that they weren't puffy anymore, the marks where the stitches had been were light pink instead of red. Mom says the scars on my legs will fade to nothing eventually. And the scar on my heart will fade even sooner. I'm not sure I believe her. I'm not sure whether to believe anything she says anymore.

THREE

The lofty pine is oftenest shaken by the winds;
High towers fall with a heavier crash;
And the lightning strikes the highest mountain.
—Horace (poet)

Reed showed up at our door four months ago, at the beginning of December. The quarterly meeting had already started. I was in my room doing homework, trying to drown out the talking with music, but it was impossible. My room shared a wall with the back room, which was where all the meetings were. I heard Angela's voice, listing off her latest ailments, always blaming the lightning. The lightning. The lightning. Sometimes they didn't even use the word, they'd just say "since *it* hit me, I have no peripheral vision" or "since *the strike*, my husband says I scream in my sleep." And always the sound of ice cubes clinking in cheap glasses filled with gin and maybe a little tonic.

There was a knock at the front door. I knew that everyone who was coming to the meeting was already here, so I thought it was Serena. She was picking me up to go out for a coffee study break. I ran to the front slider, still holding my pencil. I slid open the door, but it wasn't Serena. It was this guy who looked homeless and much older than he probably was.

"Hi," he said quietly. "Is this where the support group meets?"

I must not have answered him because he continued. "The lightning-strike survivors group?"

I nodded. I'd seen tons of them before. The newbies. The ones who'd never met anyone like them before. Whose family and friends didn't understand why a lightning strike that may have left no visible physical damage could turn them into someone else and could change them forever. I'd seen them come, and I'd seen them go. I'd never known for sure whether Mom had anything special that made her become all these people's savior. But at that moment, I hoped she did have something. For this boy. I hoped that he would get better because, underneath the grime and the gloom and the fear, there was something in there. Behind the misery in his eyes—blue like the hottest part of a fire—was a teeny, tiny glimmer of hope.

I gestured for him to come in and I pointed to the back room. He hesitated.

"Should I take my shoes off?" he asked. They were expensive sneakers—the kind that a basketball star sponsored—but they were well past the point of being worn out.

"No, it's okay," I said.

He nodded but still didn't move.

"I'm sorry," I said. "About, you know, the lightning. I mean, I assume that's why you're here."

"Thanks. You too?"

I shook my head no. "My mom. A long time ago."

He stayed put, not in any rush to get to the meeting.

I'd heard all the group members' stories—where they were, the storm, the strike, what it felt like, what happened afterward, hazy memories, and then everything after that—the stuff that came so slowly, they almost didn't notice the relationship to the strike—the physical, emotional, mental changes. They thought it was just a coincidence that they'd forgotten their locker combination at the gym, or that they'd started to lose their hearing, or that one day months later, they'd wake up with a sudden pain in their knee so bad, the only thing that could help was oxycodone. Tons of it. Or the insomnia, or the mood swings that became so erratic, their spouses would leave. Or the ability to quote entire Shakespeare sonnets they hadn't read in thirty years. Or . . . like in my mom's case, the sudden power to see soul mates.

I'd heard every possible iteration of the story since I was a little girl. I was pretty sure that I never needed to hear another for the rest of my life, unless it was my own. But something in me wanted to hear one more. His. With his old expensive shoes, slightly dulled bright blue eyes, his fit-looking arms and chest under the ratty clothes and all the dirt, it seemed like he hadn't always been this way. He'd been a rich kid somewhere with a completely different life. And now here he was in my house looking for whatever it was he needed to try to make himself whole.

"Come on," I said. "I'll take you back there."

He looked relieved. Grateful, even, that he wouldn't have to enter alone. I opened the door to the back room, with him close behind me.

The talking stopped.

"Hi, sweetheart," Mom said. As a child, I'd been to many of the meetings, despite the fact that they were no place for a little girl, but in the last few years, I'd felt less welcome. I wasn't one of them.

"This is—um." I looked at the guy. I didn't know his name.

"Reed," he said, looking down at the floor.

"This is Reed," I said. "He came for the meeting."

In an instant, Mom was out of her seat and in front of Reed. She put her hand on his cheek and she stared into his eyes.

"Reed. Please come in. We're glad you're here. You're always welcome here."

Ron got up to let Reed have his seat.

Reed looked at me as he sat and smiled, like a thank-you.

"Rachel," Mom said. "Would you get one of those stools from the kitchen?"

I nodded, and when I returned a few seconds later with the stool, Ron took it from me.

"Thanks, doll," he said. Ron's second wife had died last year. She'd also been a strike survivor—they'd met through the group—and I'd heard them all talking earlier about what a blessing it was that she wasn't in pain anymore.

Mom gave me a quick glance and I knew I was to close the doors behind me. I gave Reed a look that I hoped conveyed "good luck," and I went back to my room to finish my homework.

Twenty minutes later, there was a knock on the front door again. This time it was Serena. I grabbed my vest and went with her for coffee. I didn't tell her about Reed even though I could feel him settling on my skin like a soft, transparent film. If it had been a few months earlier, before she'd joined the cheerleading team, I definitely would have told her about him. Actually, Serena had known me so well, she might have guessed by the look on my face that something had just happened, even before I could tell her. But she didn't guess and I didn't tell her. That's how I knew that things had already started to change between us.

FOUR

It really does change you. It's an invisible burden.
People don't understand—there's no sympathy for people hurting.
—Phil Broscovak (lightning-strike survivor)

Jay and I are silent as he drives the two minutes from Comma Beach to my house. Ron's yellow Chevy and Sue's black pick-up are parked side by side in my driveway. I groan. I just want to be able to walk into my house and not have people there.

"You want to come over?" Jay asks. He isn't always the best at reading people, but he's gotten very good with me.

"It's okay. I've got my American Lit paper," I say, getting out of the car. Water drips off me; the seat is soaking wet. "Oops, sorry about that."

He shrugs.

"Are we still getting together later?" he asks.

"I think so," I say. "I'll check with Serena, but she said seven-ish."

"Okay."

"Call you later," I say, closing the car door.

I stick my hands in the pockets of my pajama bottoms and run up the front steps. But on the third step, I trip where a board is loose. Even though I get my hands out in time to brace my fall, a splinter wedges itself into my palm, and my knee lands on a sharp corner. By the time I get up and brush off my hands, Jay has gotten out of the car and is ready to inspect them and my knee. He grimaces and then looks toward the front door, but I shake my head.

"My first-aid kit's in the car," he says.

Back in the car, he opens the kit on his lap. He works on the splinter with tweezers, and I involuntarily yelp at a sudden pinch. Jay doesn't say a word. He's temporarily super-mature EMT-in-training-Jay, and not seventeen-year-old dorky-Jay. And EMT-Jay, though extremely skilled, doesn't have the warmest bedside manner. I would make a joke about it, but he's torturing me with the tweezers, so I keep quiet.

"This is in deep," he whispers, concentrating, pulling at my skin.

Just when I'm about to scream for him to stop, he says, "Got it."

His eyes are bright when he holds up the long skinny splinter. He opens a packet with a cleansing pad and dabs at my hand, then the scrape through the hole in my pajamas.

For a moment, I imagine what it would've been like if he'd been the one to stitch up the cuts on the backs of my legs that night at the hospital. He's one of the few who have actually seen my scars.

One morning a few weeks after my fall, I'd forgotten to set my alarm. So when I wasn't outside waiting for Jay to pick me up, he came inside to get me.

I'd slept in boxers and a tank, and I must've been hot because I woke up on top of the covers. When I opened my eyes, Jay was sitting on the bed next to me.

"Wow," Jay said. He was staring at my scars. The stitches had been removed a few days before. And he was tracing the scars with his fingers, barely touching them. The pink, puffy, jagged lines that covered my thighs and the backs of my knees. The physical reminders of the glass and metal.

"What are you doing?" I had asked, coming out of sleep slowly. Since my injury, I didn't wear shorts or short skirts if I could help it. Even on the hottest days in gym class, I wore sweatpants. I didn't want people looking at the scars that told the story of how naive I'd been, and how hurt.

"I knocked a few times but you didn't answer. We're going to be late," he said, but he said it slowly and quietly, like he didn't care.

"Sorry," I said.

"I wish I could have brought you in that night and watched them take it all out, and close up each wound. Like, this one here," he said, touching the side of my right knee, which made me shiver. "This one looks different from the rest. The stitches weren't quite as even as the others. It just makes me wonder. About all of it. Who was it? Did they do the best they could or were they at the end of a long shift when you got there? Was it done by a resident or a physician's assistant?"

This was why some people thought he was a freak. But it made me like him even more.

"You should get up," he said. "We're late."

"Okay." I turned over and pulled the sheet up around my waist.

He didn't move.

"Jay," I said. "Let me get up."

"Do they still hurt?" he asked, watching my fingers fiddle with the corner of the sheet.

"They itch sometimes. And they ache when it rains."

He nodded and looked at my chest—I wasn't wearing a bra under the tank I'd slept in, obviously.

"Jay," I said. "Leave my room so I can get dressed."

I smile now as I watch him dab at the scrape on my knee. He must mistake my smile for a wince of pain because he says, "Just wash this with soap later. It's really nothing."

I know it's nothing—a stupid splinter and a scrape—but it feels like it's something, because I like the way his hand feels holding mine. And that scares me to death because my heart is supposed to be broken and my world is spinning and I don't know what's real anymore or whether I can even trust my own feelings.

"Okay?" Jay asks, wiping down the tweezers with alcohol.

"Yeah."

"I wasn't really on my way to Comma," he says as he reorganizes the contents of his kit. "I stopped at your house. When you weren't home, I figured you'd be at the tree, but I hoped you weren't."

"It wasn't what you think." Of course it's what he thinks.

"I can't reconcile all that stuff with my view of how the world works," he says.

"I wasn't, I just—"

"I didn't even know you were still doing that."

"I'm not," I say quickly. "I'm not anymore. It was just—it was habit, I guess."

He nods toward the house and starts the car.

"Good luck in there. Tell them I said hi."

I walk up the stairs slowly, avoiding the broken step. Jay drives away, and my hand throbs.

When I open the door, I smell the cigarette smoke before I even hear their voices in the back room. Mom's deep laugh. Ron's raspy chuckle. Sue's high-pitched chirp.

I'm starving—working in the garage and then running for the lightning sapped every ounce of energy I had. But I don't want to see them right now, so I pass by the kitchen instead of stopping on the way to my room.

"Rach?" Mom calls out.

My wet clomping boots must have given me away.

"Yeah?"

I pray she won't make me go in there. I'm afraid they'll bring up Reed and I can't hear his name right now.

"Where'd you go?"

I stop where I am, halfway to my room. I hear her footsteps approaching and she appears in the front hall. She notices me now, soaking wet, smudged with dirt, and she lifts her eyebrows.

"What happened? I was worried," she says. She notices the hole in my pajama pants and squats down to look.

"I tried to go for a walk, but I got caught in the rain. Jay drove by and picked me up. And I tripped on the loose step on the way in. We need to fix it. Jay had his first-aid kit in the car. I'm fine." I'm babbling.

She stands back up and pushes a strand of damp hair out of my face.

"Remind me about the steps again tomorrow. Come say hello, okay? They're dying to see you. You want something to eat?"

"Sure," I say. "I'll change first."

In my room, I peel off my wet clothes, put on sweats, towel off my hair, and go to the back room.

"Look at this beauty!" Sue squeaks. She's on the couch, and Ron's next to her.

"Hi, Sue. Hi, Ron," I say, trying to smile.

Ron looks worse than usual. His skin is paper-thin and his shaggy beard is dishwater gray. The scar that runs from his hairline down the side of his face to his chin looks more pronounced now against his pale white skin.

Sue is crocheting, as always, her fingers working faster than seems humanly possible. She's wearing a crocheted pink sweater and a green crocheted scarf. It looks like she's making a purple neck warmer now.

She places it next to her, then stands in front of me, staring into my eyes.

"How are you, honey?" She puts her hands on my cheeks. I don't like it when she does that, but I would never tell her that. "Your mom's been giving me daily updates but it's good to see you up and about."

"Much better," I say, giving her a big smile. "Almost like new."

"That makes me happy. After what happened, my heart broke into a million pieces for you."

"Yeah, I'm doing okay. How are you guys feeling?" I ask, hoping to move the subject away from Reed and what happened. But it's a stupid question because now I'll be here forever.

"Okay, about the same," Sue says. "Memory's getting worse, though."

Sue is about Mom's age, but she looks like an old lady. She'd been to so many doctors to find out what's wrong with her, but once she found Mom and the survivors group, she stopped trying.

"Oh please," Ron says. "Mine's kaput. Last week I just couldn't take it anymore; I put a gun to my head. But you know what? I forgot to load the goddamn thing!"

Ron and Sue burst out laughing like this is the funniest joke they've ever heard, even though I've heard it at least forty-seven times throughout the years. But they probably forgot that he used it on me already, given their crappy memory and all.

Mom's memory is just fine. She remembers everything. She just refuses to share her memories with me. Just little things, you know, like any single detail about my father at all. I suddenly remember the box in the garage and my fingers practically tingle at the thought of looking inside. It will have to wait, though. I haven't told Mom about my plan to fix up the garage yet. I figure she'll be okay with me moving in there, but if she saw me poking around, she might want to look through things first, and I'd lose my chance to open that box.

"So, I hope you're okay with us being around a bit more the next couple of weeks—we've got the meeting to plan for," Sue says, sitting and picking up her crocheting. She must realize that I get uncomfortable when the house is full of people. She and Ron never stay the night, at least. They both live close enough to come and go.

I must have blocked out the fact that at least twenty people will be here for the lightning-strike survivors big meeting. Would Reed show up for it? If he was planning to come, Mom would have warned me. Right?

Now moving into the garage feels like an emergency.

Ron clears his throat, and I picture the nuggets of phlegm and nicotine and whatever other crap is in his body rattling around.

"So . . . how many are we expecting?" he asks, his voice raspy.

"I can't remember!" Sue shouts and they both laugh their asses off again.

Mom comes in, smiling. "What's all this?"

"Just teasing your gorgeous daughter, who seems to be doing just great," Sue says. "Every time I see her, she looks different. Or maybe that's because I don't remember what she looks like from one time to the next!"

Mom rolls her eyes, smiles. This smile isn't for me, though; it's for them—Ron and Sue, and the other survivors.

"I thought we had some fruit, but we're all out," Mom says to me. "I made you a peanut butter sandwich."

"Thanks." I half-wave at Ron and Sue. "See you later."

I grab the sandwich and a glass of water and take them to my room. My weekly American Lit paper is due tomorrow, and I haven't started. It sucks for the obvious reasons but also because my laptop froze the other night and is refusing to unfreeze.

I start outlining in a spiral notebook. I can write the paper longhand and get to school early to type it up in the computer lab. I'll have to ask Mom for a ride to school even though I hate depending on anyone for rides. And now, if I have to use the money I made last summer working at PJ's to fix up the garage, there's no way I'll be able to buy Mr. Lash's truck. He hasn't sold it to anyone else yet—it's still parked in his driveway next door—but I know he can't hold it for me forever. I start to feel panicky. What if Reed shows up for the meeting? If the garage isn't ready by the time everyone comes, and I don't have the truck, then I will be trapped at home, no way to avoid him.

FIVE

Some people are attracted to vulnerability.
—Jay-Z (musician)

The morning after Reed showed up at our door for the first time, I slept until ten. When I got up and went out to the hallway, my bathroom door was closed and I heard water running in the sink. Members were always staying over, especially if they'd had too much to drink. But they never used my bathroom. We had a perfectly good powder room down the hall, and Mom had a shower in her bathroom that they used when they needed to. This was *my* bathroom. I leaned against the wall, pissed. I was trying to talk myself out of screaming at whoever was in there when I heard the sink turn off. Then the door opened a second later.

It was Reed, with one of my towels wrapped around his waist, and nothing else. His pale chest was thin, but his arms were defined.

"Sorry," he said. His dark hair was slicked back, his face smooth and symmetrical. His eyes were still that same fiery blue, even in the bright morning light. He looked completely different from the night before, though. He was clean, he was shaven, he was really cute. I avoided looking at his eyes and his practically naked body by staring at a chip in the paint on the doorframe.

"It's okay," I said and pushed past him into my bathroom and closed the door. He must have taken an hour-long shower in there; I'd never seen it so steamy. He used my shampoo too. I was about to freak out that he may have used my razor, but then I saw a disposable men's razor in the trash can.

I wiped the steam from my mirror and looked at my eyes. I pictured Reed looking at his eyes in the same mirror only moments ago.

After I showered and got dressed, I headed down to uncharacteristic quiet. Usually the day after a big meeting, Mom or someone would be there chatting, laughing, maybe crying. But today the house was empty. There was a note from Mom on the kitchen counter.

We've gone out to The Crock for brunch. If you want to join, text me. I'll come back and pick you up.

It was signed with just a heart.

I wouldn't be joining them at The Crock, the twenty-four-hour diner in Eastham. I'd be enjoying my few moments of peace and quiet while I figured out what to do with the Saturday that stretched ahead of me. Serena had cheerleading practice and then a game, so she was out. I thought about texting Jay, but lately when we were together without Serena, it felt different. I didn't know if that was just me. And since Serena was normally the plan-maker, the one who got us together, bought movie tickets ahead of time, that kind of thing, I didn't know what to suggest we do that wouldn't seem like a date.

I poured a bowl of Cheerios and drowned it in milk. I ate my cereal staring into space, my mind wandering from pre-calc to images of Reed in my shower.

A crash and then the sound of breaking glass in the back room pulled me from my thoughts. I figured maybe a window was open and a breeze had knocked a vodka glass over, so I went to check it out. When I opened the door to the back room, I saw Reed crouched on the floor, picking up shards of glass.

"I didn't know anyone was still here," I said.

He looked up, startled.

"Hold on, I'll help," I said.

I went to the kitchen for a bag and a broom, and we cleaned up the mess.

When we were done, we both sat on the couch.

"So how come you didn't go out for brunch?" I asked.

He shrugged. "Not quite up for that."

Mom must have washed his clothes, because he was wearing the same jeans and shirt but they were clean. He looked good. Probably almost the way he was supposed to look. Clean-cut, kind of pretty-boy-ish. But I could still see that he'd been through a lot. In his eyes and in the way he moved—slowly, like the air was thicker for him or something.

"Why aren't you there?" he asked.

"Not really my thing. I don't fit in."

He smiled and his teeth were straight and white. If he'd been living in his van, it hadn't been for that long. He'd definitely been to the dentist in the last few months, I was sure of it. He probably even used that whitening toothpaste that everyone says strips your teeth of its enamel.

"I think that's a good thing," he said. "Why would you want to fit in with a bunch of people who've been struck by lightning?"

"I used to want that," I said quietly. "More than anything."

"You wanted to get struck by lightning?" He asked this like I was out of my mind, insane. He wasn't totally wrong.

"I used to try to get struck." I still did, but he didn't need to know that. It was fine to talk about it like a strange little thing I did as a kid, but now? Not so cute. "I was obsessed with the Weather Channel. I followed storms and tried to pinpoint where they'd hit. Then I'd run out to the highest, barest spot I could find, like basically covered in metal."

"I don't believe you," he said, but he didn't mean it. He believed me.

"Every time, I'd have to go back home soaking wet and make up some excuse for my mom about why I was out in the rain covered with aluminum foil, holding a shovel or a crow bar."

"Jesus," he said. "Why would you want to do that?"

"Like I said, to fit in."

"So all your friends growing up were struck by lightning? You were the only one?"

I rolled my eyes at him.

"My mom," I said, but he knew that, too. He was just making a point. "The support group is kind of her life, you know? It was weird not being one of them."

"I could see that," he said. "As a nine-year-old. But what about now? As a—"

"Seventeen," I said.

"As a seventeen-year-old. You still trying to fit in?"

"I gave up," I lied. He didn't need to know that I was still chasing lightning, but for a different reason.

"That's kind of sad in a messed-up way," he said.

I shrugged.

"Seems like your mom has enough energy and love for everybody, from the few hours I've known her."

"Yeah," I said, even though I wasn't sure I agreed with him. "She's a really amazing person."

He nodded. "You grow up thinking your parents are your world and you're their world, and that they're infallible, and then you sort of realize they're just people and they totally fail you, even though they don't want to. I guess they try, you know?"

"How have your parents failed you?" I asked. Clearly they had because he showed up here looking homeless. For all I knew, they were dead, but I decided that it was okay to ask the question since he'd brought them up.

"I failed *them*," Reed said quietly. "But then they failed me worse."

"I'm sorry," I said. And I really was. He looked away. I felt bad that I made him think about sad stuff, so I put my hand on his knee. He immediately grabbed my hand and squeezed hard, squishing my fingers together, but it felt good because it was so real. It was the most real thing I'd felt in ages—the tight, suffocating grasp of someone who was in pain. So much of everything in school and in life was so fake and by the book, but this—Reed squeezing my hand, trying not to cry—was just so real.

He sniffed, then pulled his hand away and swiped at his eyes with his fists.

"If you ever want to talk about it," I said. "I'm not a survivor, obviously, but I can still listen."

He looked at me now, his eyes clear.

"Thanks, yeah," he said. "Can I just . . . never mind."

"What?"

He took my hand and squeezed again, gently this time.

"Can I just do this for a minute? I know it's so stupid, but it made me feel better. Is that okay?"

I blushed—I totally did. I knew he wasn't coming on to me or anything—it was almost like he was asking me to scratch an itch on his back. But holding hands was usually so intimate, and with him it felt even more than that—like I was special, and he needed me, and only me, to do it. It felt good to me, too.

I leaned my head against the back of the couch. We sat there, both looking straight ahead, our hands together, resting on my knee. We stayed quiet, just breathing.

I was so relaxed, I didn't even hear when Mom came in the door.

"Oh!" she said. Reed let go of my hand, and suddenly I felt like we'd been doing something wrong even though we hadn't been.

"I ran back to see if I could convince you to come," Mom said to Reed, eyeing me a little. "We haven't even ordered yet. Come on, both of you. You've got to be hungry."

"I ate," I said.

"Well, come on, Reed. It's good to get out for a bit."

Reed looked at me.

"You should go," I said.

He nodded. "Okay."

He followed Mom out.

And I was back to where I'd been before, trying to figure out what to do with my day. But I felt different.

SIX

I don't want to be too cool.
You get so caught up with whether you're doing it right.
–John Hughes (filmmaker)

My hand is sore from writing my American Lit paper, so I massage the muscle, remembering the warmth of Jay's hand on mine as he took out the splinter only a few hours ago.

Then Serena bursts into my room.

"Hey," she says, sitting on my bed. She picks up my notebook. "Since when do you write papers longhand?"

"Laptop's frozen. Any chance you want to get to school early tomorrow so I can type it up in the computer lab?"

"Sure," she says.

I stand and I must wince when my sweats touch my skinned knee, because Serena's eyes go all soft and she says, "Your legs okay?"

"They're fine. I tripped and scraped my knee earlier," I say. "Is Jay meeting us?"

"He's in the car. We were debating whether it would be too wet, but I think we're good."

Mom's in the back room with Sue and Ron, and the door is closed, so I text her that I'm leaving. I grab the blanket and get in the back seat behind Jay.

"Whose idea was this again?" I ask, zipping up my fleece, my eyes closed to the setting sun, which provides no actual warmth. The sand is damp, but otherwise, it's as though the storm never happened. Comma Beach is ours alone and we're here ready to watch the shooting stars the meteorologists promised.

"Mine," Serena says, bumping her head against mine. "Obviously."

"Oh right. As most outrageous ideas are."

Jay is stretched out on the American flag blanket that I brought, his knees up—one crossed over the other, arms behind his head. Serena and I lie perpendicular to him, our heads cushioned on his stomach and chest.

"Your chest is too hard to be a pillow," Serena says to Jay. "But other than that, I wish we could stay like this forever. Right here in this moment."

My eyes are closed, but I murmur in agreement.

It's true. If we could stay right here forever, I would be happy. And that's how I know I'm starting to get over Reed. A few weeks ago, I couldn't have imagined ever being okay without him. But now, I feel like there's hope. Even if Reed were standing right here in front of me reaching out his hand, I'm sure I wouldn't take it. I'd stay in this exact spot. With Serena and Jay.

After the orange ball of sun finally disappears behind the water and the sky begins to turn pink and gray and white, Jay shakes his body a little, a signal that he wants us to get off him now. Serena and I lift our heads and the three of us sit up, staring at the water.

Serena hops up. "Let's put our feet in."

"You're crazy," Jay says.

"Come on." She grabs my hand, and I stand, taking Jay's on my other side.

I feel his hand tighten around mine as we put our bare feet in the freezing bay water. I glance up at him, but his profile is unreadable.

"Holy shit that's cold!" Serena says, letting go of my hand and backing away from the water's edge a few feet.

But Jay and I keep our feet in, our hands firmly clasped together. When I look back at Serena, I see her see us—Jay and me—together, as if it's something more than it is. I release Jay's hand, and he crosses his arms in front of his chest, his face unchanging.

Serena stalks back to the blanket. She starts rummaging through the cooler she brought, her back to us. Nothing is actually going on with Jay and me, but our threesome feels different now. It feels like we're grasping on to the three of us—of what we used to be—too tight.

My feet are numb from the freezing bay water, so I walk back to the blanket, Jay right behind me. Serena doles out the food she brought—turkey sandwiches, Doritos, and Pepsi. We eat and watch the sky as it transforms to dusk. After we finish, we lie back on the blanket, all in a row, and wait for the dark and the stars.

Serena is my best friend. That will always be true. We've slept at each other's houses pretty much every single Friday or Saturday since the beginning of freshman year. I know what every single expression on her face means—even when she tries to hide her feelings—and she knows mine.

But even before Reed, things were changing. In September, she reluctantly joined the cheerleading team.

She'd always been a gymnast, but last year, she grew like seven inches in two months. Her body ached all the time and she had to miss most of the gymnastics season. Once she started to feel better, she knew her height and compromised flexibility would hold her back, so she quit. Selfishly, I thought it meant we would spend more time together. But when the cheerleaders found out that she was available, they recruited her hard. Then she was even busier because her new teammates like to hang out a lot with the guys on the teams they cheer for. Some of them are like a cliché of themselves. The jock pretty boys with broad shoulders, thick calves, and gelled hair, and the cute perky ponytailed cheerleaders that go along with them. A bunch of matched sets of Barbie and Ken look-alikes.

But not Serena—she's black. Wellfleet, our small town all the way out toward the tip of Cape Cod is ninety-seven percent white (we looked it up on Wikipedia). So, when you're one of the thirty or so black people in a town, you stand out. Whenever Serena and I walk into the movie theater, ice cream shop, or Dunkin' Donuts, she starts singing that Sesame Street song quietly so only I can hear: "One of these things is not like the other." We crack up, calling attention to ourselves, and we get what she calls *the stare*.

One time I told Jay about *the stare*, and Serena corrected me.

"Uh-uh, no," she said. "*I* got the stare, not you. Don't try to take credit for my stares. They're mine, all mine."

And Jay said, "You're weird."

And Serena said, "Look who's calling the kettle black."

And then she and I looked at each other and said "Doh!" We cracked up, and Jay just rolled his eyes.

Serena told me that in eighth grade, before I moved here, she looked like she was ten with braces and crooked cornrows with little colored beads at the ends. And back then, those people she's hanging out with now—the jocks and their cheerleaders—had taunted and tormented her, pulling on her braids and calling her nasty names. Maybe they've matured, changed their ways, but I don't buy it, even if she does. Maybe it's because she's hot now—tall and curvy and gorgeous. But I know there's no way she can be herself hanging out with them. Not like she is with us.

I've tried to adjust to her new life. I go to parties with her sometimes, but Jay won't. And on the nights I don't go with her, sometimes I hang out with Jay when we can figure out what we want to do. And sometimes during football season, when Serena had late practices and games every weekend, I felt the air shift between Jay and me when we were alone, a mix of comfort and anticipation. It's weird how that happens sometimes, like you go the longest time without seeing something that's right in front of you, but then once you see it, you can't un-see it. It was easier to ignore it when Reed was here, but now that he's gone, the thing with Jay is just staring me in the face again.

SEVEN

Nothing takes the taste out of peanut butter
quite like unrequited love.
–Charles M. Schulz (cartoonist)

Reed had nowhere to go. Mom didn't want him sleeping in his van anymore, so he stayed on the pullout couch in the back room. It wasn't unusual for someone from the group to stay for a few days, or even for a week, but this was the first time I'd ever had a crush on one of them. I was in a perpetual state of distraction—I couldn't wait to get home from school, knowing that he'd be there. I sensed his presence in the house even when I was alone in my room. I looked in the mirror more frequently than I normally did.

But after about ten days, Reed said he didn't want to overstay his welcome, so he'd found a room to rent in a house near town.

The next afternoon, I opened my bedroom door and Reed was standing in front of me, his hand up like he was about to knock.

Reed hadn't been in my room before and I always kept the door closed. He looked over my shoulder a little. Maybe he was curious.

"Hey," he said. "I was just coming to say good-bye."

The word *good-bye* coming out of his mouth did something to me, made me feel a little nauseated or something. My face must have changed because his mouth twitched up in a smile.

"I'm not *leaving* leaving. Just moving into that house in town. Remember?"

"I know, I just didn't realize it was today," I said. Of course I knew it was today. But I never wanted him to leave. The house or Wellfleet. He was so different from anyone I knew. Other than being ridiculously cute, he was this mix of cool, confident jock and vulnerable, sensitive boy. Even though he was only two years older than me, in so many ways it felt like so much more. He didn't go to school. And he was on his own—he answered only to himself. And he just seemed like he'd lived more.

"You feel like walking on the beach?" he asked. "I know I'll be over here for meetings and stuff, but I'll miss being able to see the water anytime."

Was he going to miss being able to see me anytime, too? Or just the water?

"Sure," I said. Even though my voice didn't squeak at all, my body felt kind of squeaky at the idea of being alone with Reed. So I might as well have squeaked.

He was already wearing his parka, though it was unzipped. The gray sweater he had on underneath muted the color of his eyes—like seeing the blue fire through cloudy lenses. He followed me to the front hall, where I grabbed my coat. While I put it on, he zipped his up. Then, at exactly the same time, we both pulled hats out of our pockets.

"Jinx!" I said, and even though he laughed, I wanted not to have said that. I felt so *young* when I was around him, and

I didn't need to give him any reason to remember that I was two years younger than him.

My phone buzzed in my pocket. It would definitely be Serena saying she was leaving practice. She'd be here in less than ten minutes. I didn't have time to take a walk with Reed.

SERENA: Practice running a little late. Be there in 20.

ME: No prob!

No problem at all.

We walked down the beach stairs quietly.

"Be careful," I said. "Use the rope. The railing has splinters."

Now I sounded like a schoolteacher or a mom. No happy medium for me.

"Which way should we walk?" Reed asked when we got to the sand. It was cold on the beach with the wind coming from the water.

I pointed to the right. It was high tide, so the left would have some areas where the water had come up all the way to the dune.

"So, are you excited for the house?" I asked as we started walking, the damp sand making soft, squishy sounds under our boots.

He shrugged. "Yeah. It's good for me to settle in, start my new life, I guess."

"This is a good place to do that," I said.

"Yeah, I think you're right. When did you move here?"

"Three and a half years ago."

"And they've been good years?" he asked.

"Sure. It's the longest we've lived in one place. We were in Detroit most of the time, but we moved apartments a lot, and usually that meant switching schools."

"I've never had that," he said. "I lived my whole life in the same house, same school, same friends. Until now. I mean, I guess if things had gone as planned, I'd be halfway through my freshman year in college now. So I would've left home anyway."

I didn't want to pry into the circumstances of him leaving home. I felt like everything with him was too precarious to push. I stayed quiet in case he wanted to talk more about that. But he didn't say anything else.

"So," I said, finally breaking the silence. "What do you know about your housemates?"

"Well, there's Greg, Chuck, Biraj, and Clarissa. Greg's a cook at the Flying Fish, Biraj works in a—realtor's office in town, I think. Or maybe it's insurance or something. Chuck is a computer tech, and Clarissa is an artist and works at a gallery in P-town."

"Sounds like an interesting mix," I said.

"Yeah. They're all older than me, though, so it's a little weird."

"I'm sure it'll be okay. You'll be working. And you'll be here, too."

At least I hoped he'd still come hang out at the house.

"You're always so positive," he said.

"I am?"

"Yeah. I like that about you."

I felt the flush coming to my face.

"You're blushing," he said, smiling.

"No, I'm not." I totally was.

He knocked his shoulder into mine gently.

"I'm glad I met you," he said. "It's nice to have a friend. It's too bad we didn't—" He looked at the water, didn't finish his sentence.

"Didn't what?" I asked.

"I don't know. I just thought, if things were different, maybe things would be different." He laughed. "Well, that made a lot of sense."

Now I was really blushing. After he'd used the word *friend*, I'd figured that's where he'd put me in his head. But if he thought things would be different under other circumstances, then maybe he actually *liked me* liked me. Like I liked him. And now I really felt like I was twelve.

He stopped walking.

"Turn back?" he asked.

"Sure."

We talked a little on the way back. About his housemates, the other survivors, our favorite foods. But in my head, I kept hearing what he'd said. "If things were different, maybe things would be different." And I started to wonder, why couldn't they? What was stopping him? I couldn't think of anything that would stop me. And knowing he could be interested in me made my brain shoot forward to years from then. Maybe we were soul mates. Maybe we'd be together forever, have what Mom was never able to have since her soul mate died. Maybe Mom would tell me whether he was my soul mate. She always said she never would, but what if I was in love—would she tell me then?

EIGHT

You can't deny laughter;
when it comes, it plops down in your favorite chair
and stays as long as it wants.
—Stephen King (author)

After school on Friday, Serena comes over to hang out and get ready for the beach bonfire she's going to. Jay's on his way to Boston to spend the weekend at his dad's.

Serena pulls a denim miniskirt out of my closet. She's too tall now to fit into my pants, but she still likes to borrow my skirts and tops.

"You can't wear that; it's way too cold out," I say. "You froze last night at Comma. It's supposed to be even colder tonight."

"I was taking it out for you," she says. "Come with me tonight."

I shake my head no, and I can see the disappointment in her eyes. Actually, it looks more like annoyance, but I feel like lately I've lost my ability to read her expressions as perfectly as I used to.

"We haven't had any fun together in so long," she says. "It was all Reed and now it's all post-Reed gloom, and—I just miss having fun with you."

"I know. I'm sorry I'm no fun," I say.

"It's been like a month and a half and your legs are better now. You've been cooped up here with nothing to do but think about him and rehash it all. We'll have a beer and laugh. If nothing else, it'll get your mind off everything for a few hours."

I look up for a second, pretending I'm thinking about it.

"I'm just not up for it," I say. "Not yet."

She sighs dramatically and hangs the skirt back in my closet.

"I'm starving," she says. "What do you have?"

Before everything with Reed, before she joined the cheerleading team, she would've called me out on trying to fake her out, and she wouldn't have given up so easily.

"Let's go look."

In the kitchen, she opens and closes cupboards while I look in the refrigerator.

"Salty," I say, as I reach into the cheese drawer. "Block of cheddar cheese and I think we may have half a bag left of pita chips."

"Sweet," she says. "Graham crackers." She pulls a box from the cupboard. "And Nutella."

"Perfect."

I reach for two glasses and hand them to her to fill with water as I search for the chips.

And then Serena shrieks. I don't think I knew what a shriek really was until I hear Serena do it.

She's standing in front of the sink jumping up and down and flapping her arms saying, "Oh my god, oh my god, oh my god!"

She runs to the table and climbs up onto a chair, standing and pointing at the sink, still flapping her arms.

"What?"

I move to the sink and see a tiny black mouse by the drain, now soaking wet from the water she was running.

"Oh my god!" I sound a little shriek-y, too. "How did it get there?"

I turn off the water, and the mouse tries to run up the side of the deep, stainless-steel tub sink.

"Oh, poor little guy, he can't get out. You're just a little guy, aren't you, little mousy? But you scared poor Serena out of her mind. She's such a wimp, isn't she? Look at her, she went screaming and she's standing on a chair. Scary, scary, one-inch mouse."

I'm laughing while I say all this, and she comes down from the chair and peers over my shoulder.

"Yeah, I guess he's sort of cute."

"Grab a Ziploc," I say. "Let's get him out."

I grab a pair of tongs.

"You'll squash him with those!" Serena says.

I get a cooking spoon instead and while she holds the baggie over the sink, I scoop him up.

He wiggles off the spoon and we both scream as he plops back down in the sink. He runs around in circles.

"Oh my god, you dropped him," she says. "You're so mean. He thought you were trying to rescue him but you're just a mean giant who likes watching him suffer. Cruel, cruel human giant."

"You shut up," I say, and we're both laughing as he runs around the sink, slipping all over the place. "Let's try again. Hold the bag down here. I'm going to push him in."

"Okay," she says, wiping a tear from her eye with the back of her hand.

I scoop the mouse into the bag and then she's holding the bag and the mouse is jumping all over, and she's screaming again, so I grab the bag from her, run to the slider and open it, and empty the little guy out off the side of the deck. I watch him as he lies still for a second in the sand, stunned, and then he runs off.

"Is he gone?" she asks.

"Yup, he went to find his mouse family."

I go back inside and we giggle while we wash our hands.

Laughing feels good. When Serena's laughing, I know her again, and it seems like we can get past this weirdness between us.

We sit down to eat our snack, passing the block of cheese back and forth with a knife, and the Nutella with a spoon.

"Did I tell you about the garage yet?" I ask.

"Oh, yeah, that you want to move in? When?"

"I haven't told my mom that I want to do it yet. I found this box in there with her name on it and, I don't know, I just have this feeling it could be something important."

Her eyes widen, and she plants her spoon in the Nutella.

"Well, what are we waiting for?" she asks.

I feel prickly heat all over and suddenly I realize I don't want to open the box with Serena here. And I'm not exactly sure why. Serena and I share everything. But this is something I need to do alone. She stands and I'm afraid telling her this will be one more thing putting a wedge between us.

My phone rings. Mom. I answer.

"Hi, I'm on my way home," she says. "Just trying to figure out my plans for tonight. Are you staying in or going out?"

"I'm st—actually, I'm going to a party with Serena."

Serena throws her head back and reaches her arms up to the ceiling.

"Yes!" she says. "Finally!"

NINE

I waited for my first kiss.
–Carly Rae Jepsen (musician)

After Reed moved to the rental in town, I missed him. I missed the excitement of coming home from school knowing that I'd see him. He'd been gone a week and I'd only seen him twice—once he came over to bring Mom a bottle of wine as a thank-you for helping him, and once for a meeting.

The next Saturday, Mom, Sue, and Ron had been in the back room since early morning planning a special trip for the group. People had been showing up, in and out, opening the refrigerator, closing it, piling their muddy boots by the front door. Weather was unpredictable on the Cape in December—the week before had been cold, and white frost had coated all the grass, but this week was pretty mild. When Ron announced he was going to pick up a few people from the bus stop, I grabbed a fleece jacket and hitched a ride with him to town. I didn't have a plan; I just needed to get out. Serena was in Hyannis shopping with her mom, and Jay was studying for a test.

After Ron dropped me at the center of town, I went to the candy store, loaded up on all my favorites, and then headed toward the harbor. I ducked to avoid a seagull that had swooped down for something just in front of me.

It was colder in town by the water than it had been at home. A gust of cool air made me shiver and regret leaving my winter coat at home.

When I heard the van's clanging muffler, my heart felt like it was flying along with the gull. I'd gotten to know that sound so well, and every time I heard it outside my window, telling me that Reed was there, the air became thick with possibility. I was pretty sure from what he'd said to me on the beach that day he moved out that Reed felt the connection between us, too. But my crush on him had developed so quickly and so forcefully, I had no idea whether he was where I was—dying to get things started.

The van pulled up alongside me.

"Hey," Reed called out.

I pretended I didn't hear him, which was ridiculous considering there was no one within fifty feet of me.

"Rachel," he yelled.

I turned and smiled, concentrating on what I'd learned from listening to the it-girls in the locker room. 'For the best picture, you have to tilt your head down a little, smile big, but not too wide or that will make your chin sag.' One of the girls had done some catalog modeling, so I always listened when she'd tell the other girls her secrets.

"You need a ride somewhere?" Reed asked.

I shook my head, but I desperately wanted to get near him. I was too embarrassed to tell him that I was just walking aimlessly to the harbor, just needing a place to sit and eat my candy, a place that was not my overcrowded house.

"Come on, get in," he said.

Reed reached over and opened the van door from the inside. I knew by now that it didn't work from the outside.

I'd seen him open it this way before. For other people, but not for me. Not until now.

After I got in and fumbled with closing the door, he smiled at me. Once he'd settled in with his new housemates, he'd slipped into this new, confident skin. But I could tell it wasn't new at all; it was like he'd put on an old shirt he used to wear every day before and, even though it needed a bit of patching at the elbows, it still fit him perfectly. Even with that, though, I could see the holes under the patches—the pain and fear I'd seen when he'd first shown up at our door.

Now his dark hair was clean and brushed, his face smooth. He looked so good, I couldn't stop staring.

He laughed at me like he knew the effect he had on me.

"What's in there?" He pointed at the crumpled white paper bag in my hand.

"Candy."

"Hand it over," he said, so I did. He peeked in. "Ooh, caramels, Swedish fish, and what's this? You have like ten atomic fireballs. You like fireballs that much?"

I nodded.

"No chocolate?"

"There's plenty of chocolate at home. My mom's vice."

"Are you gonna share?" he asked, and I saw his eyes light up and go warm. For me? Or did he love candy that much?

"Sure."

He put the van in gear then. It made a sound like it was saying "I'm getting too old for this shit," but it obliged when he stepped on the gas.

"That's a good-looking candy-eating bench over there," he said, gesturing to an empty wooden bench as we pulled up to the harbor.

We got out of the car, and I slammed the door closed.

"Easy on her," he said. "Lola's been through a lot." He patted the back of the van like it was a butt.

"Lola. Of course," I said. I sat on the splintering bench. An old lady was on the next bench over, rustling through one of those reusable shopping bags that looked like it had been re-used a few too many times. She looked up for a second but then returned to her search.

Reed sat next to me. Close. Closer than a friend would sit? Definitely closer than Jay would sit, but Jay had personal space issues.

I held the bag out to Reed and he took a green sour worm. I dug around for a handful of Jelly Bellies.

"So what are you doing out here buying candy and walking around by yourself?" he asked.

"Not much else to do, I guess," I said.

"It's Saturday. Isn't there a basketball game or some kind of school Winter Fest, rah-rah-type thing going on?"

I couldn't tell if he was poking fun at me for being a junior in high school. I wasn't jailbait or anything. He was only two years older than me.

I shrugged. "Yeah. My best friend Serena's a cheerleader, so I go sometimes to support her, but otherwise, I don't really like that stuff."

"So you're one of those 'I wouldn't be a part of any club that would have me' girls? I see. I know your type."

"*Do* you?" I asked, and then I wondered what *his* type was. What was his group in high school, and what kind of girl did he like? I suspected, since I knew he'd played baseball, that he was one of the jock popular guys who ran the school, got any girl he wanted. He probably liked girls who were tall and pretty, with straight, glossy ponytails and big white smiles.

"I do," he said. "But it confuses me. You're cute, smart, you don't smell."

He leaned toward me and sniffed.

I swatted at his chest.

"And you don't seem particularly annoying," Reed said, scooting even closer to me on the bench. He reached into my candy bag and pulled out a green Swedish Fish, then immediately dropped it back in the bag and rummaged until he found a red one, his fingers scraping my palm through the paper bag.

"I guess I'll have to live with 'not particularly annoying,'" I said. "You, on the other hand . . ."

I crumpled the top of the bag and held it to my chest. I gave him a sideways smile—my best attempt at flirting.

"Are you alone a lot because of your mom?" he asked, his tone more serious. "The lightning-strike support group and her thing about soul mates? Do people know about that?"

I paused. I didn't realize he knew about the soul mates, but of course he did. He was in her support group. I touched my nose, like "ding ding ding" in charades. You got it.

"I could see that, I guess," Reed said.

He put his arm on the back of the bench behind my head and stretched his legs out in front of him. He was close enough now that I could feel the heat from his arm by my neck, even though he wasn't touching me.

"Yeah, she's a little nuts," I said.

"I don't think so." I could feel his eyes on me, so I turned to meet them. Fire blue. "She's passionate. Not nuts."

"Do you think she knows what she's talking about? Do you believe it all?" I asked, letting my gaze drift down to his fingers resting on his lap. He tapped his jeans lightly with his pointer finger. Over and over and over.

"I believe that she's the kind of person who would take in someone like me, no questions asked."

"Yes, I know she's a saint and all," I said.

Reed snorted.

"You know what I mean," I continued. "Do you believe the things she says? About soul mates? That she can see people who are meant to be together?"

Reed let his head fall back and looked up at the sky, which was gray and white, to match the faded sand that surrounded the edge of the concrete.

"I believe in her ability. I don't think she's making it up. Last year? Before everything? I would've said no way. But now, I believe her."

"Did she tell you? About you?" I asked. I immediately wished I could take it back. It was too personal. The question skirted too close to whatever was going on, or not going on, between Reed and me.

He touched my right shoulder with the hand that was behind me. Just a little touch—a flick—almost imperceptible. But I felt it throughout my entire body.

"I didn't ask," Reed said.

"Oh," I said, trying not to let the disappointment sound in my voice. What was I expecting him to say? *You, Rachel. She made me swear not to tell you, but she told me that I'm meant for you, that we're meant to be together. You are my soul mate.*

Stupid, ridiculous me. Stupid fantasies.

"What about you?" he asked. "Has she ever told you yours?"

I shook my head no. "She won't tell me anything about anything. Ever."

"You want to know?" Reed whispered, leaning so close to me, I could feel his warm breath on my cheek.

I turned my face so that we were looking right at each other, our noses just a couple inches apart. He didn't flinch. My heart jumped out of my throat.

Neither of us moved for what felt like minutes. I could sense something happening—my breathing sped up and he swallowed. I looked at his mouth.

And then I couldn't take it anymore.

I dropped the bag of candy on my lap, reached my hands around the back of his neck, and pulled his mouth to mine. All my thoughts flew away except *I am kissing Reed and he may be the one. This is my first real kiss. His lips feel thinner than I thought they would. Now he is kissing me too and this is the best moment of my life so far.* And then no more thoughts. I devoured him. And he was devouring me back.

Until he pulled away.

"Holy shit," he said, and not in a *holy shit, you are so amazing* way. More like a *holy shit, what is wrong with you* way. He wiped his mouth with the back of his hand and then turned away from me, looking toward the water.

I felt the wetness of our kiss evaporate from my lips in the cool air. I wasn't going to wipe it away like he did. I wanted it to sink in and change everything. I wanted him to be my destiny.

"I can give you a ride home," Reed said. He stood and ran his fingers through his hair. But he wouldn't look at me.

I couldn't say a word. Or move.

He walked toward the van.

"Come on," he said. "Let's go."

He'd started it. Hadn't he? I was the one who kissed him, but he was so close to me, and he was flirting. Wasn't he?

He'd kissed me back. He'd definitely kissed me back. His lips and tongue had been just as active as mine. He'd put his hands on either side of my face. I didn't imagine that.

I grabbed the bag of candy, letting the crinkly sound of the paper drown out my beating heart. I followed him, waited for him to open the passenger door from the inside, and then I climbed in. He put on some music. The lead singer had a raspy voice that was full of emotion. I focused on the rise and fall of his voice, the guitar, the light drumbeat. I did not focus on the fact that Reed and I were silent the entire way back to the house and that I felt like I was being put in time-out.

He pulled up our driveway and put the van in park, but he didn't turn off the engine.

I opened my mouth to tell him I was sorry.

"Wait," he said. And then he softened his voice a little. "I'm sorry. I probably shouldn't have done that."

Did he mean he shouldn't have kissed me? Or stopped kissing me?

He reached over and touched my arm. Just one quick touch.

"I've wanted to, though," he said. "I've wanted to kiss you since you held my hand that day."

I was sure he could see my heart pounding through my shirt if he looked.

"Your mom," he said. "She kind of made it clear that you're off limits."

"What?" I said, my voice shaking. "What did she say?"

"After that morning when she saw us on the couch, she said something like 'If you touch my daughter again, you're out.' Actually, that's pretty much exactly what she said."

What. The. Fuck. Mom had never done anything like that before, as far as I knew.

"That doesn't sound like her," I said.

"It was her. The look on her face is kind of etched in my memory. And I can't lose this group. Or your mom. I need them. They saved me. I wouldn't have made it if I hadn't found them."

"I understand," I said. I understood what he was saying, but I didn't accept it.

"Please don't tell her about this," he said.

I nodded and stepped out of the van. I slammed the door before I remembered he didn't like that, and I ran into the house. I didn't want Reed to see the tears that flowed freely down my face. I didn't want Mom to see them, either, so once inside, I pushed off my shoes and tried to walk silently to my room. I heard Mom talking on the phone in the kitchen, so I knew she didn't notice me.

TEN

A kiss that is never tasted, is forever and ever wasted.
—Billie Holiday

I let Serena pick out an outfit for me—jeans, not a skirt—and try to pretend I'm excited to go to the beach bonfire party. When we get there, we stand around the fire for a few minutes, scoping out the scene, and then we find a seat on a charred log. There are mostly seniors and juniors here. A lot more guys than girls. I haven't been to a school party in a while and I forgot how boring they could be. I can tell Serena regrets bringing me. I'm not fun right now. I'm sulky.

"I'll get us beers, okay?" Serena says.

"Do you want me to come with you?" I say, shoving my feet deeper into the sand, which is surprisingly cold.

"It's okay," she says. "I'll be right back."

She makes her way to the keg, and I catch a couple guys checking out her butt in her tight jeans. I can't blame them. It's one of the nicer butts that exists, but they should try to be less creepy about it. She gets in line at the keg next to Rylin, one of the cheerleaders, and Serena laughs at something she says.

She has other friends now. She's been good at still hanging out with Jay and me when she can, but I can feel her slipping away. And if I keep up this broken-heart broody thing, I'm going to lose her.

I sense someone next to me.

"Hey, Froggie," Sawyer Baskin says as he sits down on the log next to me.

"Hey, Ribbie," I say.

It's dumb. Sawyer and I were lab partners for freshman bio, and we dissected a frog together. And so, the clever nicknames. We have a couple of classes together this year, and we say hi in the halls, but we've never really hung out outside of school. He's junior captain of the lacrosse team, the quarterback of the football team, and I think he plays basketball, too. So, we don't have a ton in common. He's been with Lindsay Easton, cheerleading captain, since freshman year. And while I wouldn't classify her as a mean girl, with Lindsay, you just don't exist unless you play a sport. I was pretty sure Serena said something about them breaking up in the last couple of days, but I tended to tune out when she talked about cheerleader gossip.

I watch sparks from the bonfire leap out onto the sand. At that moment, the wind shifts, blowing the smoke from the fire directly at us.

We cough and turn our heads at the same time, but we turn toward each other and end up bumping noses.

"Ow," he says, rubbing his.

"That was your fault."

He laughs. "Okay, I'm willing to accept half the blame, maybe sixty percent because I'm good like that."

"That's very gracious of you."

"I saw you walking down by the pier the other day," Sawyer says.

I've been doing that a lot since Reed left. Taking walks on the pier to stretch my legs and help my scars heal.

"Yeah?" I say to Sawyer. "You should've said hi."

He shrugs.

"You looked like you didn't want company," he says.

He chews on the lip of his cup.

"Next time you should say hi," I say, even though he's right. I didn't want company.

We sit for a minute. There's a pause in the music while the guy playing DJ fiddles with his phone to find the next song. A few people yell at him to hurry up. Then the portable speakers crackle again with hip-hop, but with the increasing wind on the beach, the sound keeps going in and out.

"Do you want to take a walk?" he asks.

Something happens in my stomach right then. I don't know if it's rising excitement or panic. Why is he asking me to take a walk with him? Does he want something to happen? Do I?

The angel on one shoulder says, "Do not go for a walk with him. You're not *that* stupid. You never even think about Sawyer Baskin." And the devil says, "Oh, yes, you *are* that stupid. Because how can you pass up the possibility of hooking up with Sawyer Baskin? Plus, you never know . . ."

The devil wins.

"Sure," I say.

Serena wants me to stop sulking, to have fun. She would probably want me to be impulsive right now, see what happens. Sawyer's cute. He makes me smile. I deserve to have fun. She's right.

As we stand, I look over and see that Serena's still in the keg line, talking and laughing.

Sawyer and I walk away from the light of the fire. I notice that he looks back once, like he wants to know if anyone saw us walk off together. Another night, I might have taken that as a sign and changed my mind about the whole walk. Tonight, I take it as a sign, but keep going anyway.

We walk for a minute or two in silence.

"Lindsay and I broke up," Sawyer says suddenly.

"Oh. Are you okay?" I ask.

He shrugs. His shoulders are kind of hunched over a little in defeat. He seems sad. I know about sad.

"Yeah."

Now that we're a good distance away from the fire, it's dark. The moon lights up the water a bit, but I really can't see much of Sawyer's features at all.

"Yeah," he says again. "I guess I'm okay. It was time for us to break up—we've been together for a long time. It's like we haven't ever been with other people, you know? And I wonder a lot if, you know, if we just stay together out of habit."

And then he sniffles. And I know he's fighting tears. And that's when I know I'm a goner. Dammit. Boys' tears are like catnip.

"Hey," I say quietly.

He stops walking and looks out toward the water. He probably doesn't want me to look at his face if he's actually crying.

"I had a bad breakup kind of recently, too," I say. "It does get better."

Despite being out of school for a couple of days after my fall, Serena kept the details of my breakup with Reed quiet. People know I fell down stairs but they don't know the whole story.

Sawyer quickly swipes at his eyes with the back of his hand.

"Oh my god," he says. "I am—shit. I'm the biggest baby."

I press my hand against his back, between his shoulder blades. For one second, I allow myself to think of Reed. How I once held him when he cried, when he leaned his forehead against a wall and swore at life. *Okay, one second to think about Reed. Only one second. Now stop.*

Then Sawyer turns around to face me and puts his arms around my waist, pulling me into a hug. He puts his face in my hair and then breathes in deeply.

"I'm seriously so embarrassed right now," he says.

I nod so he can feel me understanding him. Yes, I know what he means. He isn't usually so vulnerable. He's the quarterback of the football team, the captain of the lacrosse team. He has an image to protect.

"Don't be. It's totally okay," I say.

I'm aware that it's sort of weird that we're hugging. I've probably never touched Sawyer Baskin before. Maybe a few high fives when we got something right in bio. But the hug continues past a normal amount of hugging time and suddenly I feel really awkward. I have absolutely zero idea if he just wants a shoulder to cry on, or if he wants to hook up. And the idea of Sawyer and me together has never occurred to me before.

"You're so . . . small," he whispers. "Like a little package."

I giggle. I think about how I'm small but Lindsay's tall, and how that must be weird for Sawyer to be hugging me, so different than Lindsay.

He squeezes more tightly around my waist and lifts me up so I'm eye-level with him, and it's so unexpected, I yelp.

He puts me down, and I start laughing uncontrollably because this whole situation is so strange.

"Okay, that was super weird," he says, but he's laughing, too. "I have no clue why I just did that."

Laughter is breaking the tension I felt about the hug.

"So," he says, and his voice is lower and quieter now that our laughter has died down. "I'm thinking I need to distract you now from how badly I just embarrassed myself."

"Um," I say. "I'm not easily distracted. How do you propose doing that?"

Now I'm shamelessly flirting. I'm basically looking up at him and batting my eyelashes. I'm practically begging him to kiss me. This whole situation is so odd, but I'm having fun.

He puts his hands on either side of my waist and then kisses me. A long, slow kiss. It seems like we're both feeling so much—sadness, vulnerability, and the excitement of a first kiss with someone new. It's all right there between us. I feel different. I'm calm. I'm not afraid of saying or doing something stupid like I often was with Reed.

But my subconscious is tugging at me, reminding me of something. An image of Jay and his dimple flashes into my mind. *This has nothing to do with Jay*, I tell myself. *Just be here. Now. Have fun.*

Sawyer kisses down the side of my neck and I shiver.

We make out for a long time, figuring out how our mouths work together. He puts his hands, which are cool from the ocean air, up my shirt and he unlatches my bra with ease. He definitely knows what he's doing, pushing my bra up and touching me in just the right way so that I can barely take how good it feels. His leg is pressed between mine, and I move and rub myself against it.

A loud burst of laughter comes from the dune behind us, and we pull apart quickly, but it's too dark to see anyone and the laughter continues, the sound moving away from us.

Sawyer pulls his hands from under my shirt and rests them on my hips. He leans his forehead against mine and smiles.

"Well, did it work? Have you forgotten about all that other stuff from before?"

"What stuff?" I say.

"Ah, very good. My patent-pending amnesia potion works then. I'll make millions."

He kisses me on the lips, but it's an ending not a continuation.

I re-fasten my bra.

We walk back toward the party.

When we get close to the bonfire, he drops my hand and moves a few inches away from me. Of course he wants to keep this quiet. If Lindsay just broke up with him, it's really too soon for him to be moving on. We needed each other tonight, but just tonight.

He looks at me and smiles kind of apologetically. I smile back, innocent like *What? We're good.*

"Thanks for listening," he says quietly. "I hope you don't think crying was just a ploy so I could kiss you."

"What are you talking about?" I say. "Someone cried?"

He laughs, and I do too.

"Are you okay to drive?" I ask Serena as we walk up the dune to her car.

"Yeah. I only had half a beer. It was gross."

In the car, we're both quiet. I replay the kiss with Sawyer in my head.

"I can't believe you haven't told me anything yet," Serena says.

"What?" I say.

"I saw you go off with Sawyer, and I saw you come back all smiley with your hair messed up." She doesn't sound excited to hear about it, though. She sounds annoyed.

"We just kissed," I say. "It was fun. That's it."

Serena is silent for a minute. I feel judgment seeping out of her, wafting over me.

"He and Lindsay broke up," I say, like I'm defending myself. I'm not sure how it's turned into this. I thought she wanted me to move on.

"They'll probably get back together," she says. "They always do."

"Okaaay," I say, drawing out the word. I don't even know what to say. She can't be so close with Lindsay that she'd be offended on her behalf. Or is she? She does spend a lot of time with the cheerleaders. Maybe they *are* that close.

"I'm just saying," she says. "If you're thinking he's your soul mate or whatever, he's probably not the one."

"Um, I wasn't thinking that," I say.

Serena has always known about Mom and the lightning, and how badly I wanted to find a soul mate like Mom did. We used to lie in bed at night and talk about who our ideal soul mate would be, if we could choose. When we were fourteen, we imagined finding perfect brothers—one for each of us—and we'd marry them and become sisters-in-law and spend the rest of our lives together. When we were sixteen, we were a bit less idealistic and romantic. Serena would point out a cute new guy at school and say something like "I'd like to mate with his soul, if you know what I mean," and I'd say,

"Oh, I know what you mean, that's one smokin' soul he's got right there."

But when I met Reed, I couldn't joke around anymore. Because I thought maybe I had actually found my soul mate.

Serena turns right into my driveway.

"So you had fun?" she asks.

"Yeah," I say. "I had a lot of fun."

"That's good. I'm glad someone has the ability to help you remember how to have fun."

There's an edge in her voice that I don't recognize. And I don't get it. Serena has been trying to get me out of my Reed funk for weeks, but now that some of it's starting to lift, she seems angry.

She doesn't turn off the car.

"Aren't you sleeping over?" I ask.

She shakes her head. "I'm just gonna sleep at home tonight."

"Oh," I say. I'm afraid if I ask why, she'll get even more edgy. "Talk tomorrow then."

I get out of the car and she drives off.

ELEVEN

Love is an irresistible desire to be irresistibly desired.
–Robert Frost (poet)

For a few days after my first kiss with Reed on the pier—which Serena had labeled "the candy kiss" because of the "aphrodisiacal powers" of the candy we'd shared—seeing him was torture. He'd come over to the house for a meeting, and we'd say hi to each other, but we didn't talk much. I felt our connection just hanging there in the air, and if something didn't happen soon, I was going to combust. I wondered whether this was what Mom had felt for my father. She said she'd known there was something special between them from the start—they'd helped rescue a seal who'd gotten stranded on the beach—and then the lightning only confirmed what she'd already known in her heart. That Carson was her soul mate.

Finally, on one of those rare nights that it was just Mom and me, I decided I had to do something about the Reed situation. We'd just finished eating dinner and were doing the dishes.

"Mom?" I said.

"Mmhm?"

"I really like Reed, and I'm pretty sure he likes me, too. And you told him we can't see each other, and you had no right to do that and it's not fair."

It had all come tumbling out and not at all like I'd planned. Instead of mature, I sounded like a whining child, which would not help my case.

Mom sighed and put a plate in the dishwasher.

Then she turned toward me, leaning her hip on the counter. She shook her head, almost imperceptibly.

"He's too old for you," she said.

"I'm seventeen, he's eighteen," I said.

"You just turned seventeen, he's almost nineteen."

"Mom." I rolled my eyes.

"He's in a different place. In so many ways. He's graduated from high school, he's living on his own, with no one supporting him. He's more of a man than a boy."

"He seems like a boy to me. He's sweet and I like him."

"He is sweet," she said. "And very broken, Rachel. He's estranged from his family, he's working through PTSD, and he needs to fix himself before being with someone else."

"Jesus, Mom. Are you looking out for me or for him?" I couldn't believe this.

"You. Both of you, really. But you. I don't want you to get hurt. And this is just a stopping place for him—he won't be here forever."

"So? I won't be here forever either, Mom!"

Mom flinched visibly and then I felt bad.

"I may go away to college, who knows?" I said, softening my voice. "Anyway, I just want to hang out with him. I'm not even talking about forever. I wouldn't have said anything to you, I would have just done it, but I know he won't unless you say it's okay."

Mom nodded. She closed the dishwasher.

"Okay?" I asked.

"With some conditions," she said. "You can be together here or go out places within a twenty-minute drive. You may not, under any circumstances, go to his house."

"Thank you," I said, and I couldn't contain my smile. "Why can't I go to his house?"

I regretted saying it instantly. Mom's face got hard.

"He lives with adults, Rachel. Young adults in their twenties who are on their own, working and paying rent, and legal to drink. I think Reed is too young to be living there, quite honestly, but I couldn't have him staying here anymore. And you're a junior in high school. Do you understand?"

"Yes," I said. "I'm sorry, I was just curious."

The next day, while I was in World History, Reed texted me.

> **REED**: So, I guess you really like me? ;)
> **ME**: ?
> **REED**: Your mom said she's lifting her sanction on seeing you.
> **ME**: She told you!?
> **REED**: Well, I asked, too.. She said you got to her 1st. Pick you up after school?
> **ME**: Yes!

And that was how it started. When I wasn't at school or studying and he wasn't doing odd jobs or delivering pizzas, we were together. I craved Reed. There wasn't any other way to describe it. After only a few weeks, it felt like we'd already been together for much longer. I knew spending so much time with him was at the expense of time with Serena and

Jay, so I invited them to do stuff with us a few times. But Jay didn't know what to say to Reed, and I could tell by the way Serena's voice changed when she spoke to him that she was still very unsure about him.

"He could be a serial killer on the run or something," she said after I'd spent nearly every minute with him for two weeks.

"Oh, come on," I said.

"I'm serious. What do you know about him?" she asked.

"I know enough."

"Enough?"

"I know enough to know that we have something special."

"So you think he could be *the one*." And then under her breath, she said, "Of course."

I didn't answer her. Instead, I said, "Maybe if you tried to get to know him, you'd see that he's really great."

Serena stared at me. Her eyes were cold.

"Or not," I said. "Whatever."

It was our first real fight, and after that, even though we continued quizzing each other on our Spanish vocab, the air hung heavy with it.

One night, Reed and I decided to go to the new Wes Craven movie.

We'd just left my house when Reed said, "Oh shit."

"What?"

"I have to go put the extra key back in its hiding place for Biraj or he'll be locked out."

He turned left toward town.

"We might still make the movie if I hurry," he said.

But I didn't care about the movie. I just wanted to be with him.

We drove through town and then past the library. After a few blocks, he pulled into a small gravel driveway. The house was a pretty shade of yellow, but it was beginning to peel. Underneath patches of melting snow, the grass was more brown than green. Whoever owned the house had tried to make it look nicer by adding two large barrels for flowers, but all that was there now were crumbling, brown bits of old geranium-looking things. They must have forgotten to ask the renters to water them.

He turned off the ignition and started unwinding a key from his key ring.

"I'll just go leave it in the hiding place and then we can get going."

He hopped out of the van and jogged to the side of the house.

I stayed where I was for a minute, and then I opened the door and followed him.

He was already on his way back, having left the key.

"Hi," I said.

"You're not supposed to be here," he said, smiling.

"I won't tell if you don't."

He put his arms around my waist and kissed me. Then he walked me backward until my back was against the wall of the house. We kissed, and even though it had been a few weeks, I still couldn't believe I was with him. I was definitely falling in love with him. It was the real deal.

"I want to see your room," I whispered.

He hesitated, so I kissed him again.

Then he nodded and took my hand.

Inside it was not what I'd expected. It was darker than I thought it would be—dark floors, dark paint on the walls. He flipped on the lights in the living room where there were two small couches, a coffee table, and a TV on a stand. Everything looked kind of drab and used, but it seemed clean.

He gave me the short tour, pointing at each room—living room, dining room, kitchen.

He led me to the bottom of the stairs.

"What's this?" I asked when I looked up.

A large sculpture-type thing hung on the wall at the top of the stairs. Its base was a large copper circle that looked like it had been part of a log holder by a fireplace. Two bottoms of broken beer bottles—one green, one brown—hung from invisible wire and glistened when light fell on them. The rest of the thing, which I thought was supposed to be a face, had pieces of rope, gnarled wood, and plastic on it, but I couldn't tell where exactly the eyes and mouth were.

"My housemate Clarissa," Reed said, as if that explained it.

As we walked up the stairs holding hands, our movement caused the glass pieces to move slightly, making the stairs seem to shimmer and glow.

"That's cool," I said. "So this is the art she makes?"

"Yeah, she makes sculptures from all recycled materials, so she collects junk. Whenever people come over to the house, they bring things to add to her collection."

On the landing was a basket that held bottles, rusted metal, rope, and wire.

"Does she sell it?" I asked.

"I think the gallery she works at in Provincetown shows some of it," he said. "I don't think she sells much, though. Her stuff is kind of—"

"An acquired taste?"

He laughed and then opened a door at the top of the stairs. His room. I stood inside the doorway and looked, but there wasn't much to see—a bed with a rumpled light blue comforter, an oak dresser, and a closet door. Before I could say anything, Reed closed the door.

I sat on the edge of the bed, bounced a little. He sat next to me and grinned.

We never made it to the movie.

TWELVE

Friendship has its illusions no less than love.
–Stendhal (writer)

The morning after my hookup with Sawyer Baskin, I text Serena to see if she wants to hang out later. She was right—I had fun at the bonfire, and I feel better. At least better enough to want to do something more than hang around the house all day, or maybe even go out again tonight. I can't remember her schedule, but I'm pretty sure she doesn't have practice or a game today. After two more texts and three more hours, I still don't hear back. I look up the cheerleading practice and game schedule. Nothing. I figure her phone is dead, which isn't completely impossible.

I try her one more time.

ME: Hey, heading to town to grab lunch.

I ride to town and eat chicken parm at Town Pizza, alone, staring at the wall, feeling dread.

Back at home, I wait to hear from Serena. Nothing. I sensed something was up last night, but now I know for sure.

ME: Are you going out tonight?

As people were leaving the bonfire last night, I'd heard people talking about a party at Tim Erickson's the next night. His parents were always going out of town.

Serena doesn't write back.

I'm still willing to believe that she's lost her phone or there's been some emergency, but I know I'm clinging. If she lost her phone, she'd call from home. If something happened to her, her mom would contact me.

At ten, Mom walks in the door, typing on her phone as she walks. She does a double-take when she sees me sitting on the couch watching TV.

"Oh," she says. "I wasn't expecting you to be here."

"Why not?"

"I just saw Serena's car parked at the Ericksons', so I figured you'd be with her. I'm texting you to tell you I want you home by midnight."

She smiles.

"No need," I say. "I'm here."

My eyes sting at the realization that Serena ignored all my texts, then went out without me. It isn't an innocent mistake, an oversight. She's shunning me. Kissing Sawyer can't be enough. I scroll through my feed looking to see if she's posted anything. Nothing since the selfie she took of us last night before we left for the party. But Lindsay tagged Sawyer in a photo of the two of them, his arms around her waist, kissing her cheek. Lindsay has written, *There's no place like home.* The photo is dated today.

It isn't surprising that they got back together, though I would've expected the breakup to last a few more days. Would Serena choose Lindsay over me if Lindsay's pissed

I hooked up with Sawyer? While they were broken up? It doesn't make sense.

I send Serena one more text.

ME: What did I do?

Nothing.

I refuse to humiliate myself any further. I don't text her, and I don't call her. I just get in bed and wait for sleep.

I wake with a start and look at the clock: 1:17. Someone's pounding at the door. I go to the front hall as quickly as I can. I want to get there before Mom in case it's Serena or Sawyer or someone coming by drunk after the party at Erickson's.

I see through the glass door that it's Sawyer's mom. I'm still half-asleep, and all I can think is that something has happened to Sawyer. Or that she's angry at me for kissing her son.

I open the door, and she storms in, demanding to see my mother. She's clearly been drinking.

Mom rushes out of her bedroom, pulling her robe tightly around her.

And now I realize this visit has nothing to do with Sawyer. Or me. Mom is already composed. She has that ability to go from deep sleep to awake, alert, and beautiful within seconds.

"Come with me, Trish," Mom says to Mrs. Baskin, pointing her toward the back room.

As I've been taught when someone shows up in this state, demanding a soul mate reading, I check outside to be sure no one's watching, and then I close and bolt the door.

Mom gives me a stern look, which means "bring us a drink" and "not a word of this to anyone."

"She goes to school with Sawyer," his mom whispers, staring at me.

"Don't worry," Mom says. "Rachel is very discreet."

And I am. I've never even told Serena or Jay who comes to the house to talk to my mom.

THIRTEEN

Mistakes are always forgivable,
if one has the courage to admit them.
–Bruce Lee (martial artist)

One Thursday, after Reed and I had been together for about two months, he picked me up at school. It had been a good day—I'd aced a history test, and Serena, Jay, and I had sat together at lunch and laughed so hard, we couldn't even eat. Being with them had felt normal for the first time in a long time and I thought maybe we were finding our way back. Or it could have just been the snow. It was dumping outside and everyone was excited about the possibility of a snow day.

Reed and I went back to his house. Since that night we'd skipped the movies, we went there most days. I didn't like breaking Mom's rule—she didn't have that many of them to begin with—but it was really the only place we could be alone.

I skipped homework—I was that sure school would be cancelled the next day. We drank tea and ate microwave popcorn and snuggled up on the couch under a blanket while we watched a movie. His housemates were all working, so we had the place to ourselves.

When Biraj and Greg came home, we went up to Reed's room—his housemates were always friendly, but he preferred it when we were alone.

We stayed in his bed for hours, lazily kissing and messing around. We ended up with all of our clothes off.

And I was so ready. Even though we'd been together only a couple of months, it felt like a couple of years. Or forever. What we had together felt so real, so big.

I told Reed I was ready, but he said no.

I turned my back to him so he wouldn't see how much it hurt.

"I can't be your first," he said. "I don't deserve to be with you at all, but I definitely can't be your first."

"What are you talking about?" I asked through sniffles.

I could hear him turn onto his back, put his arms behind his head.

"I'm a mess," he said.

"But you're not. I know you think that, but you're not."

"I am. I'm homeless, my parents hate me. Before I left, they couldn't even look at me. That's how messed up I am."

"Why? Because of the lightning?" I asked. Reed hardly ever talked about it or about his life before he came here. I knew that he was from an upper-class suburb of Cleveland. He'd graduated from high school, had played baseball, had planned to go to Union College. And I knew that after he'd gotten struck by lightning, everything had changed. What I didn't know was what he told me next.

"Because my little brother is dead and it's my fault. And when they look at me, that's all they see."

"What?" I turned toward him. His eyes were closed. I stared at his profile.

"It was my fault he was struck, and I should've been able to save him, but I didn't. It's my fault he died."

"You didn't tell me you had a brother."

"I know."

"How old was he? What was his name?"

"Ten. Max."

I put my hand on his chest.

"Does my mom know?" I asked.

He nodded, and I felt a pang of jealousy.

"Will you tell me about him? About what happened?"

He was silent for what felt like an eon.

"My parents went to Chicago for the night. They were planning to take Max with them but Max really wanted to stay home. He hated flying more than anything. My parents had been fighting a lot and I figured some time alone would be good for them, so I said Max could stay home and I'd be responsible for him—it was just one night. The next morning, the day they were coming home, some of my friends called and said there were tons of fish on the other side of the lake—our house is on a lake—so I wanted to check it out. Just a quick paddle to see if we could catch a few. Max didn't want to go with me. He didn't care about fishing and didn't want to stop the computer game he was playing. I wouldn't leave him home alone because I promised my parents I wouldn't, so I made him go with me. I was a dick. I even made him row while I sat back and relaxed. Max saw the storm clouds and wanted to go back, but I'd seen the fish jumping and I was determined to catch a few. I told him to stop being such a pussy. A little rain wouldn't hurt us. But it wasn't just rain. It was a thunderstorm."

Reed's voice was monotone and matter-of-fact, like he was telling me about a trip to the mall.

"The lightning hit the boat—it was metal—and we both ended up in the water. I knew I'd been struck—I felt the jolt and I could barely move—but I wasn't sure about Max. I tried to look for him, but my limbs felt so heavy, I couldn't swim. I hoped he'd somehow swam his way to shore, but I knew there was no way. The paramedics found him. They said if we'd been struck on land instead of on the water, he probably would've survived. He was unconscious from the lightning or hitting his head, and then he drowned."

"Oh my god, Reed. I'm so sorry. It wasn't your fault."

"It was. He begged me to turn back. He didn't even like being on the water. I forced him. And I could've saved him. I could've stopped him from drowning."

"No," I said. "There was no way you could've known the lightning would hit. And you tried to find him, you couldn't. It's not your fault."

I smoothed my hand over his cheek.

"You really didn't do anything wrong. You were just being a typical big brother bossing around his little brother, that's it."

I put my arms around his neck, ran my hands along his chest, trying to pull him to me.

"I'm not whole. I shouldn't even be here with you."

"Stop. It doesn't change the way I feel about you," I said. "You're everything. I—"

"Don't," he warned.

I'd been about to tell him I loved him and he knew it. He didn't want me to say it.

"I want you to be my first," I whispered.

"Rachel," he said, so quietly. "Don't."

Then he sat up.

"I should get you home before the roads get worse," he said.

FOURTEEN

Friendship is the marriage of the soul,
and this marriage is liable to divorce.
—Voltaire (writer)

Jay picks me up on his way home from Boston on Sunday, and we go to his house to do homework. My books are spread out in front of me on his kitchen table, and he's working on his laptop. But I can't concentrate. I'm holding back tears. I sniffle, and he looks up.

"What's wrong?"

"Serena's been avoiding me since Friday night," I say. "It's like she suddenly hates me."

"What? Why? You guys are best friends," he says. "She doesn't hate you."

"She won't answer any of my texts or phone calls. She's not speaking to me. Why did you have to go to Boston? This never would've happened if you'd been here."

He stiffens.

"What happened while I was gone that wouldn't have happened if I was here?"

Shit. Now I have to tell him. Why does it feel so weird telling Jay about Sawyer? Like I'm disappointing him. Or cheating on him. Either way, I have to tell him. I fully expect it to be Monday gossip at school. I have to tell him before he hears it from someone else.

"I sort of hooked up with Sawyer Baskin Friday night," I blurt. "It was nothing. Just one of those things."

Jay squeezes and releases his fingers, but otherwise, he doesn't move or look at me.

"One of those things," he repeats.

"It was dumb. Lindsay dumped him. He was sad. I was sad. So we tried to cheer each other up."

Jay snorts. "You couldn't have just shared a gallon of ice cream or something?"

I punch his arm lightly. It's obvious talking about this makes him uncomfortable. I never talked to him about Reed. We've never talked about crushes or hookups or anything having to do with that stuff, but he's still sitting here, so I'll take that as a good sign.

"Ice cream would've been less complicated, for sure," I say. "Apparently he and Lindsay got back together yesterday. So I'll be wearing a huge red *A* on my shirt at school."

"You might be right," he says.

"But they were broken up. I didn't do anything wrong. And Serena shouldn't even care. I'm her best friend. Do you think she's choosing Lindsay's side over mine? Has she gone over to the dark side? Do you think the cheerleaders are too powerful to resist?"

He shrugs.

"You're no help," I say.

"Maybe she likes Sawyer," he says.

Now *that* has not occurred to me.

"No," I say. "No way. Plus, I'm sure there's some sort of cheerleader code where you can't hook up with each other's exes or something."

"Do you like him?" he asks quietly.

"No," I say quickly. "I mean, I like him, he's nice, but I don't want to go out with him or anything."

"Then why did you hook up with him?"

"Are you being judgmental right now? Or is that a real question?"

"Real question," he says without missing a beat.

"You want to know why I kissed him if I didn't want anything more with him?"

He nods.

I hesitate. Articulating why is hard. Why does anyone do anything?

"I think because I just felt like it? Serena was so adamant that I stop sulking and have fun. So when the opportunity presented itself, it seemed like it would be a fun thing to do, a good distraction. It wasn't that complicated. But maybe it was—I don't know. Maybe I was trying to erase everything that happened before."

"Did it erase it?"

"No. Well, maybe. I mean, nothing has been erased, obviously. But maybe I feel cleansed in a way, like I can move forward now."

He looks at me now, holds eye contact. And I feel the thing between us that had started before Reed showed up. It's still there and it's getting stronger.

"I'm glad then," he says, then looks up at the ceiling. "You want me to talk to Serena? I don't want to get in the middle, but I will if you want me to. If it would help."

"No, it's okay."

We go back to doing homework. We order pizza, and while Jay goes out to pick it up, I stay. His house is quiet. Kyle, his brother who's one year younger than us, has a lacrosse game, and his mom and her boyfriend went to it, even though Kyle's a benchwarmer.

I suddenly wish I could rewind to Friday afternoon. Maybe I could've enticed Serena with the box in the garage. She loves anything that involves mystery and secrets. And she's always been almost as curious about my father as I am. Then I could have convinced her not to go to the bonfire at all and I wouldn't have kissed Sawyer, and she'd still be speaking to me. Now, the idea of looking in the box without her feels strange and lonely.

When Jay gets back, we eat while we work. I try to focus on my pre-calc problem set, but Jay is leaning back so far in his chair, it's making me anxious.

"You're definitely going to fall on your ass if you keep doing that," I say. "And I'm just going to sit here and say *I told you so*."

He comes forward quickly, and the chair makes a loud *thwack* when the front legs hit the floor.

"That's better," I say.

"She called me," he says.

"Who?"

"Serena."

I look up at him, but he just sits there.

"When?"

"When I was out getting the pizza," he says.

"Well? What did she say?"

"Not much," he says.

"What the fuck, Jay?"

He sighs.

"She asked if I wanted to study bio with her. I said you were over and then she said never mind."

My eyes sting and I rub them.

"I asked her why," he continues, staring at his pencil. "And she said she forgot she had practice."

"Bullshit," I say.

"I know. That's what I said."

"You did?"

He nods.

"Tell. Me. What. She. Said. Jay."

"She said, 'I can't deal right now. I just need a break.' I asked her if it's about Sawyer and she seemed surprised I knew, but she said 'no, not really.' I asked her if she liked him and she said 'no' and she definitely meant it, like she seemed pissed I'd even suggest it. But she wouldn't tell me anything else."

He still won't look at me, but I can't keep my eyes off him.

"I told her that if she doesn't talk to you about whatever's going on, then I won't be studying with her or hanging out or anything," he says.

"You did?"

"Yeah," he says. "It's too weird."

"Thank you," I say, my voice a bit wobbly. "For doing that."

I scoot my chair closer to him and lay my head on his shoulder. He doesn't put his arm around me or anything, but he relaxes his shoulder a bit so I can find a soft spot between the hard bones.

"Girls are strange," he says.

"You're telling me."

We stay like that for a while, and then finally I straighten and go back to my problem set while Jay studies for his bio test alone.

FIFTEEN

Having a pulmonary embolism is definitely easier than heartbreak.
—Serena Williams (athlete)

After the night Reed told me about his brother, I didn't hear from him for three days. He even missed a group meeting, which was a first.

"He's *ghosting* you?" Serena said when I reluctantly told her.

"No," I said. I didn't want to give her any ammunition against him. "He's probably just not feeling well. He gets migraines and stuff."

She looked at me like I was insane.

And suddenly the tears started. And then Serena's arms were around me and I was sobbing.

"I'm sorry," she said as she held me tight.

"I don't know what happened," I said. "One minute we were together and everything was great and then it was like he just shut it all down."

"Maybe you're right," she whispered. "Maybe he has a migraine. Maybe it's okay."

I shook my head because I knew. I'd seen it in his eyes when he dropped me off after the slow drive home in the snowstorm. And the entire next day when school was cancelled, I stayed in bed and waited to hear from him, but I just knew I wouldn't.

"I think he's done," I said, sniffling.

She let go of me then.

"What's his number?" she asked.

"What?"

"His number. I'm going to call him."

"No," I said.

She grabbed my phone off the bed and opened my contacts. Then she punched his number into her phone.

I stared at her in disbelief.

She stood and walked to the window, the phone to her ear.

"Reed?" she said. "It's Serena. Are you okay? Are you dying? Bedridden?"

She paused.

"Okay. Then there's no reason for you to be ghosting my best friend."

Oh. My. God.

"That's the biggest load of shit I ever heard. Don't even give me that. Do not be that guy."

She paused again, listening.

"Yes. We're good then? Okay."

She ended the call, then came back to my bed.

"Why did you do that?" I asked.

"Because. It's not fair," she said.

"So, he said it's over?"

"He gave me some shit about not deserving you, and he needed some time to think or something."

"So maybe it's not over then."

She took my hand.

"Rachel, I don't know him well enough, but I know you, and you should not wait around for this guy. He is going to break your heart. He already has."

"But he could be—"

She groaned loudly before I could even finish my sentence.

"If he's your soul mate, then he needs to get his act together fast and start treating you like the amazing person you are. If he's your soul mate, then he's fucking it up big time."

My phone buzzed.

> **REED**: Can I pick you up from school tomorrow?

My heart sped up.

> **ME**: Okay.

Serena nodded at me.

"We should talk," Reed said as I got into his van after school the next day. I'd spent all day thinking about this moment and hadn't heard a single word a teacher said in any class.

"Okay." I tried to sound cheerful, even though his voice was gloomy.

I looked out my window. Obviously, I knew he was breaking up with me, but I didn't know exactly why. My chest throbbed, and I pictured my heart just going on and doing its thing, unaware that it was about to get broken, even if my head knew.

He drove in silence and pulled into our driveway. I waited for him to turn the van's ignition off, but he didn't. Oh my god, he was going to break up with me in the car with the engine running. So he could make a quick getaway. I wasn't even worth turning off the ignition for.

"Rachel," he said.

I looked at him. His beautiful dark hair, wavy only in the front so it dropped into his eyes a little. His bright blue eyes, big and beautiful. And his lips. The lips that had given me my first real kiss.

"It's not going to work out with us," he said. And even though I knew it was coming, it felt like my heart slammed against my chest, like it was trying to get out and punch him. Because there had been a teeny tiny little voice named Hope who said "maybe he's going to say something else. Maybe he won't break up with you." But now Hope was gone, and I oddly felt relief now that I knew for sure.

"Why?" I was proud of myself for not crying. Yet. And my voice didn't even crack.

Reed put his forehead on the steering wheel.

"After the other night," he said. "I—I just realized that—I don't know—"

"Because of what I said?" I asked, and this time my voice squeaked. He didn't move, so I knew I was right. "But I didn't even say it. And, yes, I want you to be my first, but I didn't ask you to marry me or anything."

He finally lifted his head and his eyes were sad.

"You didn't have to say it. I know how you feel. I've known for a while. But I'm a wreck. I'm damaged. I don't even know if I'm capable of it. That day when we talked about Max, it was like I could see your thoughts planning our future. And I like you so much, Rachel, but I can't see a future for myself even. So, I can't lead you on like that. I'm sorry. I shouldn't have let this happen."

He said it like it was some horrible accident he'd been responsible for.

I opened the car door and ran inside the house, straight to my bed, collapsed on it face down, and cried. I couldn't hear Reed's engine anymore.

I spent ten days zombie-walking my way through the school hallways. I was glad it was so cold outside because I couldn't be bothered with makeup, a hairbrush, or even clean clothes, so every day I wore the sweats I'd slept in and a knit hat. I listlessly did only homework that didn't involve much thinking. Serena and Jay sat with me at lunch and carried on conversations, every now and then trying to include me but failing. Mom reminded me to wash my hair every other day. She told me that breaking up hurts, and there's no way out but through. Thanks, Mom.

I checked my phone constantly. I imagined Reed texting me like in a movie, "Come outside." And I'd go outside and he'd be leaning against his van, just staring at me. And we'd just do that—stare at each other. And then he'd stride to me and grab my hands and say, "Rachel, I made a terrible mistake. I was just scared of how deep my feelings are. I'm sorry. Please take me back." I played the fantasy in my head over and over all day and all night.

When Mom made me change my sheets, I found one of Reed's favorite band T-shirts bunched up at the bottom of my bed. I texted him and told him I had something I needed to give him. I didn't hear back for a full day and a half. When the text from him did finally come, I was in pre-calc. I felt my phone buzz in my pocket and I knew it had to be him. I got up to go to the bathroom, my heart pounding in my throat.

I went straight into a stall and sat on the toilet, pants and all. I needed to be by myself, completely alone to read his text. I held the phone in front of me, my hand shaking.

REED: Okay.
ME: Can I come by tonight? Around 9?
REED: Sure.

The rest of the day was a blur of teachers' voices, lockers slamming, the buses grumbling. When I finally got home, I showered for what felt like hours, and I even dried my hair and swiped a bit of eyeliner and mascara on. Reed's place was on the other side of town, toward Truro, and I wasn't exactly sure how to get there by bike on the back roads—all the times I'd been there, he'd driven and always on Route 6. I looked up the fastest bike route on Google and got going.

Getting there didn't take as long as Google said it would, so I pulled up to the old house and put my bike on its side next to the front steps. Even though the front lights were out, I could see lights on in the house. I knocked, hoping someone would hear over the music coming from inside the house. I heard movement, the sound of someone walking. And then the door opened.

A skinny guy opened the door.

"Hey," he said. "Come on in."

Maybe this was Chuck. He was the one housemate I hadn't met before. Even though he didn't know who I was or why I was here, he didn't seem to care. I followed him inside.

"What's your poison?" He turned to me for a quick second as he led me into the kitchen, which was overflowing with dishes, glasses, and dirty pots and pans.

I shook my head. Inside the living room about twelve people sat on couches, on the floor, standing, swaying to the music. It was smoky and dark, but I could see that none of them was Reed. The guy opened the refrigerator and held a bottle of water out to me. I took it. I didn't want it, but I could tell that he would keep trying until I accepted something.

"Is Reed here?" I asked.

"I assume so since it's his going-away party."

Going-away party? My mouth suddenly felt dry. I took a sip of the water and then put it back on the counter.

The guy poured vodka into a cup. I watched it *glug glug*, almost to the top. Then he poured a quarter inch of orange juice on top.

"I'm just gonna go look for him," I said, though it came out more like a whisper. He shrugged, as I left the kitchen.

Reed was going away? Was he going back to Cleveland? Did Mom know? My hand felt shaky as I grabbed the handrail and walked up the stairs. They must have had a few parties in the last couple of weeks because Clarissa's basket on the landing was almost overflowing with empty beer bottles and rusted pieces of metal.

I knocked softly on Reed's door. No answer. I slowly turned the handle and peeked in. It was dark, but I could see that Reed was asleep in bed, his hair showing above the sheets, his soft snores barely audible. I was surprised that he was sleeping while there was a party for him downstairs.

I tiptoed toward the bed and sat on the edge. Reed shifted a little in his sleep, and that's when I saw her. Clarissa.

Her brown curly hair touching the side of his face, her bare shoulder pressed against his chest. My heart stopped. The earth shifted.

"Oh my god," I said, but it came out as a horrified whisper. I stood but I kept my eyes on her, this girl Clarissa, sleeping soundly, with Reed's bare arm around her. Reed opened his eyes and his body jerked when he saw me. I wanted to run, but I couldn't move. I couldn't do or say anything.

Clarissa's arm snaked around him in her sleep, trying to pull him back down to her, but he kept his head up, his eyes on me.

"What time is it?" he whispered. "You're early."

As if my being early was the issue. Even if I'd been on time, he would've been fine seeing me right after screwing his housemate? And I knew he had because there was a condom wrapper on the floor next to the bed.

Clarissa turned her head then and her mouth puckered into a surprised "O."

Reed put his hand on my forearm. His fingers that had just been on, maybe *in*, Clarissa's body. I pulled away.

"Hold on," he said. "Let me just—let's talk, okay? Gimme a minute. I'll be right out, okay?"

I knew what he was trying to say. He wanted me to leave the room so he could get up and get dressed because his naked body and Clarissa's naked body were under those covers together. Exactly where I'd been only a couple of weeks earlier.

"Rachel," he said, when I didn't budge, when I couldn't move my eyes from the spot where her shoulder was still pressed against his chest. Clarissa had turned back around, hiding her face.

"Oh god," she said. "Fuck."

I stumbled to the door. I looked back. He got out of bed and stood, not a stitch of clothes on him.

I burst into tears and ran as fast as I could toward the stairs. Tears blinded me as I ran, sliding my hand along the wall. I felt sharp metal on my hand. It sliced through my palm, and then there was an awful ripping sound as the hook holding Clarissa's sculpture pulled out of the wall. The huge copper circle fell, crashing against my shoulder, and then I was no longer upright. I tumbled, tumbled down, slid down, bumped down the steps as the sculpture knocked over the basket of broken bottles, gnarled wood, and pointy metal objects. Everything was on top of me, underneath me, with me. Clarissa's art and junk tumbled down the stairs with me and I no longer knew whether the things slamming into me were stairs or her creations.

I heard Reed call my name as I landed hard on the floor.

SIXTEEN

Love is blind;
friendship closes its eyes.
–Friedrich Nietzsche (philosopher)

Monday is a warm, early spring day, so at lunch, I know I'll find Jay sitting on our favorite bench in the courtyard. Serena mixes up who she eats lunch with. Sometimes with us, sometimes with the cheerleaders. But since she told Jay last night that she needs a break from me, I know she won't be eating with us today. Maybe ever. And that hurts like hell.

I sit next to Jay and drop my messenger bag on the damp grass. I peek inside my lunch bag as though something has miraculously appeared since this morning. I pull out my granola bar and groan. Jay nudges me with his shoulder and offers me half of his sandwich. It's always the same—four slices of roasted turkey, one slice of Muenster cheese, and one lettuce leaf between two pieces of whole wheat bread.

"I'm good. Thanks," I say.

A few of the junior guys from the lacrosse team walk by us. Wade Rush, bulky with hair buzzed so short, you can't even tell what color it is—plants himself directly in front of me and makes a weird sound, sort of like a growl.

I probably should feel threatened, but I'm more grossed out by the smell of his breath—garlicky and sour.

"Stay away from our boy," he hisses. "He doesn't need any distractions."

Jay stands, six-foot-five and solid.

"You know," Jay says calmly. "A hard hit on the helmet can fracture the basilar bone of the skull and you can leak cerebral spinal fluid from your nose without even realizing it."

"Freakin' mutant freak," Wade says, but he wipes his nose as he walks away.

"My *hero*," I say to Jay in a high-pitched voice as he sits. The corner of his mouth twitches up.

Wade and the other guys keep looking at me and whispering as they cross the walkway to the lawn and sit with Sawyer.

"Shut it, assholes." Sawyer says. "She didn't do anything."

Serena's sitting a few yards behind Sawyer, next to Rylin. I want to catch Serena's eye, see if she'll acknowledge me at all, or that this is happening, but she seems oblivious to it, and she's not looking over here.

Sawyer gets up and walks toward us. I can feel Jay's body tense next to me.

"Don't listen to those dicks," Sawyer says. "I played shit lacrosse at the game yesterday and, using their exceptional logic, they assumed it was because of you. But it's not." He looks at Jay quickly, then back to me. "I've just got some stuff going on at home, and I don't feel like telling the guys yet."

Given his mom's visit to our house Friday night, I'm pretty sure I know what the stuff at home is.

"We're okay, you and me," he says. "I'll make sure they lay off."

Not that my life depends on whether Sawyer Baskin and I are okay, but if he wants to play the good cop to his bad-cop friends, I'll let him.

He nods at Jay, then goes back to the other guys.

"That was . . . odd," Jay says.

"Yeah," I say.

"Kyle did say the game was abysmal yesterday. But still—"

"Let's talk about something else."

"I got a 98 on my bio test," Jay says.

"That's great."

"It's not great at all," he says. "I got all the answers right but Billings dinged me two points because I didn't show my work on one problem. Does that even make sense?"

I shake my head no.

"I'm going to talk to him," Jay says.

I watch Serena as she gathers her stuff, says good-bye to Rylin, and walks away by herself. I can just make out the back of her as she enters the school building. The bell is about to ring for sixth period. I know Jay must be watching her go, too. In her too-short skirt that's way too cold for today.

SEVENTEEN

*The idea of a soul mate is beautiful and very romantic
in a movie or a song, but in reality,
I find it scary.
—Vanessa Paradis (musician)*

At the ER after my fall down the stairs with Clarissa's sculpture, the doctor pulled about seven shards of glass and pieces of copper out of the backs of my thighs and then stitched up the wounds. It felt awful, but the tetanus booster the nurse gave me almost hurt more. Afterward, she said I could get dressed and wait to be discharged.

"You know when people ask what your most embarrassing moment is?" Serena asked, handing me the sweatpants she'd brought me from home. I pulled them on gingerly over my newly bandaged wounds. "And you can never think of anything good, so you have to say something like 'I farted at gym in second grade and everyone laughed?' Well, now you really have something."

"Yeah," I said. "Except it was the worst, most painful moment of my life. Even more than embarrassing."

Serena sat on the bed next to me and put her arm around my shoulder.

"I'm sorry," she said.

"I know."

"Can I start talking shit about him now?" she asked.

"Not yet," I said.

She got up and handed me my sweater.

"Is he still here?" I asked.

Reed had driven me to the hospital. I'd lain on my stomach on the bench seat in the back of the van, and Clarissa kneeled on the floor in front of me, holding my hand as my tears rolled onto the faded gray upholstery. Given the circumstance, I wanted to tell her to get the fuck off me, but her other hand was smoothing my hair and calming me, and she seemed so genuine and kind, so I allowed myself to forget who she was.

"No," Serena said. "They left right when your mom got here."

That stung. I'd pictured Reed sitting in the waiting room, worried, feeling guilty, hoping to get a minute to come in to see me and apologize. To beg my forgiveness.

"Why did you go to his house?" Serena asked.

"I just needed to see him. I wanted to see if, I don't know, I thought—"

"I know," she said quietly. "But he wasn't. He isn't your soul mate. You deserve so much better than him. You know that now, right?"

I felt like a child being reprimanded. I didn't answer.

"I'll go see where your mom is and tell her you're ready. She's probably out there hounding someone for your discharge papers."

"Thanks," I said.

I lay on my side—it hurt to put pressure on the backs of my legs—and reached over to the nightstand to grab my phone, which had been retrieved from my torn and bloody jeans when I first arrived.

No message from Reed. One from Jay, who was out on an all-night EMS training run. If Reed and Clarissa had called 9-1-1 instead of driving me to the hospital, Jay probably would've been with the EMS team to show up. I didn't know whether that would've been better or worse.

JAY: Did they get everything out? Make sure they give you tetanus booster. Call when you can.

I smiled. That text was clearly from EMT-in-training Jay, not from Friend Jay. But it was okay. Both versions made him who he was.

ME: Got the shot. Pain in the butt.
JAY: The shot or me?
ME: Both. Thanks for checking in. Hope to leave here soon.

I put my phone next to me as Mom came in the room.

"I never understand why it takes so long to sign a few papers and get out of here," Mom said. "You got dressed okay?"

I nodded.

"It hurts?"

"Yeah," I said. "Did you know Reed was leaving Wellfleet?"

She nodded.

"Where's he going? Why didn't you tell me?"

Mom sighed, then sat on the chair next to me.

"He's going to stay with friends of Angela's in Vermont. They have a room and a job for him," she said.

"Did you tell him he had to go because of me?"

"No," Mom said, but I wasn't sure I believed her. "I made it pretty clear from the beginning how I felt about the two of you together, though."

Reed was moving away, probably in part because of me. It was officially over. He didn't love me.

"I thought he'd change his mind, but—" The tears started again.

"I know, sweetie, I know."

She sat on the bed next to me and rubbed my shoulder.

"I really thought he was my soul mate," I said.

Mom nodded. "I know," she said. "He wasn't. He isn't."

I jerked away from her. Mom had never even hinted to me about my soul mate. She'd always sworn that she would never, ever see who my soul mate was. No matter what.

"What?" I said. "I thought you can't see—or won't look—or whatever. So now you can see who it is?"

"No, honey," she said. "I don't know anything about your soul mate. And you're right—I can't see who it is *because* I won't look."

I knew I was doing that squinty thing I do when I'm starting to get angry.

"God, Mom. Then how can you possibly know that Reed *isn't* my soul mate? If you can't see, then how do you know it isn't him?"

"Because, Rachel," Mom said, her voice louder now, too. "I know because I'm your goddamned mother, that's how. I know that he's not someone you would end up with because I know you and you're seventeen years old and I'm a grown woman, and I just know. Jesus."

I started to cry.

Mom wiped my tears with her thumbs.

"I'm sorry, sweetie. I'm so sorry."

I sniffled some more.

"Your heart is broken. It will take time, but I promise you'll be okay. Your legs will heal, and your heart will, too. I promise."

"I just want to go home now," I said.

Mom straightened. "I'll go see what's taking them so long."

EIGHTEEN

I would kiss you, had I the courage.
–Edouard Manet (artist)

On the way home from my first full day of school without Serena speaking to me, Jay and I are both quiet, him concentrating on driving, me watching the evergreens zip by. We have the windows open, and the breeze is making Jay's hair stir.

"I'm going to turn the garage into my bedroom," I say.

He glances at me before turning back to the road.

"Isn't it, like, a storage room or something? It's kind of a mess, right?" he asks.

"Yeah, it's a big project. I'll have to clean out all the crap, and paint and get a rug and stuff."

"What about heat? Is there heat?"

I smile because—I don't know why—because he cares, maybe.

"There's an electric heater in the wall. I think my grandfather used to do woodworking in there."

Jay nods. "Your mom okay with it?"

"I haven't told her," I say. "And I'm not going to yet. I found a box in there."

Jay doesn't look at me, but his eyebrows lift a bit.

"I think I want to look in it before I tell her, in case she takes it away before I have the chance."

"Why?"

"I don't know. It's sealed. But I just have this feeling that it has to do with my father." The word *father* feels strange to me. Formal. But since he died before I was born, and Mom doesn't talk about him, *dad* feels too familiar.

"Am I a horrible person?" I ask. "If I look inside?"

"You're asking *me*?"

"Yeah."

He laughs, and it's cute the way his dimple bounces on the side of his cheek. I'd been noticing things like that about Jay more and more lately.

"You find a box that could have stuff in it about your mom, who you can never get a straight answer out of about your dad or anything from her past. Who wouldn't look? It seems like a logical thing to do."

"But I mean, it's sealed and the label isn't in her handwriting. Maybe she doesn't even know it's there. I thought you might think I was being dishonest, like I should give it to my mom right away."

"Oh," he says. "Yeah, maybe."

I punch him gently on the arm.

"Like I said: You're asking *me*?"

"I feel like I'm so close," I say so quietly, I'm sure he couldn't hear me.

"Close to what?" He has bionic ears.

"To knowing something. I've never really known anything. I'm just feeling my way around, you know? Banging into walls, reacting. I want to just know stuff and then get started with my life."

Jay's quiet for a few seconds.

"Would it make a real difference to you? Knowing more about him?" he asks.

"I don't know," I say. "I was never one of those fatherless kids whose mission in life is to find out everything about their biological father. It really didn't matter to me. I have my mom and she always told me that the support group is our real family. But as I get older, it's become clearer that they aren't. I mean, every one of them has been struck by lightning. But not me. I don't fit in."

"So you want to know where you fit in? You want to know who he was so you can see if you're exactly like him or something?"

I shrug. "Maybe."

He's quiet again, then says, "I don't think biology matters that much, though. I'm nothing like anyone in my family. And I don't fit in."

I snort. "Are you serious? You absolutely fit in with your family. You and your mom, you're like, best friends. And you and her and Kyle are always teasing each other and laughing. You have actual fun together."

He glances at me as he slows for a red light.

"Is that what fitting in is?" he asks.

"What do you think it is?"

"Being with people who think like you do," he says.

"But I don't think like you, do I?" I ask.

"No."

Ouch. I look out the window.

"But, I mean, that's okay," he says. "I'm not sure if it's a me thing or an Asperger's thing, but the people with Asperger's I've met online—we have a lot of similarities, so I think it's that. But you get me. Mostly. You and my mom and Kyle. And Serena, too."

I let his words sink in. And now I feel bad that I've put him in this position—where he's not speaking to one of the people who gets him most.

"What do you think fitting in means?" he asks.

"I think it means feeling accepted and loved. Being with people who care about you, with people who like you the way you are. Unconditionally."

Jay takes a left onto my road and then drives in silence until he pulls into my driveway. He puts the car in park, turns off the engine, and then looks at me, stares into my eyes. I can probably count on one hand the number of times in the few years I've known him that he's looked into my eyes for this long.

"Then you fit in with me," he says. His eyes are hot. I've never thought of eyes that way, but right now, I feel like his are burning into mine, searing. Not in a bad way—in a delicious way. I feel a rush of adrenaline the way I used to when Reed was about to kiss me.

"Jay," I say.

He keeps staring. I know if I don't say something now, he never will.

"Are we—are we feeling the same thing here?" I ask, and my voice feels suddenly not my own. "I mean, I think so, but like you said, I'm not in your head. And I don't want to mess anything up."

I feel like this moment has been building for a long time. Something had started growing silently between the two of us when Serena first joined the cheerleading team last September, but then Reed showed up and I pushed the idea of Jay and me out of my mind. In the time since Reed left, though, and now with Serena ditching us, the something is back even stronger than before.

He doesn't say anything, but he breaks eye contact, and I'm pretty sure he's looking at my mouth now.

"Is it weird that I want to kiss you?" I ask, and my pulse is racing.

Jay shifts in his seat, moves his eyes to the steering wheel. He isn't feeling it. I made up those mutual feelings in my head. Just like I must have made up Reed's feelings for me.

"Um," I say, the ball of fire in my chest signaling tears are on their way. "Let's forget I ever said that."

I turn my back to him and reach for the door handle. Humiliated. The tears burn behind my eyes.

"Hold on," Jay says. I feel his hand, heavy and warm, on my shoulder. "I just . . ." He clears his throat, but he doesn't take his hand away. "I can't. I don't know how to explain . . ."

I turn to him and his hand slips off my shoulder and back onto his lap. He looks down at it. I'm glad he isn't looking at me so he can't see the tear that leaks out of my eye. I swipe it with my finger.

I thought he wanted it as much as I did. It felt like one of those things that was inevitable, like when you bike up to the top of a hill and down is the only possible next move. So, I need to know why he's putting the brakes on just as we're about to get going down the hill.

"You don't know how to explain that you're not interested?" I say, trying so hard not to let my voice crack.

A surprised look passes over his face. "I made you cry?"

"Nope. I did that all by myself."

He takes a deep breath and then stares at me again. I know he's using all his reserves to do that. It can't be easy for him to look directly at me right now.

"I'm interested," he says. "I think about you all the time."

"Okay then," I say. "Me too." My breath comes out shaky. My heart pounds. His lips part a little. He thinks about me all the time. He does want to kiss me. He just needs prompting.

This is it. I lean forward just slightly, hoping my lips aren't chapped. I stare at his lips and I want to know what they feel like on mine.

"I can't," he says.

I freeze and lean back against the door, deflated.

"Rach, please. This is hard for me."

I look straight out the windshield.

"Please just look at me." He's never asked me that before, so I do it. His eyes are solidly on mine again.

"I want to," he says. "I really do, Rach. It's that—you know I haven't kissed anyone before. I doubt I'd be very good at it. Can we wait until—I don't know, until—"

"What? Until you can watch a how-to video on kissing? It's not something you can research on YouTube. There's no step-by-step process."

"I wasn't going to watch a video. I'm just trying to be honest."

"Sorry," I say. God, why am I being so nasty? I just want him to be unable to resist me. Why aren't I irresistible?

"Rach," he says, exasperated. "You went out with an older guy who doesn't even live with his parents. You hooked up with Sawyer Baskin. Can't you see how that might be slightly intimidating for me?"

I feel sick. I hate myself.

"That's not—that has nothing to do with you—with us," I say.

"Right. I've got to go," he says. He's dismissing me.

I open the door. I get out, slam it shut, and go inside.

After a few minutes, I hear Jay's car start and then drive off.

NINETEEN

Love is the flower you've got to let grow.
–John Lennon (musician)

Mom is in the back room with Sue. I can hear them talking about topics for the quarterly meeting. I say hi, grab a sleeve of crackers, and go to my room.

I try not to think about Jay and his "I've got to go," which sounded so cold. It's my fault. I pushed him and I hurt him.

I have another American Lit paper to write. It's due in two days, but I still haven't dealt with getting my laptop fixed, so I'm trying to finish it so I can type it up in the computer lab during my free period tomorrow. I have to find all the examples of similarities and differences between Stella and Blanche in *A Streetcar Named Desire.* Mom calls up to say that she and Sue are heading out to Eastham for a bite. Mom hates running into people from when she lived here before I was born. She usually sticks to the bigger towns like Hyannis and Orleans, but occasionally she doesn't feel like driving so far, so she compromises with Eastham.

Their voices die out after the slamming of car doors. I put up my hair and get back to work.

By the time I finish my conclusion, I'm squinting, trying to see my paper in the almost-dark. A sudden loud pounding comes from outside. It's almost seven. Too late for construction, and besides, no one here in the off-season has any money to do construction.

I head down the hall to the front door. The pounding is coming from right outside. I slide open the door and find Jay kneeling on my steps, holding a hammer above the broken step that I now realize Mom must have forgotten about.

"What are you doing?" Which is the dumbest question, because it's pretty obvious what he's doing. He gives me a look that says just that.

I sit on the top step. I cross my arms over my chest tightly—today's warmth disappeared with the sun. I watch the muscles of his shoulder move beneath his canvas jacket. Up and down goes the hammer as he holds the board in place. I just watch. When he finishes, he sits on the repaired board.

"It'll hold up for a while, but not that much longer. It's rotted out."

"Who knew you were so handy," I say.

He shrugs. "Nails, a hammer. Pretty much it. When I dropped you off before, I noticed it was still sticking up."

I laugh a little at the fact that Jay could take note of a broken step at my house while we were arguing.

"Well, thanks," I say. "You coming in? Just finished my American Lit paper and my mom and Sue went out to dinner."

He nods and follows me inside.

I make two peanut butter sandwiches and we eat standing at the counter.

"Since I'm here, I can look at your laptop, if you want," he says.

"Okay."

Jay has been in my room a million times but never after we've talked about kissing. Maybe this isn't a good idea because I still want to kiss him and it seems like he isn't ever planning to. It's not like I can undo what I've done with Reed or Sawyer.

I quickly sweep cracker crumbs off my comforter. He goes to my desk, which is just big enough for my laptop, lamp, and pencil jar. The ceiling slopes near the desk, and he has to duck when he gets near it. He looks so much bigger in my room. When he sits on my chair, I'm almost afraid it'll break under his weight.

He turns the computer on and it dings. I sit on my bed and read over my paper. Jay types, clicks, and clicks some more.

"All good," he says after a few minutes.

"What was wrong with it?" I ask.

"No idea, but it's fixed now."

"What if it happens again? How do I fix it?"

He smiles. "I don't know. If it happens again, I guess you'll just have to call me."

I smile back and then it hits me. The just-a-friend Jay from before this afternoon probably wouldn't have come over to fix my stairs or my laptop. He's here now as the maybe-something-more Jay, the one who said he wanted to kiss me but is now making things strange and awkward by not kissing me. I let my realization be enough for me. For now.

I walk him to his car. Then I go back up to type my report.

The next morning, I wait at the end of my driveway for Jay. It's chilly, and a fine mist is frizzing up my hair. When he finally pulls up, I'm shivering. I get into the car quickly, relieved that he has the heat on full-blast.

"You're late," I say.

"The bus always comes on time," he says, and I see the little dimple above the corner of his mouth appear.

Even before, when it was Jay and Serena and me, it was always just the two of us on the way to school since Serena has her own car. But it feels different now, being alone in Jay's car with this new thing between us. It's like this crisp, fresh feeling in the air, like the first day there's a cool breeze and the leaves make a certain rustling sound and you know fall is on its way.

Jay pulls into the junior lot and clears his throat loudly, startling me. We got to school without my even noticing.

"You zoned out," he says.

"Yeah." I smile. "Just feeling pretty good today, I guess."

"Good. That's good."

Kids are streaming in through the front doors, which means that the homeroom bell is about to ring. We both get out of the car and close our doors at the same time.

Jay slings his backpack over his shoulder.

I see Serena, Rylin, and Lindsay in the sea of people. All three are staring at their phones. Serena looks up at us, and for a second it looks like she's about to say hi but then stops herself and looks back down at her phone.

Some of my good feelings disintegrate.

When we reach the top of the steps to the open door, the noise and chaos spill out, exactly the way we left it the day before.

I stand with Jay for a minute while he lets his eyes adjust to the fluorescent light, and the blur of the moving swarms of people. He's doing the trick he told me about where he tries to click off his ears to the buzz of everyone.

I follow closely behind him toward our lockers. When he's in this mode, he won't talk. He walks quickly, staying close to the wall until we get to our row. After he opens his locker, he turns to me.

"Okay," he says.

"Okay, what?" I don't remember if we'd been in the middle of a conversation when we entered the building.

"I want to try. Today. I was afraid. It was dumb and I—"

"Wait," I say. "Are you talking about what I think you're talking about?"

"Is that bad? You changed your mind?"

"No. Of course not. It's just the timing is weird right now."

He looks in his locker, starts moving things around. A group of girls down the hall laugh loudly, almost screeching, and then a teacher comes out of his classroom and tells them to move along to their homerooms.

I duck under Jay's arm and block his locker so he'll look at me. I'm only inches in front of him, so I have to tilt my head back to see him.

"Yeah, okay," I say.

"Pizza for lunch? We'll talk then?" he asks.

I nod enthusiastically.

"Meet you at your car after fourth," I say, and I head to class, smiling.

TWENTY

Pizza makes me think that anything is possible.
—Henry Rollins (musician)

After fourth, I head out to Jay's car so we can go out for pizza and our "talk." I finally remember where he parked his car this morning, and, of course, as punctuality isn't Jay's thing, he isn't here yet. I should've met him at his locker. Now I'm stuck waiting in the cold. After yesterday's warm weather, we're back to the regular April that feels like winter. I pace around his car.

A loud *beep-beep* sound of a car unlocking nearby makes me jump. You're only allowed to go off school grounds during the day if you're eighteen. Everyone does it anyway, but I don't want to be the one who gets caught.

"Didn't mean to scare you." Sawyer Baskin is walking toward me, his keys in his hand. He points at his car, which is parked a few spots away.

He stands in front of me.

"Listen," he says. "I'm sorry about yesterday. Wade's always looking for a fight. He's like in a constant state of 'roid rage."

"Well, that's a scary thought. Does he really take steroids?" Truthfully, I don't care that much, but I'm curious because I didn't think anyone actually did that.

"Nah, he's clean. I'm just joking. But really. I'm sorry. About that and Lindsay and everything. I've always thought you were cool and, I don't know, I just don't want you to hate me."

"I don't," I say.

He smiles, and I experience a sudden flash of touching that tiny gap in his front teeth with my tongue.

"Oh, hey," Sawyer says, but he isn't looking at me. Jay's coming toward us, looking frazzled, his key in his hand.

"Hey," Jay says, not making eye contact with either of us, and unlocks his car.

"See you later," I say to Sawyer.

I get into Jay's car, hoping his temperamental heater will cooperate.

We park in the Fairhaven Pizza lot. On the way in to the restaurant, two guys walk by us. One of them stares at Jay, then turns to his friend and says something that sounds like "Hey, that's K.O., isn't it?"

The friend looks at us and shrugs before getting into his car.

The muscle in Jay's jaw works up and down.

"Do you know those guys?" I ask.

"No." He holds the door to the restaurant open for me.

"Why'd they call you K.O.?"

He shrugs and goes right to the counter and orders, so I order, too.

We settle at a table with our slices of pizza and sodas.

I look at the peeling wood paneling next to me, the scratches in the table. Fairhaven needs a facelift. Since I started thinking about re-doing the garage, I've been noticing things like this more and more. The way places are built. What can be done to make them look better.

I pick a piece of pepperoni off his pizza.

"You could've just ordered pepperoni yourself," he says.

"I wanted plain."

"Then why are you stealing my pepperoni?" he asks. "You used to be so good at sharing."

He pushes his pizza toward me.

"No thanks," I say.

He shrugs, pulling the plate back in front of him.

His phone buzzes five times. He looks at it and groans.

"Kyle's such a pain in my ass," he says. "He wants me to drive him and his dickhead friends places. He's starting to act like them now. Neanderthals in shoulder pads."

I stare at him, annoyed that he's avoiding the subject we came here to discuss: us.

Jay kneads the back of his head. "Rach, you know I can't do that. Well, I *can*, but I don't have the energy for it right now."

"Do what?"

"That thing where I have to figure out what you're thinking. You have to tell me or I'll just assume everything's okay and I'll start talking about Kyle and yesterday's ride on the ambulance or how I just saw a guy without a helmet on his motorcycle and I know we'll be picking him up at some point in the next year, hopefully not as a DOA. But if I talk about that stuff then you'll get more pissed but pretend you're fine, and then you'll raise your voice at me and I'll freak out a little and then I'll shut down and . . . you see where I'm going with this?"

"This is why I love you," I say—and immediately wish I could take it back. That's the kind of thing you can say to a friend, but not a friend who you've talked with about the possibility of kissing each other only the day before and haven't figured out what it means yet.

Jay's cheeks redden a little.

"I mean, because you're no bullshit," I say. "Anyway. I'm annoyed because you're avoiding the conversation we should have about this whole thing." I gesture between us.

"Oh that," he says. "Yeah. I want to do this whole thing." He mimics my gesture.

"Me too," I say.

"Great, that conversation is done. Moving on. What else should we talk about?"

I laugh so loudly, the woman behind the counter stops talking on the phone for a second.

"Um . . . so. I want to know why that guy out in the parking lot called you K.O. And if it's something mean, I'm going to find him and scrape his eyeballs out."

Jay takes a bite of pizza and stares at the wall behind me.

"I know what you're thinking," I say.

"No, you don't."

"I do. You're thinking about how to reattach eyeballs."

Jay's mouth drops open.

"See?" I whisper. "I knooowww your thooouuughts." I make it sound like a ghost. "Tell me why they called you K.O."

He clears his throat.

"Knock Out. That's what they called me," he says. "You know the story. I'm sure Serena told you. About the kid Jeremy Robins?"

I have a vague recollection of Serena telling me something when we first started hanging out with Jay. Something about people thinking he was violent. But Serena had told me it was bullshit and ancient history.

"She told me something about a fight in middle school," I say. "That it was a pretty bad one, but the other kid had started it and none of it was your fault."

He smiles a little.

"Glad that's how she saw it," he says.

"I would've interrogated you a lot sooner if I'd known it was that big a deal or that you got a nickname from it—she made it seem like it wasn't, or at least that it was so long ago it was all forgotten. So . . . out with it."

"In sixth grade, I brought a stethoscope to school to show, um, to show, Serena, actually. It was a real one. My pediatrician gave it to me. Jeremy Robins grabbed it out of my hand and held it up above my head, so I couldn't get at it."

"He was holding it above *your* head?" Jay is six-foot-five, and I know that he's always been the tallest kid.

"He was the one kid in the grade as tall as me. He bullied everyone, but I guess someone must have told him to pick on someone his own size. He was getting me going, and I was headed toward a meltdown. I had some pretty big meltdowns at home—like I kicked a hole in my wall once—but I'd always been really good at school. That day, though, something about the way Jeremy was teasing me, I couldn't control myself. So I head-butted him, and he hit the floor. And it knocked him out."

I choke a little on my soda. "You head-butted him?"

"Yeah," he says.

"Didn't it hurt you?"

"What difference does it make whether it hurt me? The point was that I hurt *him*. Badly."

I stare at him.

"I was completely, like, in a different zone—so yeah, at first I didn't feel any pain. Later, when I had this screaming headache, I figured I deserved it."

"So, what happened to Jeremy?"

"They moved to Boston right after."

"And that was it?" I ask.

"Not really. For a while, his parents thought that he could have brain damage, since he'd been unconscious for so long. Kyle always joked that they just tried to blame his natural stupidity on me, but I never thought that was funny. They tried to sue us."

I gasp.

"They lost the suit, but it cost my parents a lot of money, and it was all over the papers and people didn't want their kids near me."

"Oh my god," I say, thinking of poor Jay being treated like a leper.

"Kyle defended me," he says. "My mom and dad went around talking to parents, making sure they understood that I wasn't a violent person. I felt bad for them. And then, once we started high school, it kind of blew over. Well, I thought it did anyway. I still think about it sometimes, but I figured no one else does. Sixth grade was a long time ago. But every now and then I hear someone say K.O. or Killer."

"So who were those guys outside?" I ask.

He shrugs. "I don't think I've seen them before. No idea."

"Did you ever talk to Jeremy again?" I ask.

"No," he says.

"Do you ever think about talking to him? To clear your conscience or whatever?"

"Well, the truth is," he says, "I'd probably want to do the same thing again if it happened today. I mean, I wouldn't actually do it—but I'd want to head-butt him again. Definitely. I can't really clear my conscience."

I think about that for a second. Another reason why I love Jay. Honest. Few regrets.

"So then, why do you think about it at all?"

"I guess because I feel bad I put someone in the hospital, that I hurt him, even though he was an asshole. And I think about how I couldn't control my meltdown, how after that day . . ."

He takes a sip of his drink.

"After that day, what?"

He picks up the crumpled napkin next to his plate and puts it down again.

"You were going to say something else," I say.

He shakes his head and sighs, like I'm driving him crazy with all the questions, but he continues. "I think after that, things changed with my dad. I think he started to be afraid of me or something. It's never been the same after that. And maybe that's . . . maybe that's why they got divorced. Because of me."

I laugh. "Classic!"

He looks at me like I've slapped him. I stop laughing.

"Come on, Jay. Every kid thinks their parents get divorced because of them," I say. "It's classic. It's cliché. And it's never true."

"But in my case, it might be," he says. "You laughed at me."

"Sorry. It was a knee-jerk reaction. Maybe I was being spiteful. A defense mechanism, I guess. Maybe you should talk to your dad about how you feel."

Jay stares out the window.

"See, now you're mad at me," I say.

"No, I'm not," he says. "I'm thinking."

"About what?"

"About what you said. It's complicated. I'm trying to figure it out."

"Do it out loud." I have to say that to Jay sometimes, or else he'll just sit there silently staring off into space for eons.

"Fine. You said you were being spiteful, which is confusing since I don't think you really want me to feel bad, and I was talking about my parents' divorce, which is pretty personal and difficult for me to talk about."

Dammit. "Jay—"

"But then you said you were defending yourself. So who are you defending yourself against? Me? I don't *think* I did anything for you to defend against."

I nod. I want to apologize, but I wait.

"So, if you're not defending yourself against me," he continues. "And the only other person here is you, it must be you. You're trying to defend against your own sadness because you don't have a dad at all. No grandfather, no family other than your mom. No brother, no sister, no cousins. And the way you're doing that is by getting angry. But maybe that anger is really jealousy. So, you're jealous of me because I have a family. A brother. Cousins, aunts, uncles. Two parents. Well, three, if you count Gabe, even though he and Mom will probably never actually get married."

I half-smile, feeling a lump rise in my throat.

"I'm not even sure I knew that's what I was doing," I say. "But you're probably right."

"It was too harsh, wasn't it?" he asks.

"No," I say, but my eyes start to water. "You're right. I think you nailed it."

"So, you're jealous."

"I guess."

"You'd rather know your father and have divorced parents than just one parent," he says.

"I think I would. But, Jay, we don't have to compare who has the shittier deal."

"You have the shittier deal," he says.

"We don't have to compare."

"You definitely have the shittier deal."

"Can I have your pepperoni?" I ask.

"Yes."

TWENTY-ONE

If you don't go to a dance, you can never be rejected,
but you'll never get to dance, either.
—Maeve Binchy (writer)

When I get home from school Friday, I realize I've survived an entire week of being Serena-less. Every time I caught a glimpse of her in the hallway or heard her voice, I wanted to go to her, to ask her why she's doing this and when she'll be done with it, but I didn't because I have a little bit of pride. Each day she continued to ignore me, I tried to convert my feelings of missing her into anger at her, but it never worked. I just miss her.

I have the house to myself, so it's the first time I've had a chance to check out the box in the garage since I found it. I drop my bag on the kitchen table, find a half-empty can of mixed nuts in the cupboard, and take it into the garage. The sealed box is pushed into the far corner, right where I left it. Mom never comes in here, so I'm not surprised that nothing's been touched since I found it more than a week ago. I stride over to the box like there's no reason not to, crouch down, and pull at the flaps until the old packing tape rips free. I cough a little at the musty, dusty smell from inside. On top is a plain envelope with NAOMI written on the front in blue pen. I take it out and hold it, turning it over. It's sealed, as though it's never been opened. I peer back into the box.

There's a black Nauset sweatshirt, a few vinyl records—David Bowie, Depeche Mode, Prince—a small stuffed elephant holding out a red heart that says I'M YOURS, and a Ziploc that holds about six Loony Toons character Pez dispensers. I push the sweatshirt aside and underneath is a red leather box, a little smaller than a shoebox. The lid is embossed with the words LOVE NOTES. It's the kind of thing you'd find in a Hallmark store.

Just as I reach in to get the red box, I hear a car in the driveway.

Quickly, my heart racing, I drop the envelope back on top of everything, close the flaps of the cardboard box, grab the can of nuts, and rush back to the kitchen at the same time Mom opens the front door.

It must be one of her short Fridays. Mom gave one of the other bank tellers some of her hours to help pay for some medical expenses. I'm not sure why she did—it's not like we don't need the money. Especially now that I'm using my savings from my job at PJ's last summer for the garage, I have to depend on Mom for spending money until the restaurant reopens for the season next month.

"Hi," she says. She looks frazzled. "You have a good day?"

"Kind of boring." I fill the tea kettle with water. "You?"

"Let's just say, TGIF, and that it was a short day," she says, brushing hair out of her eyes.

She walks past me to the garage door, which I'd forgotten to close.

"Why's this open?" she asks. "You looking for something?"

For a second, I consider lying—"Yeah, I couldn't find my brown boots, so I thought maybe they'd gone in a donation box by accident." But I decide to go with the truth. I've got to tell her at some point.

"I want to fix up the garage so I can move in," I say.

Mom doesn't look at me. She stays quiet, standing in the garage doorway, looking in.

"What?" I ask, finally.

"Why do you want to do that?" Her voice sounds almost hurt.

I shrug. "Just, you know, it's quieter. And I thought it would be fun, something new. I don't know."

"Were you going to check with me?" she asks. Her voice seems curious, though, not angry.

"Of course. That's what I'm doing now. Is it okay with you?"

She closes the garage door and looks out the back windows to the water. Her eyes are shiny.

"Yes," she says, quietly. "It's okay with me."

"I'm sorry, Mom. I didn't mean to upset you. It was just an idea that—"

"No, it's okay. It just hit me that you've only got one more year of school and then you might be gone and I just wasn't ready to think about that."

"Don't count on me going anywhere," I say. "You might have to kick me out, especially once I'm in the garage—it'll be like my own apartment."

She smiles. "In that case, let's make it amazing so you stay forever."

"Deal," I say. "I'm using my own money, though."

She squeezes my shoulder, then goes off to her room to change.

Now that it's the weekend, she'll be home and I probably won't have a chance to look at what's inside that red box, or that envelope. The thought of waiting until Monday almost hurts.

I call Jay and tell him I need company.

"Come over," he says.

I hang up and ride my bike over to his house.

When I get there, I go through the kitchen door and basically run right into him. He must have been standing in front of the door, waiting for me. I rest my cheek on his chest, and he puts a hand on top of my head.

"You okay?" he asks.

"Yeah." I put my arms around his middle and sink into him. He hugs me back then, his arms tight around me. Jay's hug is so strong and secure, it feels like he's infusing me with healing.

His brother Kyle comes in from the TV room, and when he sees us, he groans.

"Gawd, get a room," he says.

We pull apart. Jay's neck is pink.

After Kyle grabs a bag of chips and returns to the TV room, Jay and I look at each other.

"Do you want to hang out upstairs?" Jay asks.

"Yeah, sure."

When we get to his room, he closes the door and we stand a few feet apart.

Jay stares straight into my eyes, like he's asking a question.

"Now?" I whisper.

He shrugs and the corners of his mouth turn up a little.

So, this is it. The point of no return. We are going to kiss.

We walk toward each other, and I know we're both feeling shy and strange. When we get close enough, I go up on my tip-toes and put my arms around his neck, and he bends way down and puts his around my waist.

"Okay," he says, his voice shaky.

It was always clear I'd have to be the one to start the kiss.

And so, I kiss him. It's just one touch of our lips at first. Hesitant. And I know that Jay's brain is probably on overdrive, and I hope he's not thinking too much about the mechanics of the whole thing or about what I had to eat or something.

His arms tighten around me, and I'm surprised at how soft his lips are as he presses them against mine a few times, more than pecks but less than making out.

He pulls back a few inches.

"Is this right?" he asks.

"Yes," I say. "Definitely."

He nods, and we kiss again. And he's more sure now, and I know he's figuring this whole thing out. Our lips match and move, press together, pull apart, press together again. Soft, juicy, tingly. And yes, now he's really figured it out. And when our tongues meet inside our mouths, it's like—

"Wow," he whispers.

"I know."

"It's . . ."

"Amazing?" I ask.

"Weird," he says, at the same time.

I narrow my eyes at him.

"The idea of touching someone else's tongue with mine has always freaked me out," he says. "But in reality? It does feel kinda weird, but also really good."

"Well, but I'm not just someone," I say, smiling.

"No," he says. "You're not."

He pulls me closer. I think about what he must be noticing—the bumps of my chest against him, my pounding heart, how I have to pant a little for air. That sigh of relief I couldn't help when I felt how soft his lips were. I know he notices it all.

After a few minutes, my neck hurts from having to reach up so high to kiss him.

"Can we sit on the bed?" I ask.

He nods and backs up, sits on the edge.

I climb onto his lap.

We go back to kissing and he slides his hand up my shirt, his fingers moving slowly on my bare back. I think about how he must know, biologically, what is happening inside my body that makes me radiate so much heat that I'm almost sweating. I take my shirt off in one quick move and then for a second I just sit there, topless other than a light blue bra. The way he looks at me makes me feel so pretty. I've never seen this look on his face—part freaked out, part pleased confidence, and totally absorbed in me. For a second, I picture how I'd feel taking my jeans off, exposing the scars on the backs of my thighs that I keep covered all the time. But I'd be okay. It's Jay. He knows what they look like already. And he knows how I got them.

He kisses my neck and he's breathing harder now and it all feels so good. And then he pulls away. He quickly moves his hands from my back to the bed.

"What's wrong?" I whisper.

"Nothing, I . . . um . . . I think we should stop."

"Did I do something?"

He shakes his head no. "I just think we should stop."

I look down at his hands on the bed on either side of my legs, and I want to grab them and place them on my back again, but I see that they're shaking a little. His neck is red. But he doesn't move.

"Are you okay?" I ask. "Your hands are shaking."

He balls them into fists.

"Yeah, I'm fine." But he won't look at me. "I just . . . don't want to do this anymore."

I unwrap my arms and legs from around him, get off the bed, and stand in front of him. He stares at a point on the floor.

"Oh my god, you don't want to do this, and I just basically jumped your bones. I'm—I'm sorry. I didn't—" My voice shakes and my chest hurts in that *oh shit, I'm gonna cry* way.

"It's not that I don't—" he says.

In the years I've known him, I've gotten to know the complicated way Jay's mind works pretty well. Except now I have no idea what he's thinking because this whole kissing thing is new.

I turn away from him and tug my T-shirt over my head. The back-hem catches on the clasp of my bra. I hear Jay shift his weight like maybe he's going to get up to help me, but I yank the shirt down before he has a chance. He takes a breath the way he does when he's about to start talking for a long time.

"What exactly does jump—"

"Jump your bones," I say. "Meaning I tried to get it on with you."

"Yeah, I know what it means but . . ." He pauses. Even if he tried to stop himself, he couldn't. "But why bones? Why not body or flesh? It doesn't make any sense. I wonder if it's connected to the word *boner.*" I can sense him itching for Google.

"I thought you wanted this as much as I did," I say. "I thought you were into it. I'm so confused. And embarrassed. I have to go."

I start for the door.

"I did want this," he says. "I do—I just—"

I turn to face him, tears stinging my eyes.

"Rach, wait. Don't cry."

I know that this is just him, that I need to be patient. I know I should stay and we should talk about it. I know all of this, but I'm embarrassed and hurt and I just want to leave. So I do, my boots clomping down the steep, uncarpeted stairs.

Kyle is at the kitchen counter drinking milk out of the carton.

"Hey, Rach, you leaving?"

I grunt a yes, making sure he can't see my watery eyes. Kyle is probably the only person in the world who'd have a clue what just happened up there in Jay's room, but there's no way I'd talk to him about it. I pull my phone from my pocket, wishing I could call Serena. She may not know what Jay's deal is, but she'd say something to make me feel better. I can't believe she doesn't know what's going on in my life. I ride home, tears from sadness and from the wind in my eyes mixing together as they slide down my cheeks.

TWENTY-TWO

People are trapped in history and history is trapped in them.
–James A. Baldwin (writer)

I must have fallen asleep when I got home from Jay's because something tickles my arm and I jerk awake suddenly. Mom is sitting on the edge of my bed, her hand resting on my shoulder. She's staring out the window, but she says *shhhh* automatically like she's in a trance. Her bracelet bounces on my shirt.

I haven't seen that bracelet in ages. It brings back memories of when I was little. I close my eyes, and the image of an apartment we lived in overtakes me like a powerful smell—exposed brick clashing with drop ceiling tiles stained from the apartment above. Mom tried to make the place feel warmer by hanging colorful tapestries in blue, red, and gold, but it always seemed like just a brick wall, like we were living outside instead of inside.

I was eight, I think, when I finally asked Mom the question that had been on my mind for weeks, since I'd found out that Rudy Clintock had two dads. Not only did I not have two, but I had none. It seemed like almost every kid had a dad—at the supermarket, the park, school, walking down the street. Everyone but me. The closest thing I had to a father or grandfather was Ron from the support group; he brought me candy and toys and called me *sweet little one*. But he was so old. And I knew the basics of how babies were made—the summer before, a survivor had come from California and stayed with us for three weeks. Her ten-year-old daughter told me that and other stuff I thought was really gross at the time. One thing that stuck with me was that a man's penis had to go in a woman's vagina to make a baby, and I was positive Ron hadn't done that with Mom.

"Mommy," I had asked. "Why don't I have a dad?"

Mom had run her fingers through her hair, the bracelet jangling.

"Remember I told you that your dad died before you were born, love."

"So he put his penis in your vagina?" I asked Mom finally, shifting so that she wouldn't see my face turning red.

Mom had burst out laughing. I hadn't heard her laugh like that in so long, I started laughing, too. It was one of my favorite memories, Mom and I laughing over something funny I'd said, even though I didn't really know why it was funny other than that I'd said the word *penis*.

Then she explained egg and sperm, fertilization, embryos. And she told me that an egg gets fertilized by the sperm in the uterus and becomes an embryo. And that my dad died when I was still just an embryo. With all the scientific talk, I'd forgotten my original question. Maybe she'd intended to distract me from more questions about him.

"So if a dad gives the sperm and then dies, there's no way to have a dad at all? Couldn't you get me a dad? Like, what if you got married?" My mind had started racing with images of this "new" dad. He'd swing me up onto his shoulders and we'd feed ducks at the lake. And I'd laugh and scream.

Mom hesitated.

"Why don't you have a boyfriend?" I continued. "You should go out on dates." At recess, Miss Lensner was always telling the other teachers on the playground about the date she'd gone on the night before. Usually they were "duds," but once in a while, she'd say "this guy could be the one." But it seemed like every man Mom knew was either married or old or so messed up by lightning, they weren't options. No man had stepped foot in our apartment other than Ron, and the other survivors, and occasionally, the plumber or cable guy.

Mom shrugged. "I don't need anyone else. I have the survivors, and I have you."

Had I noticed then that I'd come second, after the survivors? Had I noticed that she'd said what *she'd* needed, but not what maybe *I* had needed?

Then Mom said, "Your father and I were soul mates."

"What's a soul mate?" I'd overheard Mom using the phrase before, but I'd never understood what it was.

"It's someone who is your other half, the person you're meant to be with forever."

"But," I said, "how do you know who your soul mate is? And what if your soul mate dies? Can't you just get another soul mate?"

Mom laughed, like I was being silly again. But I really wanted to know the answers. I stared at her until she looked at me. She spoke quietly.

"I know who my soul mate is because the lightning showed me. And no, you can't get another. You only have one."

I felt the sadness settle over us.

I had one more question.

"Can't you love someone enough to be with forever, even if they're not your exact soul mate? Like what if your soul mate's dead, like yours, can't you be with someone else who you love maybe second best?"

"No," she said, but her mouth didn't close after she spoke the way it did when she was denying me candy or pop tarts.

I think I knew right then that she was hiding something.

I shift in bed a little and turn toward her, the bracelet clinking as she moves her hand away.

"Hi," Mom says quietly and kisses me on the cheek.

I stretch and yawn.

"I feel like we haven't had much chance to talk. How's school going?" Mom asks. She's right. We haven't really talked much lately about anything real. Not more than logistics—grocery lists, laundry—and notes left for each other: "I'll be home at 9," "the hall toilet is having issues, so use mine until we can get it fixed."

I'd fixed the toilet after watching a YouTube how-to, and I was pretty proud of myself. I hadn't even needed any parts for it.

"School's okay," I say. "World History is awful still, but the rest of my classes are okay."

Mom rubs my back, and her bracelet is cool on my neck when she reaches the collar of my shirt.

"Serena still being a sell-out?" she asks. That's what we started calling her. The sell-out who chose to ditch her best friend for the party kids.

"Yeah," I say.

Mom smiles weakly and shakes her head.

"You and Serena were so close. I know you miss her. She must miss you, too."

"She dumped me. Because I hung out with her friend's *ex*-boyfriend one night. It wasn't even *her* ex-boyfriend, which I would never do. The whole thing is so incomprehensible. I still don't get it."

Mom nods slowly.

"What?"

"I don't get it either. It seems like that can't be it. I just wonder," she says. "I wonder whether maybe you did the dumping without even realizing it."

Isn't my own mom supposed to be on my side?

"You didn't make much time for her when Reed was here," she says. I bristle hearing her say his name. "You can't drop out of a friendship for a guy and then come right back where you left off. Friendships have to be nurtured."

"Okay, so it's all my fault that she's hanging out with all those shitbrains."

"That's not what I said. I'm just reminding you that if you do work things out with her, you'll know better about how to make it work. Friendships are more important than you can imagine."

I nod, wanting this conversation to be over.

"So," Mom says as she pushes herself off the bed and stands next to me. "How about some dinner for the two of us? Take out or go out?"

"Go out."

She leans over and tickles my armpits. I scream and squirm and laugh.

"I'm going to pee!"

Only a handful of restaurants stay open off-season, and most of them are in Provincetown or Orleans, but since it's already late, we go to The Wicked Oyster. I'm relieved that Mom is willing to loosen up on her desire to stay out of Wellfleet as much as possible. Going there is always "too much water under this bridge," she usually says. And then I get frustrated because she's always so cryptic, and she never shares what water she's referring to.

"I'm sorry I haven't been the best mother lately," Mom says, her eyes darting toward the front door every time it opens.

"No, Mom, I'm fine."

"I'd always wanted more for us." Her voice catches for a second and I worry she's going to cry. "I was so selfish dragging you around, changing schools practically every year, living in those awful apartments."

We hardly ever talk about life before coming here. When we do, she always gets sad and regretful, which always makes me sad. So I'm determined to lighten things up.

"Mom, how else would I have learned to fix a toilet or kill a cockroach? Come on, you've allowed me to learn some incredibly valuable life skills."

Mom laughs, and that's what I need.

"I love you, Rach."

"You too, Mom."

The door squeaks open behind me. Mom's eyes flick up and then quickly back to me and they hold something now. Anxiety, fear, nervous energy.

I hear the voices of two men behind me talking about the Bruins, a corner shot in the last twenty seconds.

Instinctively, I turn. Mom kicks me under the table. I snap my head back around and smother the word "Ow!" when I see the look she's giving me.

"Hold on," one of the men says.

Even though her face is calm, I can practically see Mom's pulse jack-hammering underneath her necklace. She smiles.

It's her "beautiful Naomi" smile that makes people stop dead in their tracks. That smile is usually reserved for high-stakes moments like parent-teacher conferences and getting out of parking tickets.

"Naomi Ferguson," one of the men says. "Wow. I'd heard you'd moved back a few years ago, but I haven't seen you in all that time, so I figured it must've been a rumor. Yet here you are!"

He's big and bulky, brown hair braided down his back, with wispy curls by his ears. The other man is shorter, wiry, bald—the shaved kind, not the hair-loss kind.

Mom stands and gives them each a quick kiss and hug.

"It's been a long time," Mom says in her charming Naomi Ferguson voice.

The big guy puts his hands on Mom's shoulders and looks at her like he's in a bakery choosing which cupcake he wants out of all the perfect cupcakes. The other guy stands back and watches.

"This is my daughter, Rachel," she says. "Rachel, these are my old friends Tommy McKee and Rafe Zamora."

"Who you calling old?" Mr. McKee says. He's the big one with the braid, Mr. Zamora is the shorter bald one.

"Beautiful like her mother," Mr. McKee says. People like to say stuff like that, but I know it's just words. My mom is Naomi Ferguson, the most beautiful woman in any room. I'm just an imitation model, same basic parts, but Mom was painstakingly handmade and I was assembled by a factory machine.

Mom pushes a piece of hair behind my ear, something she'd do when I was a little girl and people would comment on how I looked like her.

"I know it's been a few years, but I'm sorry about your father," Mr. Zamora says quietly, looking down at his hands.

Mom clears her throat.

"I heard you were good to him. Thank you," she says.

He shrugs. "I did what anyone would do."

I see Mom's face change like he's said something offensive. "I did what anyone would do." Right. Except for Mom. She didn't do it. She didn't take care of her aging father. The people of the small town had done it for her. I wonder if that's what Mr. Zamora has implied. Because I'm pretty certain that's how mom took it. I wonder if that's why she feels so uncomfortable in town, knowing she'll see the people who watched out for her father because she hadn't been here to do it.

Mr. McKee keeps shaking his head back and forth, his big smile never disappearing.

"It's been, what—almost twenty years since you left?"

"Something like that," Mom says, then looks down at her plate. "Eighteen, I think."

"So you're living in your dad's old beach house?" Mr. McKee asks, and he looks around as if he might pull up a chair and sit down. "We have a lot to catch up on."

"We'll leave you to your dinner, though," Mr. Zamora says.

"Yeah, but then come have a drink with us. It'll be like the good old days." Mr. McKee laughs. "Except now we can legally drink beer."

He winks at me.

Mom laughs. "Another night, for sure."

"Rafe and I are here most nights. Right over there," he says, pointing at the bar, "is where we bachelors hang out."

Mr. Zamora smiles. His bald head makes him look like a tough guy, but his face looks sweeter when he smiles.

"It was nice to see you, Naomi," he says, quietly. He nods at me. "Rachel."

They move on to the bar and greet the bartender. Mr. McKee yells at him to change the damn channel. Mom sits back down. Her hand is shaky as she reaches for her glass of wine.

TWENTY-THREE

Three things cannot be long hidden:
the sun, the moon, and the truth.
–Buddha (sage)

At two o'clock that night, I wake to the sound of Mom crying. Next to her low, raspy rumble of a laugh when she's with the survivors, it's the most familiar sound I know. Mom sniffling and crying. I get up and knock on her door. When I was little, she'd take me into bed with her and wrap her arms around me like a teddy bear. I'd feel her tears on my hair, the fast rhythm of her heart against my back. I used to think of Mom as two separate people—daytime Mom, who was lovely and confident, filled with laughter and strength; and nighttime Mom, who cried herself to sleep, the tears making a river of sadness run through the middle of her bed.

"Mom?" I say softly as I open her door. "Can I come in?"

She sits cross-legged on her bed, and I stifle a gasp when I see what's on her lap—the red leather LOVE NOTES box I'd seen in the garage. The lid is off and inside is what looks like a stack of letters. Next to the box, I see the envelope I'd held—the one that says NAOMI in blue pen on the front. The top of the envelope is sliced open now, and I can see the fold of paper inside.

She must have gone in and found the cardboard box after I told her about wanting to move into the garage. I wonder whether she'd been able to tell that I opened the flaps. It feels like a rock has settled inside my stomach when I realize that I've lost my chance to see what was in the red box, to read what was inside the envelope.

How many minutes have I spent thinking about my father, Mom's soul mate? After everything with Reed, I'd started to doubt Mom. It was like some fairy tale, the soul mate who died before they had a chance to really be together. It seemed like a convenient story for Mom to tell me as a child to gloss over some other horror. I'd seen movies; I'd read books. The child conceived by rape or incest whose mother tells her that her father was actually a prince from another land. Lately, my cynicism has gotten in the way of my trust. I want to know what's in that box.

"Did I wake you up?" Mom sniffs.

"No, I just couldn't sleep," I say, trying to keep my voice steady.

As I sit on the bed next to her, she turns a photo over, then puts it and the envelope into the red box, then closes the lid. She takes a tissue and wipes her eyes.

"You know how wine loosens my tear ducts," she says now, attempting a smile. "Just looking through some old things."

Mom puts her hand on my knee.

"But I'm okay," she says. "Sometimes, when I run into someone from back then . . . it just brings everything back."

"The men at The Wicked Oyster?" I ask.

Mom nods. "They were part of the crowd I hung out with here."

Mom hugs the red box to her chest.

"What's that?" I ask, seeing something shiny on her nightstand. It's a small scallop shell. A loop of fishing line is threaded through a hole in the bottom. In the dim light, the shell seems to glow, like when the bay sparkles in the sun. It's like most dry scallop shells—faded purple and bone, the inside a deeper shiny purple.

"We found this," Mom says, picking it up. "The two halves were still together even though the scallop was long gone. We broke it apart and each kept a half. Like those heart friendship necklaces. We laughed so hard because we knew it was such an unoriginal gesture of young love, but we did it anyway. I wonder if . . . Here. You should have it," she suddenly says. "Maybe it'll bring you luck."

She puts the necklace over my head and slides the fishing line through the hole in the shell so the knot is at the back of my neck. The shell rests in the spot between my collarbones.

"Thanks," I say, closing my hand lightly around it. "I love it."

I hope she'll take something out of the box to show me, but she puts it on her bedside table.

"Mom?"

She looks up.

"Do you think your father and I would've gotten along?"

A few fresh tears pool on her bottom eyelids.

"Of course, he would have loved you. My dad was a tough man, but you would've gotten to the soft core inside, I'm sure. If I'd let him, he would have loved you with all of his heart."

She reaches for another tissue and dabs her eyes.

"I don't know why I thought it wouldn't matter," Mom continues. "I figured if you didn't know him then you wouldn't miss him. You used to love it when we had the support group meetings. They were our surrogate family."

I feel a sharp sting in my chest. They weren't my surrogate family. They were hers.

"My father and I were very different people," she says. "We couldn't be in the same room without exploding at each other."

"I could've come by myself to see him," I say.

"You're right," she says. "I could've sent you here for the summers. I think I would've missed you too much, though."

I would've missed her too much, too, probably. For a while, when I was little, everything was perfect. We were everyone's ideal of the single mom and daughter team. We lived in a small apartment in Detroit until I was in first grade. Mom kept the books for some of the stores in our neighborhood while I was in school, so we had enough to live, eat, and have some extras. And we did everything together. But one day, at the dentist, everything changed. Mom was flipping through a magazine in the waiting room, and she saw an advertisement for a lightning-strike survivors' convention. Mom tore the page out of the magazine. I gasped because I didn't think you were supposed to do that. And I remembered that for the entire time the dentist was drilling and poking at my teeth, Mom was staring at that page she'd ripped out.

A month later, we checked in to a Ramada in Nashville, Tennessee. After the first day of the convention, Mom realized that it was really no place for a six-year-old. The things they talked about in the sessions were scary and sad, and I had to see a lot of grown men and women crying their eyes out, cursing God, and doing really weird stuff. But it was too late—I was there and Mom didn't feel comfortable leaving me with one of the hotel babysitters, so for three more days, I saw and I heard it all.

On the third night, Mom told me what happened after she was struck by lightning—how it transformed her into someone more than just herself. How she was able to see anyone's soul mate almost as simply as the rest of us could see someone's eye color. At the time, I didn't understand. I'd never even heard of a soul mate before. But as the years went on, I began to understand, and I was naive enough to think that maybe I was capable of having a soul mate, too.

After that convention, we traveled around a lot to meet up with other lightning-strike survivors. We moved a couple of times to be closer to some who Mom connected most with—Sue, Ron, Angela, and a few others. We lived outside of Chicago for a year, in Minneapolis for two, half a year in Columbus, and then back to Detroit. Since we moved to Wellfleet three years ago, Ron and Sue had both moved to Massachusetts to be closer to us.

I can tell Mom's finished talking now. She wants to be alone with these letters.

"You sure you're alright?" I ask.

She nods.

"Go back to sleep." She kisses me on the top of my head, and I go back to bed.

TWENTY-FOUR

In dreams, anything can be anything, and everybody can do.
We can fly, we can turn upside down,
we can transform into anything.
–Twyla Tharp (dancer)

When I wake up the next morning, Mom is still sleeping. She must have been up most of the night looking through her red box and crying.

I go to the kitchen and put on the kettle to make tea. Today is Saturday and I'm planning to spend the entire day making headway on my new room. I stand in the door to the garage, imagining it clean, with fresh paint, a fun shaggy rug, a bed. I can see the Before and After as if I'm watching it on TV. It's just getting from one to the other that's hard to picture. I'll need a pad of sticky notes and a Sharpie to label a few of the obvious things to toss that have been in the garage since we moved here—a broken bike, a few mildewy beach chairs and umbrella, some boxes filled with donations—clothes, shoes, pots and pans—that my grandfather must not have gotten around to giving away.

The tea kettle whistles and I rush to grab it, hoping the noise hasn't woken Mom. But a minute later, she comes out of her bedroom, her eyes still a bit puffy. I pull a second mug out of the cupboard for her.

"Morning," she says.

"Hi."

"So much for the weekend. Bruce asked me to come in to organize some files or something," Mom says.

"Doesn't he have a secretary for that?" I ask.

"I guess they're for a big client and he doesn't trust her with it."

"Well, I guess that's a compliment," I say.

"It is. I just wish he could give me my compliments during the week instead of on Saturdays."

She stirs milk into her tea.

"I want to sort through all the stuff in the garage and label it," I say. "I'd like to have the room ready before the meeting." She flinches, but then she nods. She has to understand how much it sucks for me to be home during the meetings. And during all the preparation they do for it.

"I'll bet Donny Lash would take some of the heavy stuff out of the garage for us," she says. "I'll give him a call if you want."

"That would be great," I say.

"I'll do whatever I can to help," she says.

After Mom showers and leaves for work, I stretch out on my bed and power on my phone. I'd turned it off after I left Jay's yesterday. I knew that if he called or texted, he'd want to talk about what had happened, and I wasn't ready yet.

There's a text from last night at nine.

> **JAY**: I'm incapable of doing anything the normal way. We know this. 😒 🐶

And one from this morning, just twenty-five minutes ago.

JAY: What are you up to? Are we okay?
Come over?
ME: We're okay. I'm sorry I overreacted.
I'll come in the afternoon.

I know that if I go over there, we'll probably kiss again. And if he stops it again, I'll probably cry again. I roll onto my stomach and press my cheek into the pillow. I think of our kiss—the good parts—how perfectly our lips fit together. I try to imagine how Jay replayed it in his mind. I know he must have, and I hope he thought about the good parts, too.

I pull on sweats and an old Detroit Lions T-shirt, put on sneakers, and get some duct tape. I find a pair of gardening gloves so I won't slice my hand on any of the rusted equipment. The garage door opener is broken, and I have to use all of my strength to pull it up. Once I do, I feel like the air is already making the room feel cleaner and fresher. I start shoving stuff toward the entrance so it will be obvious and easy for Mr. Lash to take it. I look around and realize there isn't much to save. A set of metal shelves hold old gardening tools, tarps, a few inflatable rafts that are probably from the 1980s. A few snow shovels and a rake are worth keeping, but everything else looks old and broken. He should probably just take everything. I look over the boxes, blowing dust off the tops to see whether anything is written on them. Most are labeled LEDGERS with the year—and they range ten years. I open one and flip through some of the books, but they're all filled with numbers, my grandfather's old accounting ledgers. I'll double-check with Mom, but they're probably trash.

After two hours, I'm dirty and sweaty and sneezing from all the dust. I pushed almost everything to the front of the garage to haul away to the dump—either for trash or for the give-and-take shed. All that's left, other than the boxes for Mom to look through, are the black metal shelves that need to be painted but are sturdy enough to use, a few shovels and tools, and a bike pump. I pull the garage door closed.

My phone buzzes, so I take off my gloves and check it.

MOM: Donny said he could come by at 1—that okay?
ME: Perfect. Thank you.

I take a shower, already feeling the satisfying muscle soreness in my shoulders and legs from hard work. I like that feeling much better than the tingling aches I get sometimes now from the scars on the backs of my legs.

I get dressed and check my phone.

JAY: Timing?
ME: 2? I'll come there.
JAY: 👍

I'm practically bouncing, so excited about my new space. And, even with the weirdness of yesterday with Jay, a little flutter hangs out in my abdomen since I know that the potential for more kissing awaits me.

I hear the crunch of tires on the shell driveway, and then there's a knock at the front door.

"Anyone home? Naomi? Rachel? You there?"

Everyone leaves their doors open, especially on warm days—not many of the houses on the water, including ours, have air-conditioning. Even though I've lived here for three years, the city girl in me still feels strange with the door unlocked all the time. So I'm relieved when I see it's just Donny Lash.

"Hi, Mr. Lash," I say as I open the screen door for him.

"It's Donny. Please. I can't be Mr. Lash. I'm not ready for that. I may never be."

He chuckles. He's older than Mom, but he has a young face—ruddy from years of working out in the sun, a big belly that sticks out over his jeans.

"So, Naomi said you have a couple loads of junk you need me to take?"

"Yes, thank you so much. I'll go open the garage door for you."

After struggling to pull up the heavy garage door, I'm surprised to see the silver pickup in the driveway—the one I'd been hoping to buy from him. And climbing down from the driver's side is Rafe Zamora, the man we saw at The Wicked Oyster last night. He smiles.

"Hi, Rachel," he says.

"Hi," I say, wondering why he's here.

"I can get that door working for you," he says. "It would only take a few minutes—I can come back another time with the right tools."

Donny is at Mr. Zamora's side now.

"My truck had a flat," Donny says. "And since Mr. Zamora's borrowing this one for a few weeks, he came to help me out. But don't worry, I'm still saving this heap for you."

"You can call me Rafe," Mr. Zamora says. "No 'mister' for me either."

I nod but I probably just won't call either of them anything. I call Mom's lightning-strike group members by their first names, but I've known them forever. Other adults, it feels too weird.

"I understand if you have to sell the truck to someone else," I say. "I'm not even sure I'll be able to buy it now that I'm spending my money on fixing up the garage."

"No, no, it's yours. And we'll work out a payment plan. Take as long as you need. I don't like seeing you out riding that old bike on these roads. You need some solid wheels. Give me about a month, then it's yours. Now, show me what we're taking off your hands today."

I point out the stuff I'd sorted—the junk pile and the giveaway pile. They load it on the truck, Donny chatting and Rafe adding in *uh-huh* and *no way* at the appropriate times.

So many questions itch at me. If Rafe knew Mom back then, before I was born, then he must have known my father. I want to ask him what my mom was like back then, if he knew her before she was struck by lightning, about Carson, about my grandfather. But I know that now isn't the right time. If he actually comes to fix the garage door, I'll have another chance.

After I get them glasses of cold water, they take off with all the junk piled in the bed of the truck that might be mine in a month.

I sweep out the empty garage and struggle to pull the overhead door closed.

TWENTY-FIVE

I'm a human being and I fall in love
and sometimes I don't have control of every situation.
—Beyonce Knowles (musician)

I hear cars pull into the driveway, then car doors and then Mom's, Ron's, and Sue's voices in the front hall.

"Did Donny come by?" Mom asks, throwing her work bag on the kitchen table. Sue gives me a hug and then she and Ron settle in on the couch, ready to hang out for the rest of the day.

"Yeah, he took pretty much everything," I say. "And that man from last night—Rafe Zamora—helped. He's borrowing the silver truck."

Mom's eyebrows draw together in confusion, but I can't read anything else in her face.

"Okay, well. I'm going to Jay's," I say.

I ride my bike to Jay's. I picture sitting at Jay's kitchen table, the way it used to be—Jay, Serena, and me. All of us distracting each other. Serena would read out class notes in the teacher's voice, showcasing her talent at impressions. Jay would entertain us with fascinating information from his anatomy textbook. And whenever we were working quietly for too long, I'd get up to get us snacks. I miss the three of us.

I ride through town, which is quiet for a Saturday. Even though it's breezy and cool, I'm almost sweating by the time I get to Jay's. I lean my bike against the porch steps and climb them to the side door.

The kitchen windows are cracked open and I hear shouting. The fight is between Jay and Kyle, but I hear their mom, too, saying things like "Boys, come on," and "Jay, stop!"

I look through a windowpane in the door. Jay's face is right in front of Kyle's, which means he's bending down to look at him.

"You have no idea what you're even saying," Jay says. I can't see Kyle's eyes, but I imagine they look scared. I've never seen Jay this angry, and it *is* scary.

"You're not always right," Kyle shouts in his face. "You think you are, but you're not."

Jay shoves him. Kyle loses his balance, the kitchen table catching his fall, but barely.

"That's it!" their mom yells. "Out!"

They both walk toward the dining room and push each other as they go through the doorway. I'm amazed that Kyle would even try to go after Jay—Jay's like three times his size.

"Jay," his mom says, as Jay finally lets Kyle go ahead of him. "Come here please."

"Which is it, Mom? Go or stay?" I've never heard him raise his voice to her before, and it isn't pretty. He's standing close to her, his fists clenched by his sides. And he's big. So, so big.

I see her body tense, but her voice is calm.

"Stay. I want to talk to you."

Kyle, waiting on the other side of the doorway, shrugs and storms off.

Jay stares down his mom. She points at a kitchen chair. He sits.

I should probably leave at this point, but my eyes are glued to Jay. I've never seen him come undone like that.

"Have you been taking your meds?" his mom asks quietly, sitting down next to him.

"Yes," he snaps.

"Have you been eating enough?"

"Yes."

"Do you want to see Dr. Bond?"

"No."

"Then what is it? What's going on? You've been off for a few days." She touches his elbow gently.

He yanks his arm away and stands, scraping the chair on the tile floor. He turns and walks to the stairs, his shoulders sloped.

His mom sits for a few seconds, her face blank, and then she gets up and collects dishes from the table. I open the door, knocking on the window lightly as I do.

"Hi," I say quietly.

"Oh, hi, Rachel," she says, smiling at me sadly. "Did you hear all that?"

"Some."

"Any idea what's going on with him?" she asks.

I shake my head no.

"He told me you were coming, so I know he's expecting you," she says. "You can go up. But if he's still in that mood, just come on back, and I'll keep you company until it passes."

"Okay."

When I get upstairs, Jay's door is closed. I knock softly.

"What?" he says.

"It's me."

There's silence for a few seconds before he says, "Come in."

He's sitting on the floor, his back against the bed. His legs are crossed like a pretzel.

"Are you doing yoga?" I ask. I'm feeling shy, maybe because the last time I was in his room, I was half naked, getting rejected. Or because I'm not sure what to say to him after seeing that other side of him down in the kitchen.

"Breathing."

I sit next to him, tentatively touch his knee.

"How long have you been here?" he asks.

"A few minutes."

"So my mom told you I kinda freaked out?"

"Yeah, well, I heard a little from outside."

He cringes.

"What's going on?" I ask.

I watch his profile as he stares straight ahead. A look on his face of . . . regret? Shame? I'm not sure.

I put my hand in his hair. He closes his eyes. I should be more protective of my heart, but it's like now that we've broken the seal, I can't imagine not touching him. I get up on my knees and I stroke the back of his neck with my fingertips, concentrating on the thickness of his hair, the way it curls at the back. I can feel his tension, so I reach around and start to dig my fingers in a little, to work the knots in his neck and shoulders. With his eyes closed, I can look at him as much as I want without making him uncomfortable. I study his eyelids, the dark eyelashes pointed toward the top of his cheeks. His nose, big, but not too big for his face. There's some stubble on his cheeks, chin, above his lip. Just a hint.

As my eyes settle on his lips, I feel warmth everywhere. In my chest, across my arms, down to my abdomen, and below. I continue rubbing his neck as I lean toward him. He opens his eyes and puts his arms around my waist.

I press my lips on his and he kisses me back. I feel all the softness and wet warmth of his mouth. I could die from how good it feels. He pulls me closer and I make a wish that we can just do this forever. His hands travel under my shirt, up my back to my shoulder blades. I don't break the kissing, but I slowly move so that I can sit on him, straddling his still-crossed legs. He makes a little grunt in his throat when I settle myself on him. I can feel him through our two layers of jeans. He wants me. As much as I want him.

We're breathing so heavily suddenly, it's like we're running a marathon. But then he pulls his lips away from mine.

"You okay?" I whisper.

He doesn't answer, just nods slightly, his eyes closed.

I wait. Then he gives a little sigh and starts kissing me again.

I want to take his shirt off, to feel his bare chest and back, but then I'd have to break our lips apart to get it off, and I can't risk that, so I just slide my hands under his shirt and I feel his body, so big, warm, his skin so soft. He flinches a little when my fingers trail his side, a ticklish spot. His hands move down the back of my jeans over my underwear, and now he's holding my butt with both hands, pulling me closer.

Just then Jay's door opens, and I jump.

"Oh god," Kyle says, covering his eyes and closing the door.

"Oh my god, I thought it was your mom," I whisper to Jay. If she'd seen us, I would have died right there.

"Jesus," Kyle says through the door.

I sit next to Jay and lean back against the bed, close my eyes, take a breath.

"What do you want?" Jay asks.

Kyle opens the door a crack but doesn't come in.

"Hi, Rachel," he says without looking at me.

"Hi," I squeak out.

"Dude, I was going to see if you were okay, but I guess you're more than okay," he says.

"Yeah," Jay says. "Sorry about before."

Kyle opens the door more and looks at Jay.

"Did you just apologize to me?"

"I guess I did," Jay says.

"Wow, I gotta go mark the calendar."

He closes the door and we hear his heavy footsteps run down the stairs.

"That's so embarrassing," I say.

"I'm sure he knew something was going on with us."

"There's something going on with us?" I ask, punching his arm lightly.

He smiles.

"But," he says.

"Ugh," I say. "Please no buts today. I know we have to talk about it at some point, define it, whatever. But not today, okay?"

"Rach." He takes my hand in his. "It was because of this. I think my anger burst before was because of this."

I shake my head.

"That doesn't make any sense," I say. "Why would this make you angry?"

"Not angry, but I freak out from frustration or anxiety or anything negative, too. It's not always anger."

"So this is negative?" I ask, feeling that familiar dull pain in my chest. The one I get when my heart's being broken.

"This is what I wanted to talk to you about before," he says. "When I'm with you like this, I feel out of control."

"For me, that's a good thing," I say. "I feel free."

"I don't. Losing control is what happened before with Kyle and like with that guy Jeremy in middle school. And it's like I can see myself freaking out but I can't stop it. And when I'm with you like this, kissing, I feel out of control. It's scary for me."

I let the air out through my almost closed lips. I lean back against the bed, staring at the ceiling, which has a small crack just above my head.

Jay goes on.

"I work hard to stay in control. Even with the meds, it's a struggle. And the feelings that come up when this happens," he says, gesturing back and forth between us, "they're so much like what I've been trying to control."

I nod, afraid that if I talk, the tears will come.

"I want this," he says. "But you heard me before with Kyle. I wanted to rip his throat out because he said artificial turf is the same thing as sod. And when I told him he was wrong, he tried to argue with me. And *that's* why I nearly punched him. That's not normal. Even for me, it's not normal. Not anymore. I thought I was done with those kinds of reactions. But something is making them come back. And I think it's this."

"Maybe it's something else," I say, but I don't know why I'm bothering. Jay never loses an argument.

"Can we just be the regular us again for the rest of the day?"

I nod.

"Let's eat something," he says.

We go down to the kitchen, and he opens the refrigerator. I admire his broad back as his shirt exposes a bit of skin when he leans down to get lettuce from the bottom drawer.

"What were you talking with Sawyer Baskin about the other day? In the parking lot," he asks.

"Nothing. He was just apologizing for Wade. Why? Were you jealous?"

"Yeah." I knew he'd tell the truth.

"Good," I say. "But you have nothing to be jealous about."

He shakes his head slowly as he starts making sandwiches, and I know he's distracted by the number of slices of turkey he should use on mine.

The way Jay makes his sandwiches has nothing to do with being anal or neat or anything. I know this because with everything else, he's messy. The floor of his room is always covered in clothes, books, and empty potato chip bags. I've watched him shove his laptop into his backpack, and then later pull out crushed homework assignments and turn them in wrinkled or even ripped. But Jay once told me that when everything else is so unpredictable, he likes to have the turkey sandwiches as the one thing that will be exactly the same every day. For a while, when we'd go out for pizza during lunch period, he'd still bring his sandwich. But in the last few months, he's been okay with ditching the sandwich on those days.

He puts our plates down side by side at the kitchen counter, and we sit on the bar stools. He leans over, takes my hand in his, and squeezes. Not a sexy, *let's get it on some more right here in the kitchen* squeeze, but more like *I'm glad you stayed and you're here eating a sandwich with me* squeeze. I squeeze back.

TWENTY-SIX

I believe in love at first sight.
You want that connection,
and then you want some problems.
–Keanu Reeves (actor)

On Monday, I take the bus home from school because Jay has a doctor's appointment. After his anger burst on Saturday, his mom convinced him to see his therapist for a check-in. I'd forgotten how awful the bus was—hot, bumpy, and loud. And so, so long. By the time I walk home from the bus stop at Route 6 with my bag loaded with books, I'm sweaty and starving.

No one's at the house. I go into Mom's bathroom to see if her skirt and blouse are hanging up on the shower-curtain rod. She always does that so the wrinkles will steam out while she showers. The clothes are gone, which means she's at work. Mom can't resist rushing off to the aid of any strike survivor within a ten-hour drive, even if it's in the middle of a workday. So any day she doesn't lose her job at the bank is a good day in my book.

In her bedroom, I look for the red leather box and find it immediately on the floor shoved between her bed and nightstand. It's not even hidden.

I open the box and peer inside. There's a stack of a few folded papers and a couple of envelopes held together by a rubber band. A photo is pushed up against the side of the box. I pull it out, careful to remember exactly where it was so I can put it back the same way. It's a picture of Mom. Even though it's in color, the photo looks like it's from another era. She wears no makeup, her hair's windblown, and her face looks fuller than it does now. She's smiling. She looks happy. I turn the photo over. *I miss you. –N* is written on the back.

I pull out the letters. This is it. If I look at these letters,. I'm betraying Mom. But I need to know more. After Reed, I don't even know if I believe in soul mates anymore, but if these letters can tell me anything about Mom and Carson and how all this started, and how it ended, I want to read them. I want to know why it was so hard for her to move back here, what she was running from when she left. I want to know more about my father, more than just the tidbits Mom has given me over the years—handsome, a football player, smart, thoughtful. There has to be more.

I peel off the rubber band, which is loose with age, and unfold the top letter, my heart pounding.

Dear Carson,

Hi! I figured I wouldn't hear from you, being a boy and all. So, I'm writing to you. You don't have to write back. I'm sure you won't.

It's weird to be back in Connecticut and back in school. Even after all these weeks, I think about you and everyone there every day. I've never had friends like you guys. I wish I could live there all year and go to school with you.

My dad and I fight all the time. He doesn't let me do anything, he's so much more overprotective here. He seems so unhappy and angry all the time, and I'm the only one around, so it's like living with Eeyore. I can't wait to get back to Wellfleet. I know it sucks to be a single dad, but I wish he could just pretend it didn't suck that bad, you know?

The good news is that we rented the same cottage from last summer, and this time for five weeks. We'll be there starting July 21st. So, I'm excited about that!

How's football? How is everyone?

Write back if you want. Or you don't have to.

I miss you.
Love,
Naomi

Her handwriting is different than it looks now. It was loopy, bubbly, younger. Her whole voice sounds young, and I realize that when she wrote this letter, she was probably younger than I am now. The next in the stack is a photocopied letter with typed pages stapled behind it.

Dear Naomi,

I'm glad you're coming back this summer. It will definitely be fun. I'm sorry your dad is being a jerk. I hope that gets better. It's almost like summer never happened here. Football practice is brutal but at least I'll get a lot of playing time this year. Maybe you can come up one weekend and see a game. I'm sure you could stay with one of the girls, or even at my house if your dad says it's okay.

So, you were always asking about my writing and I never showed you anything—I guess I was worried that nothing I'd written was good enough for you to see. But I wrote something for English class last month—the assignment was to write a story about something important that happened over the summer. Anyway, my English teacher submitted some of them to our school's literary magazine, and they published mine. It's about that day we met—with the seal rescue. It's kind of embarrassing. When you read it, you'll see why. But I guess since it's in a publication and everyone here has already seen it and given me shit about it, I might as well show you. So . . .here it is.

Carson

The next sheets are photocopied pages from the *Nauset Literary Magazine.*

THE SEAL

By Carson Hayes

He didn't often go to the beach in the summer. Mostly the locals left the beaches to the tourists. But his football coach told them to run on the sand for at least half of their runs over the summer—something about give and turf and ankle-strengthening.

Luckily, it was an overcast day with rain on the way, so Lecount Hollow Beach was practically empty. And it wasn't too hot.

After he ran, he bent forward and let the sweat from his hair drip onto the sand. Then he sat on the towel he'd left on the beach.

He stared at the ocean and wondered how he'd become so immune to its beauty. That wasn't supposed to happen. And then, out of the corner of his eye, something moved, and he looked, and there was a girl about his age. And something happened to him when he saw this girl on the beach. He stared at her—her thick wavy brown hair, her muscular legs and small feet, her navy blue bikini top that was sprinkled with tiny white dots. She was small, and for the briefest moment, the image of lifting her in his arms and holding her flashed into his head, and he nearly felt the light weight of her against him.

The girl was sitting with a man—her father. He was packing up their things—umbrella, chair, cooler. The girl stayed sitting on the sand, hugging her knees to her chest, her eyes focused on the water. The father said something, and she nodded, not looking at him.

"One hour then," the father said. "And wait in the parking lot. I don't want to have to come back down the dune."

Then the man trudged across the hot sand, making his way up the dune.

The boy lay down on his side so he could watch the girl less obviously. She was so still, he couldn't even tell if she blinked at all. He stared and memorized for so long, he must have fallen asleep, because the next thing he knew, he opened his eyes and she was gone. He watched the spot where she'd been, willing her to come back. He could almost see the indentation in the sand where she'd been sitting.

Then he heard a sound. At first he thought it was the cry of a seagull, but then he saw that it was the girl, and she was crying. The beach was practically empty now—it was already five o'clock. She was close to the water's edge, kneeling with her back to him.

He stood and walked toward her. He heard her clearly now, sniffling and talking softly.

"I'm sorry," she said. "I want to help you, but I can't if you won't let me near you. I don't know what to do."

And then he saw that she was talking to a small seal whose flippers were tangled in yellow fishing line. It was barking and flapping itself up and down like a seesaw.

The boy crouched down next to the girl. She turned to him, her skin blotchy from crying, her dark blue eyes pained.

"Shhh," he said. "You'll scare her."

He hadn't meant it to sound so harsh, but it was true. If the seal thought it was in danger, it would go back into the water, and then they'd never be able to help it.

"I'll go for help," he said. "There's a pay phone in the parking lot."

He started to stand, but the girl shot out her hand and grabbed his wrist. He felt the pleasant shock of her skin on his.

"Don't go," she said.

"One of us has to."

"Okay." She nodded.

He ran as fast as he could up the dune and to the pay phone. Once the operator connected him to the Wildlife Rescue, he told them about the seal and asked them to hurry to Lecount Hollow Beach.

When he got back to the girl, she was exactly where he'd left her. He was afraid she'd be gone, like maybe the whole thing had been a dream.

"They usually come pretty quick," he said to her quietly. "Let's go over here." He pointed to his towel. "If we stay too close, we'll scare her and she'll go back into the water."

"How do you know it's a she?" the girl asked, her voice cracking a little.

They walked slowly back to his towel, and she turned several times to make sure the seal was staying put.

"I guess I don't," he said. "I just always think of sea animals as she's."

She smiled, and it lit up her dark blue eyes. "I always think of them as he's."

"Oh, come on," he said. "Even dolphins?"

She nodded.

"Dolphins are totally she's," he said.

She sat down on half of his towel, making sure that they could still see the lump of the seal down the beach. She smoothed out the other half of the towel for him to sit on, which he did. Her hair smelled like coconut.

"Do you live here?" she asked.

"Born and raised."

"I've never met anyone my age from here before."

"You mean us Wellfleet 'townies'? We like to keep hidden in the summer," he said. "You people can be pretty obnoxious sometimes."

"Hey," she said.

"I only speak the truth."

"Thanks for not making fun of me about crying over a seal."

"Why would I make fun of you? It's sad."

The seal was quiet now, lying still.

"Will she die?" the girl asked, and he noticed that she'd called the seal a "she."

"No. The rescue team will cut off the line and get her back in the water, no problem. But if we'd scared her and she went back into the water now, she might die. She can't swim with her flippers like that."

Soon after, the rescue team came—a guy held the seal down while a woman cut through the line with a sharp knife. Once it was free, the seal moved like an awkward caterpillar into the water and swam away. Everyone clapped and cheered.

The rescue team left, and then the girl looked at her watch.

"I promised my father I'd wait for him up in the parking lot. He's probably already there."

The boy said good-bye, but he felt a heaviness that he'd never felt before.

He was afraid he'd never see her again.

"Hey," he said. "I work at the Newsdealer. Come say hi sometime."

The girl's face lit up. "I will."

She waved as she went up the dune.
The boy watched her go.
Later, he would realize he felt different.

My chest is tight with longing. When I turned seven, Sue and Ron took me to the aquarium while Mom was at work, and they bought me a stuffed blue seal in the gift shop. When we got back to our apartment, I showed Mom the seal and she told me a story about a real-life seal whose flipper had been tangled in a net on the beach and that she and a friend helped get the seal safely back into the water. I'd loved that story, and it made Mom into even more of a hero in my mind than she already was. The seal was immediately promoted to the top of my stuffed animal hierarchy. Something about reading Carson's words, knowing that Mom was telling the truth about the seal, made my heart feel a little too big for my chest.

I wonder why Mom has never shown me this, why she's never shared anything real about Carson with me.

It's getting late; I can feel the room darkening little by little. Mom will be home from work soon. I decide to allow myself one more letter for now, maybe two.

TWENTY-SEVEN

It is not love that is blind, but jealousy.
—Lawrence Durrell (writer)

The next few letters are all from Mom to Carson.

Dear Carson,

I'm sorry I didn't get to say good-bye to you. I know you were at the hospital. My dad told me you were in the waiting room. I wish I'd told him it was okay for you to come in, but I felt so strange and I was afraid to see your face—that what I'd said on the beach had scared you away. It scared me. And I'm the one who said it.

After you left, Dad packed up the cottage, and as soon as they discharged me, we drove straight from the hospital home to Connecticut. Dad didn't trust the doctors in Hyannis—he wanted to take me to our doctor at home. So here I am.

I have a ruptured eardrum, which will heal, and I have a few burn marks on my hip from where the lightning exited my body. I'm not in pain, but the doctor said some people have other issues as they get older—like nerve pain and memory loss and depression. They don't understand a lot about the effects of a lightning strike. It's different for everyone. None of this scares me. What scares me is what I saw after the lightning. I didn't tell my dad or the doctors because I think they'd try to lock me up. But I know I'm not crazy. Something happened right after I was struck. I was trying to tell you but then the paramedics came. I could tell by the look on your face that you weren't really hearing me, or you thought I was just in shock or something. I wasn't. I saw what I saw. And I still do.

I felt the jolt right when everything turned orange for that brief second. I know you weren't struck, but I know you saw it too and heard the crash, the explosion. Afterward, with the rain falling and my hands in the wet sand, your face leaning over me, it got really quiet. Probably because of my eardrum, but it was more than that. It was like the world stopped moving for just a millisecond, enough so it could show me.

It was like a vision or prophecy, but it wasn't something I saw or heard. It was like suddenly, I just knew. *Like I know my own name. The lightning made me know that you are my soul mate. I know that sounds crazy. I've never been much of a believer in soul mates, I've never yearned for a prince charming or anything. That's why I know that this is real. Because it didn't come from me. It came from somewhere else. I think it was the lightning, Carson. I'm so scared. And I'm scared telling you this because I think you'll push me away but I need you to help me understand what this means.*

I know I'm only sixteen and you're only seventeen and we've only kissed once, and this is probably way too heavy from a girl you thought would be a little summer fling, but I needed to tell you. I'll understand if you don't write back, but I hope you will.

Naomi

Dear Carson,

I was so happy when I got your letter. Thank you, thank you for believing me. I know it's weird. And I'm wondering if there's something wrong with my brain. It's happened two more times since I wrote you. Once when I saw this girl at school—I don't even know her name—but everything got very still and she looked at me and I just knew *who she was meant to be with. And I don't even know the guy, it was just, I can't explain it, I knew. The other time it was one of my dad's work friends. He and his wife were over for dinner and it happened again. And I knew that he and his wife were not soul mates, and I could see who was his soul mate—and it was a man! And Carson, I wanted to tell him. I wanted him to know. But again . . . my dad would think I was crazy. Everyone would. Thank you for believing me.*

My dad said I could call you next week, but only for a few minutes. He's really strict about long distance calls.

Naomi

Dear Carson,

I know it's hard for you to talk on the phone with classes and practice and everything. Call whenever you can. Is the phone you called from before in the dorm lounge or do you have one in your room? I'll send you a care package and you can share it with your roommates. I'm glad they're not all football players too, or I'd never be able to make enough cookies for all of you. I'm not sure if we'll get any of the West Alabama games up here, but I'm sure we can find a sports bar to watch you play. You've worked so hard for this. You deserve to play. It's not your fault Gus was injured. Stop feeling guilty. Please.

Dad and I finally finished unpacking the new house. It's amazing—it's right on the bay—I can walk out my door and down the steps any time I want. I can tell already that we will be happier here. School starts tomorrow. I can't believe I'm going to be a senior at your high school and you're gone. Too ironic. But it doesn't matter, right? Forever is a long time. What's a few years?

I love you,

Naomi

Dear Carson,

Maybe I wasn't being fair when I got so angry, but you said you'd be home for the whole week of Christmas, and I only got to see you twice. It's not enough. I just feel like I'm waiting for life to start. I'm back here in a permanent state of waiting . . . waiting for you to call, to visit, to graduate.

Yes, Rafe and I have been spending time together. I know that makes you feel strange, but nothing has happened between us. It's not what you think. He's your friend and you owe him an apology for what you said on New Year's Eve. I've never seen you act that way.

I think maybe I just need a break from waiting.

Naomi

Rafe. Rafe isn't a common name. There couldn't have been more than one Rafe who lived here then, right? So now I know for sure. Not only did Rafe know my father, but he was his friend. And something may have been going on between Mom and Rafe while Carson was away at college. Or at least Carson had been suspicious.

Carson,

I'm not good at writing letters. But you won't answer my calls and you probably never will. I just want you to know that you were right—I do love Naomi. But she's still waiting for you. She won't be with me until you let her go. It's not fair, man. For any of us. Just let her go. Let her be happy.

Rafe

Oh my god. Mom was with Rafe while she was still with Carson. And she lied to Carson about it. I feel bad for Rafe, but I also want to kill him. But then I open the last paper in the stack.

Carson! I just got your message. I've been trying to call but I can't get through. Obviously, I'll talk to you before you get this, but I'm writing it anyway. Yes, yes, yes! I will move to Detroit with you! I can't wait. I'm so happy you got this job! It's finally here. The beginning of our forever!

I love you so much,
Naomi

Now I'm completely confused. And there's only one more letter left to read. It's the envelope that's marked NAOMI. The one that had been sealed when I first saw it in that cardboard box, but now has been opened. I slide my fingers inside the envelope, grasping the paper.

But just then, I hear tires crunching on the shells in the driveway. I quickly put the letters back in order, wrap the rubber band around them, and replace them in the box, then put the box back where I found it. My heart races as I run to my room and close the door, pulling my laptop out of my backpack and jumping onto the bed so I'll look like I've been doing homework since I got home.

TWENTY-EIGHT

Opposition is true friendship.
–William Blake (poet)

The next day, it's too cold to eat outside, and I'm not in the mood to sit in the loud caf, so Jay and I plan to eat in his car. I want to tell him about the letters.

I stop in the bathroom before heading out to the parking lot. As I flush, I hear the generic sound of kids in the halls going from class to lunch as the door to the bathroom opens. Then the noise muffles as it closes, and I hear Serena's voice.

"But you said you'd come for Memorial Day," she says. Her voice sounds soft and high-pitched, babyish, the way she always sounded when her mom told her she couldn't go out on a school night.

"I know, but—" She's quiet for a few seconds. "She'd be fine with it. Or you could stay at a hotel."

Serena sighs.

"But August is so far away. Yeah, okay. I'll talk to Mom. No, I'll tell her." She sniffles. "Bye, Dad."

Now I feel weird having heard her conversation with her dad, who lives in Canada. They're close, but she hardly ever sees him. I step out of the stall. When Serena sees me behind her in the mirror, she looks momentarily confused. She turns around and wipes a smudge of mascara under one of her eyes with a tissue.

"Hi," she says.

I miss her. I miss her voice and her laugh. I miss everything about her.

"You okay?" I ask, moving to the sink to wash my hands.

"I guess. My dad's not coming in May like he promised."

"That sucks," I say.

This is the first time we've spoken since she dropped me off after the bonfire that night. Eleven days but it feels like years. I'm not sure if our friendship is salvageable, and if it is, I wouldn't know what to say to make things right. I don't even know what happened between us.

"Canada doesn't celebrate American Memorial Day, obviously," she says. "So he can't leave work."

"I'm sorry."

I grab a paper towel to dry my hands, and she leans her lower back against the sink and watches me.

"So," she says, the way she used to when she was getting ready to share some good gossip.

"So," I say, and I can't help smiling a little.

This has been one of our rituals from when we first met, right after I moved to Wellfleet. Mom and I had gone to the market—one of the few times Mom agreed to shop in town. I'd just grabbed a box of tampons off the shelf when Mom called me over to the end of the aisle, introduced me to Serena, and said we'd both be starting ninth grade at Nauset. Her mom had been Mom's hygienist when she'd gone to the dentist the day before, and they thought it was hilarious that they were now running into each other at the market.

Our moms had kept chatting, while Serena and I stood next to each other, silently.

Finally, Serena said, "So . . ."

And I'd said, "So . . ."

She'd smiled. "So, light flow, huh?"

And then we'd burst out laughing and that was the start of the two of us. And then, because Jay's locker was in the same row as mine, after school he started walking with me to Serena's locker and then we'd all go out to the buses together. And that was the start of the three of us.

And I miss us. I want to tell her that, to tell her how much I miss her, and us. I want to tell her about the letters I found. And about Jay. I want to ask her why she suddenly stopped answering my calls and texts—was it really because I'd gone off with Sawyer that night? Did Lindsay and those girls talk her into ditching me? It's hard to imagine anyone convincing Serena to do something she doesn't want to do, so there has to be something else. But I can't find the right words to ask any of these questions.

She doesn't smile back at me.

"So, you and Jay," she says. "That's a thing that's happening?"

This isn't what I expected her to say. Not at all. And definitely not with that icy tone.

I try to mask my surprise with an indifferent shrug.

"So, maybe he's the one?" she continues. "Or are you just messing with him?"

"What?"

"After how things went down with Reed, I just figured you wouldn't be ready to get back into that soul mate game. Kind of risky," she says. "The two of you."

My mouth drops open in shock. She's never been so . . . mean before. I'm unable to speak.

She tosses the crumpled tissue in the garbage and leaves the bathroom.

I fume as I walk out of the school building and head toward the parking lot. I shiver, but I'm not positive whether it's from the cold air outside or what Serena said.

When I get to Jay's car, I'm relieved he's already in there with the heat going.

"Serena just accosted me in the bathroom," I say, slamming the door.

He stops unwrapping his sandwich.

"What did she say?"

"She asked if we were together."

His eyes widen, but he doesn't say anything.

"I didn't answer her," I say.

He looks relieved.

"So, you're glad I didn't tell her?" I ask.

"Yes," he says.

"Fine," I say, a little hurt.

"What, did you want me to jump up and down because Serena noticed we might be doing whatever this undefined thing is that we're doing? How did you expect me to react? Maybe you shouldn't have told me."

"You're right. I shouldn't have told you. But I have history with her and I—"

"I have history with her, too," he says.

Jay misses her, too. He misses the three of us as much as I do. She'd probably have some interesting way to define our undefined thing. Maybe she would've told us what to do about what's happening with us. And maybe he knows that.

TWENTY-NINE

Love is friendship that has caught fire.
It settles for less than perfection and makes allowances
for human weaknesses.
–Ann Landers (advice columnist)

As soon as I get in Jay's car after school, he asks me what's wrong.

"Nothing," I say.

"I can tell by your face. Something's wrong. Are you still upset about Serena?"

"Not really."

"Is it because of what happened at my house the other day? I thought we were okay."

"No, we're good."

"Did something else happen?"

"I guess I'm just stressed out. The meeting with everyone coming, and I don't know if—" I didn't realize that I was this worried about whether Reed would show up, but I am. I don't want Jay to know that, though. "I don't know if the garage will be ready on time. And the letters. It's kind of freaking me out a little. But I'm okay."

"Maybe reading them isn't good for you," he says. "You need to protect yourself."

I laugh. "We've kissed twice and suddenly you're this fully evolved, understanding . . . man-person?"

"Man-person?"

I shrug.

"Maybe I am evolving," he says and smiles. A wide, toothy one. "I do feel a little different. After the other day."

"Like, different toward me?"

"No. I mean, yes, but I mean like just the way I'm thinking about things. You. Life. About the things I said about control, letting go, that kind of stuff."

"Whoa," I say. "I'm listening . . ."

"I talked about it with Dr. Bond, but I haven't fully formulated my thoughts about it yet. I want to be sure I get it right before I share it."

He takes off his seatbelt and twists toward me. He picks up my hand from where it rests on my knee and holds it in his big hands, which are warm. Hot, even. My hand completely disappears into his. And I feel held and calm.

"I'm going to help you move into the garage, if you want my help," he says. "But if it's not ready before your mom's meeting, you should stay with me."

I'm not someone who's ever needed to be taken care of really, but it feels good anyway. I know that Jay knows that about me. He doesn't think I'm needy; he's just showing that he cares.

"Okay," I say.

He turns his face forward again, looking straight ahead.

"I know I'm the one who needs to change or do whatever it is to make this work, Rach."

His voice sounds pained.

"I don't want you to change," I say. "I want you to be you. And if we want to stop doing this undefined thing, we can. We're still just us."

He takes his hands away from mine and rubs his palms on his jeans.

"I don't want to stop doing the undefined thing, do you?" he asks.

"No."

He clears his throat.

"We'll meet halfway," he says.

We sit for what seems like forever. Just sitting, not looking at each other. The silence builds tension. A sweet, jumpy tension. I hear him breathing, and it sounds heavier than normal. My entire body tingles with this little game we're playing with each other—or at least that's what I think is happening.

Suddenly, I feel like I'm breaking out in a sweat, my body flushed with heat, wanting his touch. But I'm not going to kiss him. No. I will not be the one this time. It can't be me.

I try to breathe out a bit of the ache, resigned that nothing will happen. That the tension will ratchet up and then nothing. And then I hear him shift in his seat, his hand reaches behind my head. He nudges me so that I turn my face toward him.

"Rach," he whispers. "Come here."

He pulls my head toward him so gently it's almost like a suggestion, not a real thing. A question. Just an idea.

I meet him halfway, just like he said. I move my face toward him a bit, my lips closer to his. And I wait. I can almost feel the nerves coming off him in waves. I want nothing more than to relieve his anxiety immediately. To grab him, pull him to me, press my lips to his instead of the other way around. It would be easier that way. For both of us. But I wait. It has to be him this time. I know it. And he knows it.

I close my eyes. Maybe that will help. If I'm not watching him trying to get this thing done—and before I can even finish my thought, his lips are on mine. So lightly, almost like a caress more than a kiss. I open my eyes a bit and see that he's pulled back just an inch or two.

Please, please, don't stop there. But I don't say it. I just close my eyes and wait more.

It takes him a bit longer than I'd like, basically until I'm ready to kill him, but then he does it. Still soft at first, but when I respond, encouraging him with my lips, he kisses me harder, and his kiss is deep and sure. I'm alive, and for the moment, nothing else matters but what is happening with our mouths and the sensations in the rest of my body. And that Jay wants it, too.

Jay and I decide to postpone homework. Neither of us wants this afternoon to end. We grab some sandwiches for dinner from the General Store and decide to eat on the beach at Newcomb. It's warmed up a little since lunch, so we won't freeze. Plus, the two of us are so hot for each other right now, cold isn't even in my vocabulary.

Route 6 is jammed going east toward Provincetown, so we go the back way. We drive down Ocean View slowly, Jay's left hand loosely on the steering wheel, his right hand interlaced with mine on my lap. I stare at our hands—the way my small fingers fit between his huge ones, the way my pale skin blends with his slightly darker skin. I'm thinking about how strange it is that something as simple as clasping hands together can feel so good, inside and out.

And then a flash of silver catches my eye. Donny Lash's truck—possibly my future truck—is turning into the Cahoon Hollow Beach parking lot. I'm pretty sure I can make out Rafe's bald head in the driver's seat. But it's the shadow in the passenger side that makes me sit up straighter and lean forward for a better view. It's Mom's profile, her wavy hair in a ponytail bobbing up and down, her hands gesturing as she speaks.

"Wait. Turn around," I say to Jay.

"What's wrong?" he asks.

"Can we just—will you pull into Cahoon? I think my mom—I just need to see something."

"What is it?" But he turns the car around and pulls onto the dirt road.

"There, go right, to the Beachcomber lot," I say.

The truck is parked right next to the restaurant, but its engine is still running.

I point at the far end of the lot. "Just pull up over there," I say, still staring at the two heads in the truck.

Jay does what I ask, but I can tell he's reluctant.

"Are we spying on your mom?"

"Sort of, I don't know. She said she'd be home all afternoon with Sue and Ron planning the meeting."

"Maybe she's just getting dinner and bringing it back."

Rafe and Mom are looking at each other—I can see their profiles perfectly now.

"Maybe. But he isn't a survivor. He's from before my mom moved to Detroit. He's in the letters. He was my father's friend and—"

Just then Rafe lifts his hand and puts it on the side of Mom's face. I can't see Mom's expression, but she definitely doesn't move away. In fact, it looks like she leans into his hand.

"Rach," Jay says. "I don't know—this is weird. Can we leave?"

I nod because I have no voice.

Jay drives out of the parking lot, back onto Ocean View.

"I need to get back to my house," I say when my voice returns.

I need to read the last letter. I need to know exactly what happened between Mom and Carson, and who Rafe is to my mom. Because if she was in love with Rafe, and Carson wasn't her soul mate, then my mom has been lying to me my entire life.

Jay doesn't push back about changing our plan. He doesn't say anything. He just nods and turns toward Route 6.

We ride in silence for a few minutes.

"I'm sorry," I say finally. "I just need to do something."

"It's okay," he says.

When we pull into my driveway, Mom's car is gone but Ron's and Sue's are there. So she must have met Rafe somewhere and left her car there while she was in the truck with him.

"What do you want me to do?" Jay asks, his voice even. "Should I go?"

I hesitate.

"It won't take long, if you want to come in."

Jay puts his car in park, but he doesn't move to take off his seatbelt. My door is already open, one foot on the sea shell gravel.

"I'll come back in an hour," he says. "Is that okay?"

I pull my foot back into the car, lean over, and kiss him on his cheek, which is rough and warm. I want to keep kissing him, but I know I have to do this first.

"Thank you," I say.

I try to sneak into the house, but I'm not quiet enough.

"Naomi?" Sue calls out from the back room.

"No, it's me," I say, poking my head into the room where she and Ron and Angela, who just arrived from Virginia, are on the couch, a bunch of papers on the coffee table in front of them.

"Hi, Angela," I say. I try to make my voice sound excited to see her since it's been a few months.

She comes over and gives me a hug. Her perfume smells like peonies.

"Hi, sweetie. It's so good to see you," she says. I can tell by the pity in her eyes that she's about to say something about Reed.

"Naomi just ran out for takeout," Sue says, saving me. "We thought you were her getting back."

"Just me."

They smile at me and I rush off to Mom's room and close the door. I pray the traffic is bad enough to keep her away a little longer.

I pull out the box, which is right where I left it, and reach for the envelope at the bottom of the stack.

THIRTY

If you read somebody's diary, you get what you deserve.
—David Sedaris (writer)

Just as I pull the envelope out of the box, I hear cars in the driveway. Mom. I slide the envelope into the waist of my jeans, and put the box back.

I walk to the back room, hoping I appear calmer than I feel. Mom's pulling takeout food from a bag as Ron, Sue, and Angela *ooh* and *aah* over everything she's gotten.

I hear a bang from the garage.

"Rafe is here fixing the garage door," Mom says, and, though no one else would notice, I see a little pink on her neck.

"Great," I say, trying to make my voice sound normal.

"You want fried clams? I got a couple of extra orders."

"No thanks," I say. "Jay's supposed to be here any second."

I go out the front door, thinking I won't see Rafe if he's by the garage, but just as I slide the door closed, he's walking back to the truck.

"Hi," he says to me. "It was stubborn but that overhead door should be running smoothly now."

"Thanks, that was really nice of you," I say.

"Can I give you a ride somewhere? I know how Donny feels about you riding your bike out on the roads."

"That's okay, my friend is picking me up soon."

"Good, that's good."

He looks uncomfortable. And I can tell it's not a feeling he's used to. My idea of asking him about Carson and my mom—I can't do it. He's standing right there and he probably has answers, but I can't do it.

"That's an interesting necklace," he says. "Is it from the beach down here?"

I reach up and touch the necklace—the scallop shell.

"I'm not sure. My mom gave it to me."

He nods. "It's a pretty one."

I smile. "Thanks again for picking up the stuff and fixing the door."

"Anytime," he says. "See you soon."

He gets in the truck and drives away.

I walk to the end of the driveway and sit on a grassy spot. I pull out the envelope and hope I have enough time to read the letter and get it back into the box before Jay comes.

Naomi,

I know I wasn't being fair this morning. I thought after everything we've been through, after all these years, there'd be nothing left to stop us from being together. I know we're young, but I thought we could've gone to Detroit together, had this baby, and started our family. I was picturing us with a baby in that second room of the apartment I leased.

But I want you to know I heard what you were saying. It took me a couple of hours before I allowed myself to understand, but I do now. I know you're not ready—we're not ready—to have a baby. I know you've been trying to figure out who you are since the lightning—aside from my soul mate, aside from the girl who can see soul mates. I get that now. And I get how having a baby at this point in our lives would just make it even harder for you.

I went to your house, but you were already gone. I drove straight to Hyannis, to the clinic. I was hoping to catch you before you went in, so I could take you in for the appointment. I heard the protesters chanting their judgments, saw their awful anti-choice signs. And then I saw you. You were with Rafe. You were holding his hand.

I went toward the two of you. I was going to push him away and take you in myself.

But as you walked by the protesters, I saw Rafe pull your head into his chest and cover your other ear with his hand so you wouldn't hear the nasty chants. I saw you put your arms around him. I saw him kiss the top of your head as he opened the door to the clinic and walked inside with you.

You broke my heart, Naomi.

I don't understand. All these years, everything has been about you. The lightning told you we were soul mates and I believed you. I've waited for you, waited for you to say it's the right time for us to be together. It was inevitable that we'd end up together, you said, but you weren't ready to start the rest of your life yet. Is this why? Because you love someone else? I believed you when you said the baby is mine. Then why aren't we having this baby together? Or at least, why aren't

I at the clinic with you right now? Why are you with him and not me?

I'm afraid of the answer. I'll admit it. I'm afraid I've wasted the last seven years waiting for you. I'm afraid to ask you if you love him. Because I think I know the answer. I saw the way you looked at each other.

I'm done waiting for you, Naomi. I'm done.

I'm leaving for Detroit tonight. I'm not waiting around for you to decide whether to join me there. I've decided for you. Don't come.

I'm packed up and ready to go. I'm leaving this box of your stuff and the letters I've kept. My mom will drop it off at your house when she has a chance.

I'll go my way, you go yours. I won't be like your dad—I won't tell you you're crazy. I believe that getting struck by lightning gave you this power. I was there. I saw something change in you right after you were struck, when you said that we were soul mates. I still believe you saw it. But I'll say this: The lightning must have gotten it wrong this time.

Please don't contact me.

Carson

I'm numb as I put the pieces together. Carson must have died hours after writing this letter—Mom told me he was killed by a drunk driver on his way to start a new job in Detroit.

Mom had an abortion and then Carson was killed later that night.

Carson couldn't have been my father.

It's possible Mom had a fling and I was just a fling baby, but something about the way she and Rafe looked in the truck today—I just know. Mom and Rafe were in love with each other.

Rafe Zamora is my father. He has to be.

Mom lied to me. About everything.

I put the letter back in the envelope. I run into the house, calling out that I forgot something, and return the letter to the box, which was never meant for me to open. When I get back out front, out of breath, Jay's car is there, idling.

THIRTY-ONE

Truth is like the sun.
You can shut it out for a time, but it ain't goin' away.
–Elvis Presley (musician)

For days since I read Carson's letter, I can't think about anything else. But I can't talk to Mom about it. I want the truth, and I know she's not going to give it to me. I don't want her lies anymore.

I wish I could talk to Serena, tell her everything, and ask her what to do. I can picture the glimmer of anticipation in her eyes, like she'd be excited about the adventure, a truth-seeking mission.

And that's when I realize exactly what she'd say. It's so obvious. There's someone other than Mom who knows the truth.

Rafe Zamora.

Serena would say to start there. So I do. I look for him. The man who was with Rafe the night Mom and I first saw him said they'd be at The Wicked Oyster pretty much every night after work. On Thursday night, I go, but he's not there. He's not there on Friday night either.

On Saturday, the third night I go to the restaurant, Rafe is there, sitting at the bar eating a burger, watching the Bruins game. I want to turn and leave, not do this at all. But I need to. I need to know for sure.

As I approach the barstool next to him, the bartender raises his eyebrows at me. *Don't even think about ordering a drink, little girl*, his eyebrows warn.

Yeah, yeah, okay.

The wooden barstool wobbles as I pull it out and climb up on it awkwardly.

The bartender fills up a water glass and puts it on the bar in front of me.

Rafe takes a sip from his beer. I feel him look sideways at me. He must be wondering why someone would sit right next to him when there are plenty of other open seats at the bar. When I meet his eyes, they widen slightly.

"Rachel," he says. His voice is easy, as though he says my name every day.

"Hi," I say.

I'm trying to act normal even though there is no normal when you're about to basically accuse someone of being your long-lost father. I want to get a better look at him now—would I be able to tell just by looking closely? Is his forehead a little too short like mine? Are his earlobes attached or detached like mine? I wonder about my sanity. I feel like I'm on the verge of hysteria.

He smiles, though it doesn't reach his eyes. He turns and looks behind me.

"She's not here," I say. "It's just me."

He seems to recoil a little, and I suddenly realize what a seventeen-year-old girl sitting next to a middle-aged man at the bar might look like.

"Oh my god, I'm so stupid." I don't mean to say it out loud, but obviously I have because Rafe looks very confused. All of my planned conversation openers go out the window. My words ram forward like a bulldozer.

"So I'm here to ask you one question," I say.

He nods, taking a sip of beer.

"Are you my father?"

He freezes, swallows, then starts coughing uncontrollably.

I push my water glass toward him and watch him, helpless. Rafe takes a sip, holds his finger up to me—*hold on*—pounds his chest with a fist and clears his throat.

"Why are you asking me that?" His voice is hoarse from the coughing.

"Well, are you?"

He clears his throat again and shakes his head no slowly, so slowly it's almost imperceptible. It could be a *no, I'm not your father* shake or a *no, this can't be happening* shake.

This goes on for 3,700 hours, and then he finally answers.

"No. I'm not your father."

I feel like a balloon has popped in my chest and all the air has been let out. But I don't know whether it's relief that I now have an answer or disappointment in the answer itself. Had I wanted Rafe to say yes? And what if he had? Then what? We'd quickly catch up on the last seventeen years, go to a father-daughter dance, and live happily ever after?

"Are you sure?" I ask, my voice cracking.

His face changes then, like he's super sad.

"I'm sure," he says quietly.

Rafe looks into my eyes, like he's carefully weighing a decision.

"Hasn't your mom told you about your father?" he asks.

"Yeah. But not much. Nothing at all, really. Just his name and that he died in a car accident."

"So, if you knew that, then why did you think—"

"Because I know that my mom had an abortion right before he died. And you took her to the clinic."

Rafe coughs again, takes a sip of water, then clears his throat.

"If your mom told you about the clinic, then you must know what happened."

I shake my head no. "She wasn't the one who told me."

"I'm not sure I understand, but you should ask her about it," he says, wearily. "It's really between the two of you."

"Please," I say. "Tell me the truth."

"I can't be the one to tell you, Rachel. I'm sorry your mom hasn't told you everything."

He stares straight ahead, takes a long swig of beer, swallows. He looks at the TV for a minute, flinches when the Bruins miss a shot on goal. That's it?

I slide off the stool and walk about three feet before I hear Rafe say, "Rachel, hold on." I'm not even positive he's said it because he's still staring up at the TV.

I go back and stand next to him, watching his profile, the haphazard scruff on his neck going up and down as he swallows, and then finally speaks.

"I'm not your biological father."

My eyes sting. "Yeah, you mentioned that already."

He made it clear. I don't have a father. My father is dead.

"But," he goes on as if I hadn't said anything, "but I wanted to be your dad. I begged her. And I'm not someone who begs. I wanted to be your dad more than I've ever wanted anything in my life. Even Naomi."

I can barely get my next question out. "Then why weren't you?"

He rubs the back of his neck.

"It was complicated and it wasn't my decision to make."

I stare at a splotch of ketchup on his plate. After a few moments, I feel him looking at me.

"Let her tell you," he says. "She owes you an explanation."

I leave the restaurant and keep walking. I walk to the Harbor, watch the moorings bob in the little swells. I don't stop for too long, I need to keep moving. It doesn't matter how much I walk, though, because I can't digest any of it. I can't make the right connections in my head. I feel empty and stupid. I can't believe I allowed myself to think for a minute that I had a father who was alive. Of course Rafe isn't my father. That would've been too perfect, right? Too neat. The storybook ending—he was right under my nose the whole time!

I walk. Sweat trickles down my spine.

Jay's on an EMS shift, so I can't call him. But it's Serena I really want to talk to anyway. I imagine telling her about Carson and Rafe, the surprised look she'd have on her face—her eyes wide, her head shaking back and forth. I don't know what she'd say, though. And that makes me want to tell her even more.

As I cross back into town, someone in the street shouts my name.

It's Sawyer Baskin in his shiny black RAV4.

"Hey, do you need a ride somewhere?"

I wipe sweat off my forehead with the sleeve of my sweatshirt. "That's okay. Just walking off some steam."

He laughs.

"That's exactly what you looked like. Anything I can help with?"

I try to decide whether he's being suggestive—like he could help me blow off some steam in another way. Probably not. I hope not, anyway.

I shake my head no.

"You sure I can't give you a ride home?"

I consider that for a moment. I don't really have a plan for getting home.

"I'm heading over to your neighborhood anyway," he continues. "Erickson's. You could come with me. If you want. Just a few people. Not a party or anything, just a low-key thing."

"Ha ha." He has to be joking.

He turns down the music in his car.

"Sorry," he says. "That's too weird?"

He scratches the back of his head, and when he stops, his hair juts out at odd angles.

"I'll drop you at home then?" Sawyer asks.

Now that I've stopped walking, the exhaustion kicks in and I want nothing more than to be driven to the door of my house.

"Okay," I say. As I open the passenger car door, he leans over, shoving a few things off the seat and onto the floor.

His car smells like vanilla. Last summer, he'd given Serena and me a ride home from a beach party, and it had smelled like bonfire and stale beer.

He starts to drive and a football bobbles back and forth over my feet.

"You can just toss that into the back seat."

The leather is bumpy. It's not like I've never held a football; school, beach, whatever—there were always balls around. But most of them are Nerf or squishy or kid-sized. I'm not sure I've actually held a game-size football in my hands. I picture Sawyer, his fingertips pressing into the stitches as he backs up, looking for a teammate to pass to. I try to hold the football up with one hand like he does in games. But it's too big. It slips out of my hand, bounces on my lap. Sawyer smiles as he reaches over and grabs it. He holds it up in his right hand, palm down, and it's like he put crazy glue on his hand just before. He drops it behind him and it lands on the back seat.

He glances at me before turning his eyes back to the road, and I'm sure I blush.

"When we get to your house, we can have a quick toss, if you want."

I hear the smile in his voice, that question mark, like *am I making an innuendo? I could be, if you want me to be. But if not, then I'm definitely not. You choose.* He's flexible that way. A few weeks ago, I might have chosen innuendo. But now, I'd just go with straight-up. Sawyer is cute as hell but he isn't who I want.

He slows down before Tim Erickson's house. It's just a quarter of a mile down the road from mine. There are four cars in his driveway.

"You sure you don't want to come?" Sawyer asks. "It's early. No one's really here yet. Just a few of the guys—" He notices my sneer. "The good ones, I mean. Not the dickheads who were giving you shit."

I almost challenge him on that one—aren't they all dickheads? But I'd be wrong. Not all of them are. Sawyer isn't, and neither are the guys he hangs out with most—Jeff, Brad, Erickson.

"Come have a beer out on the deck. It's been proven that just one beer consumed in fresh air can ease a great deal of stress."

He does his cute little persuasive smile then—the same one he probably uses to get anything he wants. I won't fall for that, but at the moment, he's making it sound pretty refreshing. And it's a nice night. And I need a distraction from my confrontation with Rafe, which hasn't solved anything and has only left me with more questions.

"Okay, one beer."

"Cool," he says. "I'll drive you home whenever you want."

I roll my eyes because my house is totally walkable from Erickson's—I won't need a ride home. And he knows that.

Sawyer opens the hatch of his car and hands me a bottle of vodka to carry and then pulls out a case of beer. When we get inside the house, I realize that the four cars outside were misleading. There are at least 15 people, maybe 20. I scowl at Sawyer, but he doesn't seem to notice. I follow him into the kitchen and put the vodka on the counter. I say hi to Erickson and Jeff as Sawyer drops the beer cans two by two into a cooler filled with ice. While he tells them how he'd found me lurking around town, I assess the scene. Mostly guys. A couple of girls I know from classes. And then I see Serena. A tight, low-cut shirt, stretch jeans, tall boots. She doesn't see me because she's walking toward the hallway at the opposite end of the house.

"This was a mistake," I say under my breath. Erickson and Jeff have disappeared, so it's just Sawyer and me again.

"Too late," he says. "You're here. Ready for your deck beer now?"

He digs to the bottom of the cooler and hands me a cold can.

I follow him out to the deck.

THIRTY-TWO

It is one of the blessings of old friends
that you can afford to be stupid with them.
—Ralph Waldo Emerson (writer)

Sawyer was right. Having a drink outside is nice. The beer is cold and the bubbles pop on my tongue as the cool air tickles the skin on my neck in a pleasing way.

Just below the deck is a long winding path down to a small pond. Erickson's house isn't on the bay side of the road like ours. It's right on Clover Pond. And it's one of just a handful of houses with rights to the private pond. I've only seen it from the road and always thought it was just a non-descript tiny pond, but from up here on the deck, I can see, even after the sun has set, that it looks like a three-leaf clover and the water is so clean, the shadow of the moon makes it look silver.

I hear shouting and laughing down at the water. I barely make out shadows of people wobbling around on a floating dock in the middle of the pond.

"People are swimming?" I ask.

"Yeah, stupid fucks," Sawyer says. And he's right. It's too cold to swim.

I sit on a plastic chair that's meant to look like one of those heavy wooden Adirondack chairs. Two girls are nearby, whispering in hushed tones.

I hear a few words: "Amherst, Boston U."

"You going away to college?" Sawyer asks, perching in front of me on an overturned plant pot.

I shake my head and finish my beer.

He reaches into his jacket pocket and pulls out another for me.

"Thanks."

"So you'll stick around here?" he asks.

"I don't know. We moved around so much before we came here, I kind of want to stay put for a while."

It's funny how conversations are so different in the summer than during the school year. No one here talks about school or college during the summer.

"Home is good," he says.

"Yeah." I think about the garage, my future home. "Home is good."

"I want to go to Colorado," he says.

"That's far."

"Skiing, snowboarding, beers outside, that's what I want. And to get out of this small-town, townie-tourist shit."

"Seems like you'd be going from one tourist town to another," I say.

He looks at me, surprised. "I never thought of it that way."

"I didn't mean to make you rethink your life plan," I say, and he laughs.

"Nah," he says. "Denver's a city."

I nod.

"I'm out," he says, holding his beer upside down. "You want another?"

I shake my head no.

"Be right back." He goes inside.

I listen to the echoing sounds of splashing and laughing and yelling from the pond below.

And then I hear Jeff's voice in the kitchen. "You're so playing with fire bringing Rachel here, dude. Lindsay's gonna mutilate you."

"Shut up," Sawyer says. "She's just a friend."

"You don't have to convince me, dude. I don't care. Linds, though? She might need convincing. Rylin and her are on their way here now. Might want to do some advance damage control."

Sawyer swears.

And that's my cue to leave.

Just as I stand, someone pushes me from the side. Hard. It's dark and it happens so fast, it takes me a minute to understand that a guy has pushed past me yelling. He'd come from the path below. He's in underwear and is dripping wet, his feet making slapping sounds on the deck as he makes for the door.

"Call 9-1-1! Where's a phone? Someone call 9-1-1!"

There's commotion in the house. People move in all directions—going outside to see what's going on, heading out to leave before the cops come.

The guy gets to the phone before anyone else and makes the call.

"Hit his head," he says. "A lot of blood." He shouts Erickson's address.

"We need towels for Brad," the guy says. "Lots of towels to stop the bleeding."

He looks at me because I'm closest to him. So, I move into action. I run to a hallway where I assume the bedrooms are and find a linen closet. I grab a stack of white towels and run back outside to the deck.

Sawyer is there now, too. Two guys carry Brad up the path. It's dark, so I can't see well, but I can tell that Brad's head is bleeding heavily.

The two girls who were talking about college cry, saying "oh my god" under their breath.

The guys lay Brad down on the deck.

"Brad!" A girl yells from inside, then runs and gets on her knees next to him.

I try to reach around her to get a towel under Brad's head.

"Katie, move out of the way!" Sawyer says, and she scoots away, sobbing.

Brad is unconscious and the blood from his head immediately turns the white towel red.

"Fuck," I say. My hands are shaking.

Sawyer takes another towel from me and holds it up against the gash in Brad's head. His hands are shaking, too.

"I don't know what I'm doing," he murmurs. "When are they getting here? Fuck. Hurry up, you fuckers."

I look behind me and see Lindsay has arrived and is at the sliding door, her hands in her hair, her ponytail messed up.

The guys who carried Brad stand shivering in their underwear, dripping with freezing pond water.

"Where's Erickson?" Sawyer shouts. "Someone go find Erickson."

Sawyer must see Lindsay standing there but he doesn't say anything.

The wet guys go inside.

I notice Brad is kind of poking out of his underwear, so I throw a towel over his middle.

Sawyer looks at me.

"Can you help me put more pressure on?" he says quietly.

I crouch down and hold my hand over his, pushing the towel tighter to Brad's head. I wonder why Lindsay isn't helping. She's a lifeguard in the summer. She must know what to do. I know nothing.

"Holy shit!" Tim shouts as he runs outside, shirtless and his pants unbuttoned. Serena follows right behind him looking more disheveled than when I'd seen her walking down that hallway. Serena used to joke about Tim Erickson and his skinny, pale, stoner vibe. Her eyes widen when she sees the whole scene, including me.

Then there's commotion from inside and the EMS team pushes through the small crowd gathered at the sliders. The third EMT is Jay. Of course it's Jay. He works the overnight shift every other Saturday.

Jay does a quick double-take when he sees me. I don't even want to imagine what must be going through his head seeing me with my hand on Sawyer Baskin's, even if we *are* just trying to save a life.

One of the EMTs nods at Jay as if to tell him this case is all his, and Jay goes to work.

"Give me some room, guys," Jay says gruffly as he looks at Brad's head and starts pulling things out of the bag he carries, including a flashlight. Sawyer and I stand and move back a couple of feet. I watch Jay's hands work as he puts gloves on, un-velcroes a blood pressure monitor, rips a bandage open. I have a good view of his face as he works, and even though I know he's seventeen, he has such an intense look, he could easily be ten years older.

Sawyer, standing behind me, puts his hand on my shoulder. I flinch slightly since Sawyer and I aren't friends who touch. And I wonder whether he has blood on his hands and whether it's on my sweater now. I look at my own hands. In the dark, I see a couple of faint reddish smudges.

Jay opens a smelling salt under Brad's nose, and Brad starts to wake up.

"What happened?" Jay asks. He looks right at me, and then at Sawyer's hand on my shoulder, and his eyebrows scrunch up.

I take a step forward, releasing myself from Sawyer's grip.

"He fell—" I start to say.

"Jay?" Brad says.

"You were unconscious," Jay says. "You'll be okay, but you need to stay awake."

Lindsay has moved to Sawyer's side and has her hand on his arm.

"Do you know what happened?" Jay asks. "What did you hit your head on?"

Brad mumbles, "I don't know."

"What did he hit his head on?" Jay asks the crowd.

Nobody answers. It's quiet while he works for a few more seconds.

"Somebody answer me. Who saw what happened? What did he hit his head on?"

Yeah, he definitely seems older. I can't tell if people aren't talking because they're kind of afraid of him or just in shock by the situation.

"I think it was a rock," one of the guys in wet underwear finally says. "It was dark, he slipped when he was getting out of the water. It was either a rock or a tree root."

Brad reaches up to touch the wound on his head.

"Don't touch it," Jay says to him. "It's gonna be fine. Here, just tell me what you were doing before you got hurt. You were swimming? What else? What did you do today?"

The other two EMTs—a man who's about Mom's age and a girl who seems to be only a few years older than us—push the stretcher forward, and the three of them roll Brad onto it.

Afterward, the man nods at Jay, which I can tell means Jay did a good job handling the situation.

"My mom is going to kill me," Brad groans. "I'm supposed to be at a movie."

Jay stands to take hold of his side of the stretcher. He's so big. He almost looks like he's a different species altogether—like everything about him is fifty percent bigger than the rest of humanity. Tall. Thick. Dense. And he's calm the entire time. All business.

Then he turns and looks at me. His face is all hard planes, no hint of his dimple. I want to say something but I'm mute.

And then the three of them carry the stretcher with Brad on it out to the ambulance.

Tim has his shirt back on and is reassuring the police officer who'd come along with the EMS team that everything is under control, and he promises to have everyone out within fifteen minutes.

Serena is right next to me now. She leans toward me, her mouth near my ear. "He's just a rent-a-cop. Erickson knows him, but come on, let's go."

She pulls me by the elbow and leads me in a fast walk down the deck steps and around the back of the house, feeling our way through pine trees in the dark until we get to the road. The silent blue and red flashing of the police car and the ambulance at the Ericksons' house are behind us.

We stand in the dark road, both of us out of breath.

"What the fuck happened?" she asks. Her eyes glitter in the dark.

Then she scrunches up her nose and leans toward me, like a dog sniffing.

"Ew, you smell like a brewery," she says.

I back away from her.

"Ew, you hooked up with Tim Erickson," I say.

She straightens and for a minute I think she's going to push me or punch me or something. But then she throws back her head and laughs. Her laugh has always been contagious, so then I'm laughing, too.

Even as I'm laughing, I'm also praying that this moment will never end.

But of course the moment has to end. Serena's phone buzzes, and after she checks it, her smile fades.

"It's all clear now," she says.

I nod.

"You good?" she asks, and I see in her eyes that she maybe doesn't hate me.

I shrug. "You?" I hope she can see that I don't hate her either. That I would forgive her for leaving me in a millisecond.

She shrugs, too.

She's so familiar, such a part of me. I never wanted to let go of her. I want her back.

"Maybe we could talk at some point," I say quietly.

She nods slowly.

"Yeah," she says. "Yeah, okay."

She turns and walks back toward the Ericksons' house, and I walk the other way to my house.

THIRTY-THREE

Mothers are all slightly insane.
–J. D. Salinger (writer)

After Serena leaves me in the road, I rush home. I need to wash my hands. I know Mom and them are taking the weekend off from planning, so I'm expecting Mom to be in bed or reading on the couch, but as soon as I slide the front door open, she jumps up from a chair at the kitchen table, her hair falling into her eyes.

"God, Rachel," she says, a cross between relief and anger in her voice.

"What? I'm not late," I say. I don't really have a curfew, but I never come home after midnight anyway.

She follows me to the kitchen sink. I start pumping soap onto my hands.

That's when she notices the blood.

"Oh my god! Are you bleeding?"

"It's not my blood. I was at Tim Erickson's and a kid fell and hit his head. I was helping."

I start scrubbing my hands, but the water isn't warm enough yet to get out the dried blood.

"What? Jesus. Is he okay?"

"I think so," I say. "He went to the hospital."

Mom sighs loudly. "Okay. I was so worried."

"Why? It's only ten-thirty."

"Let's talk," Mom says. "I've been calling you."

"Sorry," I say. "I guess my ringer's off. I saw Sawyer in town and I went to Tim's with him."

My hands are pretty clean now, so I turn off the water and grab a dishtowel to dry them.

"Rafe called," she says.

I freeze.

"He told me you were at The Wicked Oyster," she continues. "And he told me what you said. What you asked."

"Oh."

"And?" she asks.

It seems like now that she knows I'm safe, she's angry. But I'm the one who should be angry. I feel like everything she's ever told me is a lie.

"I have to change," I say, noticing the brownish-red streaks on the knees of my jeans. "I'll be right back."

I go to my room and change into pajama pants and a tank top. I come back to the kitchen table and sit across from her. This is it. The moment when she'll finally tell me everything.

Mom takes a shaky breath, like she's gearing up for something big.

"How did you know about the clinic?" she asks.

I hadn't expected questions; I'd expected answers.

I pull my elbows off the table and stare at her.

"Why did you lie?" I ask. "You had an abortion and then Carson died. There's no way he could have been my father."

Mom shakes her head no.

"I didn't lie to you. How did you know about the clinic? I want to know how you know. Now."

I clear my throat.

"I read the letters in your box," I say.

Mom turns away, like she can't even look at me.

"You went into my room and looked through my things?"

"It's just that you're so secretive and I wanted to know everything." I start to cry. "But now I only have more questions."

Mom stands and starts walking to her room. I follow her down the hall, crying, apologizing. I feel a heaviness in the bottom of my stomach. It will only get bigger until it takes over my body. Mom slams her bedroom door behind her.

I go back to my room and fall face first onto my bed. I've done something unforgivable. And I can't undo it.

And Jay probably thinks something happened with Sawyer again. And Serena has a guy and a whole new life and is doing fine without me.

I'm alone. I've lost everyone.

I text Jay.

> **ME**: Please call as soon as you're done with your shift. I really need to talk to you. Nothing happened with Sawyer, if that's what you're thinking.

My pillow is soaked with tears. I'm too spent to undress, so I flip the pillow over, slide under the comforter, close my eyes, and wait for him to text back.

On Sunday, the sunlight wakes me up at seven-thirty. I'm sweaty and my face is tight with dried tears. I find my phone under my pillow. There's nothing from Jay.

Mom's bedroom door is open. I knock on the doorframe as I peek in, but she isn't there. Her bed is made—a little rumpled, like she sat on top of it but never got under the covers. I look out the window—her car is gone. I check the kitchen, but there's no note. She left the house at some point between when I fell asleep and now. I can only imagine how angry she is.

I take a long shower, turning the water to almost-scalding. I'm torn between feeling guilty about what I did and being angry that she's never told me anything, that she may have lied to me my whole life about Carson being my father. As the water pelts down on my head, my shoulders, anger wins out over guilt. I'm tired of the secrets, the survivors and their neediness, Mom and her half-truths. I don't care how angry she is at me; I'm even angrier at her. And now I have even more motivation to get the garage livable. It's the closest I can come to moving out.

When I get out of the shower, I check my phone. A text from Mom that says only *Went out early. Be back later.* Nothing from Jay. I hope it's because he's sleeping after an all-night shift and not that he's pissed at me for being at that party.

I don't know what to do with myself. It's spitting rain out—a gray, cold wetness that seeps right into me—so I don't want to be outside.

I go to the garage, figuring I'll clean up more stuff, but most of it's done. The next steps are painting and then moving stuff in. I haven't picked out paint yet, but I have sandpaper and putty, so I start sanding down some of the bumps and filling in the cracks in the walls.

A car pulls into the driveway and a door slams.

Mom comes in the front door.

I go out into the hallway to see her walking back out again, some bags on the floor. I follow her out.

"Hi," I say, following her to the car and pulling more bags out. "You went shopping?"

Mom smiles. "I did. I went nuts. And I want to do more. So, help me with these bags and then I'm taking you to Snowe's to get stuff for your room."

I want to ask her why. Is this some sort of apology for keeping secrets and lying to me? Or is it a way of smoothing everything over so she can avoid talking about it some more?

We finish unloading the car and then put all the food away in the cupboards and the refrigerator.

"Mom," I start. "About Carson. The letters."

Mom holds up her hand.

"Soon. But Snowe's sale ends today. I want to get there. Go put on some real clothes. Come on."

"Okay," I say. But it really isn't.

THIRTY-FOUR

There is nothing new in the world except the history you do not know.
—Harry S Truman (US president)

On the way to Snowe's, Mom keeps up a running monologue about everything but the letters. She doesn't even pause to let me talk at all.

I still haven't heard from Jay by the time we get to Orleans, and I find myself checking my phone every few minutes.

We pull into the Snowe's parking lot.

"What do you think about pale green for the walls," Mom says, putting the car in park.

"Yeah. The rug I liked at the thrift shop has some green in it."

Her phone rings.

"It's Sue. Hold on—hi," she says, as she answers, "Sue, just a sec, okay?"

Mom puts the phone down on her lap.

"I won't be long, okay? You mind going in and getting started? I'll be in in a minute."

"Sure," I say and get out of the car.

I feel the dry heat blasting as I step into Snowe's.

I go straight to the paint swatches and start flipping through them absently.

"Rachel," I hear behind me and spin around. It's Kyle.

"Oh, hey," I say.

"My mom dragged us to help pick out curtains for the basement," Kyle says. "Fun, right? You painting?"

I nod. "The garage. I'm making it my room."

"Sweet. We can help, if you want. Jay and I painted most of the rooms in our house. And the outside. That was a disaster, though. I'm never painting outside again."

He must notice me looking behind him, because he says, "I was sent for a measuring tape. My mom and Jay are over by the blinds. Come on."

I don't know how Jay will react to seeing me. I have no idea where I stand with him after last night. Even though I texted him that nothing happened with Sawyer, he may not believe me. I prepare myself for the worst.

I follow Kyle down the bathroom fixture aisle and to the window treatment section. Jay's standing with his mom. Even though she's probably almost six feet tall, she looks borderline small next to Jay. She holds out two fabrics, one in each hand. Jay studies the fabric like he can see beyond plaid or stripes. My gaze lowers to his chest. The shirt he's wearing is tight, one of those wicking-material running shirts. I've never seen him wear anything that clung to his body like that—he usually wears plain cotton T-shirts that hang to his hips. But right now, I can see the outline of his pecs, the bumps of his shoulders. I force myself to count to ten in my head and think of window treatments.

"Look who I found in the paint aisle," Kyle says. Jay and his mom look up. The resemblance between them is obvious—the strong jaw, wide-ish face, the spray of freckles across their noses.

Jay's eyes flick to my face, down, back up, then to my ear.

"Hi," he says, quietly.

"Hi," I say.

His mom looks at Jay, then at me, and smiles, but it looks forced. Or sad. Maybe Jay told her he was mad at me. Jay shuffles his feet a little and keeps his eyes down. Then, as if he suddenly remembers his tight shirt, he crosses his arms in front of his chest, and his ears and neck flush red.

"What are you doing here?" he asks. I know he doesn't mean it to sound accusatory, but I see his mom reach to squeeze his elbow.

"Came to get paint samples. My mom is all geared up to get going."

Jay looks at me, his eyes right on mine, questioning.

"Yeah, I know," I say. "She's suddenly very gung-ho about it."

"That's good," he says.

I shrug.

"Kyle, let's go look at . . . patio furniture," their mom says.

She grabs Kyle's arm and starts pulling him in the other direction. Jay rolls his eyes.

"You're so embarrassing, Mom," I hear Kyle say. "I mean, seriously."

"What am I supposed to say? 'I can cut the tension between these two with a knife—let's give them some space?' Which is more embarrassing, do you think?"

"Okay, now you're just being dramatic," Kyle says, but the corners of Jay's mouth turn up, just a teeny bit.

His mom smiles at him. I can see the love between them. The honesty. The three of them, really. They like each other. They know each other well.

"There you are, Rach, sorry that took so long, I—" Mom comes up behind me.

"Naomi," Jay's mom says. "I haven't seen you in ages."

They start chatting, and Kyle pulls out his phone.

Jay and I just stand there across from each other.

"Brad okay?" I ask.

He clears his throat. "Yeah. A few stitches."

"What are you up to later? Do you want to—"

"I'm helping my mom around the house. I can't."

I nod. I'm afraid my voice won't work or I'll cry.

"Mom," Kyle says loudly. "I've got practice. Can we make a decision on this stuff and get out of here?"

"We should get moving, too," Mom says.

"Talk later?" I say to Jay when I'm sure I can speak.

He nods.

Mom follows me back to the paints. She goes to the greens, mechanically pulling paint swatches out of the display.

"This one is nice," she says, pointing at one that's called Envy. And then another called Gentle Stream.

"That one," I say. I grab two cans of Gentle Stream, primer, some brushes, and a paint roller and we go to pay. I hear Kyle on the phone walking out the door, so I know they've left.

In the car, Mom is quiet for so long, I wonder whether she's forgotten I'm here.

"Mom, can we talk now?"

She nods, but then says, "When we get home, okay?"

She sighs loudly and I know she's going to get lost in her thoughts now.

I pull out my phone to text Jay.

ME: I really need to talk to you.

But he doesn't respond.

THIRTY-FIVE

Friendship often ends in love,
but love in friendship—never.
—Albert Camus (philosopher)

When we pull into our driveway, I'm staring at my phone, waiting for Jay to text me, so at first I don't see what causes Mom to say, "Oh, shit."

I look up and immediately feel all the blood rushing out of me, turning me into a pale, empty shell of a human being. Reed's van is parked in front of our house.

"Stay here," Mom says, cutting the ignition and opening her door. "I can't believe this. I told him not to come."

I watch Mom stomp off to the van and knock on the window. She stands there for a second and waits, then goes into the house. Our door is always open in case one of the survivors needs a place to be, but Reed should know better than to go in. Mom looks like she's ready to kill someone.

After a few minutes with no word from Mom and no text from Jay, I decide not to wait in the car anymore. I have to face Reed at some point. He's here. What choice do I have?

I slide the front door open as quietly as I can, my heart pounding.

I hear Reed's voice coming from the deck at the back of the house.

"I *know*, but—"

"I know you're hurting Reed. But it's extremely selfish of you to be here. I told you not to come. You can't stay," Mom says.

"The thing is, though, the van won't start. When I saw you weren't home, I was going to go to see my old housemates, but the van's dead."

Hearing his voice makes my chest hurt.

"I'll call for a tow," Mom says, her words clipped by annoyance. "But it's Sunday so they probably won't be able to have a truck here until tomorrow. I can drop you off in town. In the meantime, steer clear of Rachel."

"How is she?" Reed asks quietly.

Mom pauses. "She's fine. But you being here—I don't know. Jesus."

I walk through the kitchen and make sure the screen door to the deck makes lots of noise as I slide it open, announcing my presence. Mom and Reed turn to me. For a moment, time freezes as Reed's eyes find mine. Even with the sun making me squint, I can see how blue they are. His hair is longer, a bit of it pulled back into a short ponytail or maybe it's a little bun. Some curls come out and brush the side of his face. A ponytail? I didn't think I liked that on guys, but on Reed it looks good. On Reed, anything looks good. Dammit.

"Rachel," Mom says. Her voice sounds apologetic. She knows this is right up there with the most uncomfortable moments of my life.

Reed puts his back against the railing and leans his elbows on it.

"That's not very sturdy," I say.

So that's the first thing I say to Reed after all this time.

He straightens and puts one hand on the railing.

"It's okay, Mom. I'm okay," I say.

She looks at me carefully.

"You don't have to talk to him," she says. "You don't owe him anything."

I see Reed flinch a little out of the corner of my eye.

"It's okay," I say.

She nods. "I'll be in the kitchen."

After she goes back inside, I turn to Reed.

"Rachel," he says.

"My mom told you not to come but you did anyway?" I ask, not bothering to hide my hurt.

"I thought maybe enough time had passed and it would be okay to come just to the meeting. I don't know. I guess it was stupid."

I lean my elbows on the deck railing—not too close to him—and stare out at the bay. I don't care that the railing isn't sturdy enough. Despite the chill in the air, the water looks like summer—shimmering, sparkling in the sun.

He puts his hand on my shoulder. The weight of it seems to burn right through my shirt, but I shiver anyway.

He takes his hand away.

"Can we—" He sighs.

Was he going to say "Can we get back together?" or "Can we be friends?" or "Can we be civil?"

"Can we what?" I snap and turn to him.

He looks down at his feet, and the familiar straight line of his nose pains me.

He meets my eyes, and we stay like that for a few seconds. I'd always said that I'd never get tired of looking into his eyes.

"I'm sorry, Rachel," Reed says, his voice so quiet. "About all of it."

What is *all of it*? Letting me see him in bed with Clarissa? The fall? Splitting town without saying good-bye? Or is he sorry about all of it, like even what we had together before that?

A piece of my hair whips around in the wind and catches me on the cheek. I push it back. I shake my head. For a long time after he left, I'd wanted this moment. How many times had I imagined Reed showing up, apologizing, saying he wanted me back? How many times had I imagined the first time we'd touch after so long, what it would feel like to have his arms around me again, squeezing tight? How many times had I imagined him tracing his fingers over my scars, telling me he wished he could take that night back? I'd wanted this moment. But in the last few weeks, I'd stopped.

"Can we start over?" Reed asks.

"Start over where?" I don't want him anymore, but I still want the satisfaction of hearing him say he wants me back.

"Like the very beginning," he says. "Like when we first met. Before anything happened."

It's like a punch to my chest. That is not what I thought he was going to say. Even though I'm all mixed up in Jay, I still never want the "let's be friends" speech from Reed.

"I had no business being with you, Rachel," he says.

"What the hell are you talking about? Actually, never mind. Don't tell me. I get it." I turn to the water again. I can't face him. The rejection still stings too much.

"I'm sorry about what happened that night," he says. "And leaving without saying good-bye. I couldn't deal. But you knew that. You knew who I was."

"Oh, so I should've known you'd be in bed with your housemate when you knew I was coming over, and it's my fault that you left town while I was having shards of glass and metal removed from my legs? It's my fault because I should've known that you were too fucked up, so I shouldn't have let myself fall for you? Is that what you meant? What a stupid thing to say. Coward."

"Don't be mean," he says.

I can't stop the quick burst of disbelieving laughter.

"I hope your van gets fixed quickly," I say.

I go to my room and close the door. I text Mom.

ME: Tell me when he's gone.

THIRTY-SIX

Whoever does not have a good father should procure one.
—Friedrich Nietzsche (philosopher)

I stay in my room for what seems like forever, waiting for Mom to text me that Reed's gone and that she's ready to tell me everything about Carson and Rafe. I remember how broken my heart was along with my body, and the defeat after Mom told me Reed wasn't my soul mate, but she wouldn't tell me who was or even if I had one.

I hear Reed's voice, but then after a while, Mom's car starts up and the house is quiet.

She texts me fifteen minutes later that she's dropped him off in town, and she asks if I need anything. I don't feel like answering.

I hear a soft knock at the front door. So soft, I'm not sure if I actually heard it.

When I get to the door, I see Rafe walking back to the truck, like he's given up on anyone answering.

"Hi," I say, opening the slider.

He turns.

"Oh, hi," he says. "I wasn't sure if anyone was home."

He looks at Reed's van, the only car in our driveway.

"It's just me. My mom's out."

Something like disappointment flashes across his face.

"Okay," he says. "Well, I was hoping to talk to her. Maybe you can let her know I stopped by."

"You could call her," I suggest.

He nods.

"I could," he says. "I also wanted to give her something."

"Hold on," he says and jogs over to the truck. He opens the driver's side door and reaches in, then slams the door closed as he comes back to the steps. He's holding something in his hand.

"I thought she should have this," he says. He opens his hand, and resting on his outstretched palm is a scallop shell.

He looks up at the shell around my neck before looking into my eyes.

"Oh" is all I can say. "Where did you get it?"

Hadn't Mom said that Carson had the other half? Had Rafe taken it after Carson died?

"I've always had it," he says quietly. So Mom lied. Or . . . wait. I think back to when she gave me the shell. She never said that Carson had it. She said "he." She talked about young love, so I'd assumed she'd meant Carson. But it was always Rafe who'd had the other half.

Since I'm just standing there with my mouth open, Rafe takes my hand and drops the shell into it. My fingers automatically clasp tightly around it, and I feel the edges dig into my palm.

"Why don't you want to keep it?" I ask.

"I've held onto it long enough," he says. "It's time to let it go."

He turns to leave.

"Wait," I say. "Let it go? Or let *her* go? You're giving up on her?"

Why do I feel like he's somehow giving up on me, too—on us?

Rafe looks at me curiously.

"That's it?" I continue. "I still don't know what happened, but I know you were together before I was born. And I saw you two in the truck the other day. You won't even give it a shot?"

Rafe looks down at his feet.

"It's more complicated than that," he says. "I think you know that. It's been eighteen years since she left. Things change."

"Sometimes they don't," I say.

"She left," Rafe says forcefully. His Adam's apple moves up and down. I feel like maybe he swallowed the word *me—she left me.*

"She's been single ever since," I say.

Rafe shakes his head and goes back to the truck.

"You're a good kid, Rachel."

He gets in the truck and starts the ignition.

"Are you leaving town?" I ask him.

"I'm not going anywhere."

"Then, here," I say. I shove the scallop shell at him through his open window. "You can give this to her yourself."

He shakes his head, but he takes it from my hand, then drives away, the truck scattering pebbles and smooth white shells as it goes.

I sleep for the rest of the day. At one point, I feel something on my shoulder and realize it's Mom pulling the covers up over me.

"It's late. You're still in your clothes," she whispers.

"I don't care," I say, turning over. She rubs my back for a second and then leaves.

I pull my phone out. Jay still hasn't texted me back. I throw the phone on the floor and fall back to sleep.

THIRTY-SEVEN

Vulnerability is basically uncertainty, risk, and emotional exposure.
—Brené Brown (author)

I still haven't heard from Jay by Monday morning. I shower and get ready quickly in case we're in a big enough fight that I have to catch the bus to school. I try calling him. He picks up on the first ring.

"Hi," he says, his voice hard.

"Hi. I just didn't know if I should take the bus or what," I say.

"I'm on my way to your house." He doesn't sound surprised that I doubted him showing up, which is not very reassuring. For a second, I'm tempted to go the passive-aggressive route and say "Forget it, I'll take the bus," but I know that would prolong the negativity and, of course, I don't want to take the bus.

Reed's van is still in the driveway, and I panic. Mom didn't say that he'd come back, but then again, I was half-asleep when she'd come in. Is he sleeping in the van right now or did he stay with his old housemates last night? Either way, the van is here, so that means he's still in town. Somewhere. I'm very aware of the scars on my legs, even though they're completely healed now. My heart clenches and doesn't release.

As Jay's car finally comes toward me, suddenly everything feels so hopeless. I want Jay, I love him, as a friend and maybe more, but everything is so complicated. The idea of kissing stresses him out. But then I think about his soft lips, his hands tracing lines up my back underneath my shirt, and I shiver, remembering his touch. He didn't seem stressed out right then.

He pulls into the driveway and I see his eyes widen when he notices Reed's van. As I open the car door, he nods his head at the van and raises his eyebrows at me.

"He's—" I throw my head back against the seat. "I don't know. He's not at the house anymore, but his van won't start. It hasn't been the best couple of days."

"Sorry," he says and puts the car in gear.

We drive down my road in silence. When we get to the turn for Route 6, I realize he isn't planning to say anything else.

"Why have you been avoiding me?" I ask.

He shakes his head. I groan.

"You're mad because I was hanging out with Sawyer?"

Traffic on 6 is heavy, and it's obvious it'll take eons to pull out onto it. He puts the car in park and turns to me.

"Yeah," he says. "That was pretty much a shocker."

His tone is harsh and it hurts.

"And you went to a party at Erickson's house with all those assholes who treat you—and me—like shit."

"I didn't go *with* them," I say.

He puts the car in gear and pulls out onto Route 6.

He's silent.

"And you were looking pretty cozy with Sawyer—"

"No, it was just—we were trying to stop the bleeding before you came and—"

"I know," he says. "I just didn't like seeing him touching you. I know I'm overreacting. You can go to parties, whatever. You can do whatever you want. It surprised me. To see you there. After everything."

"It wasn't some big statement or anything. I'll tell you what happened," I say, trying so hard to see things from his eyes. "I was in town and Sawyer drove by. He offered me a ride home on his way to Erickson's. So, I took it because I didn't have my bike and you were on a ride and I didn't feel like calling my mom. And I'd had a really shitty afternoon—I haven't even told you about that yet—and a beer sounded good, so I thought I'd have one and then walk home from there. I'd only been there like twenty minutes and I was about to leave when the thing with Brad happened."

Jay nods like it makes sense, but I can't tell if he's still mad.

"I wasn't on some secret mission to get popular or screw Sawyer or whatever you're thinking," I say. "I had just found out that my entire life my mom has been lying to me about everything, and I wasn't ready to go home and face her yet. It was just a beer. It doesn't change anything. You know that, right?"

He keeps quiet, but the tension in his jaw has released some.

"I don't know if you're done with me now or what," I continue. "Do you still want this?" I suck in a breath because I can't believe I'm asking this. Never ask a question you may not want the answer to, I remember hearing somewhere.

"Rach."

But he doesn't say anything after.

"Oh," he says suddenly. "We have to stop for her."

I look out the window and see who he's talking about. Serena, waiting at her bus stop. He pulls off onto the shoulder, and Serena waves. My stomach feels hollowed out and nervous seeing her. And the timing sucks.

"Hi," she says, as she slides into the back seat. "Thanks. My mom had to take my car and I was dreading the morning bus."

Her citrus shampoo is so familiar, I want to eat it. But all I do is say, "Hey."

And Jay says, "No problem."

I look at him, wondering about our unfinished conversation. As usual, his face is unreadable, but I want to think he's apologizing with his eyes. For foisting Serena on me. Maybe for not returning my texts this weekend.

The three of us had spent a lot of time in Jay's car since he got it last spring, going into town, to movies, to pizza. Singing, yelling out the windows, laughing. But now everything is different. Those three friends are gone—like we were a flashback montage in a movie. Now we're practically strangers.

Serena leans forward a bit.

"Are you going to the lacrosse game?" she asks.

"No," I say as if it's the last thing on earth I'd do, which it kind of is.

"Actually," Jay says, clearing his throat. "Kyle's coming off the bench today. He asked if we could go watch. My mom and Gabe left this morning for New York, so they can't make it."

"You should definitely go," Serena says. "Most teachers probably won't give homework tonight since we have the superintendent's day tomorrow."

"There's no school tomorrow?" Jay asks.

With everything this weekend, I'd forgotten, too. Normally, I'd be happy about a day off, but tomorrow everyone will be at the house for the meeting.

I stare at Jay's profile. Lacrosse game?

"Nah," I say. "I'm just gonna head home. I'll take the bus if you go."

Jay glances at me as he pulls up to a red light. I know that expression. It's the *Don't make me handle this alone, I need you* expression. It's true. With all the noise, chaos, uncertainty, probably the only way he agreed to go in the first place was because he knew I'd go with him.

When we get to the lot, all the junior spots are taken. I know that Jay's calculating how long it will take if we have to park in the beach lot and walk. I see him clench and unclench his teeth, holding in the anger.

"There's a spot!" Serena says, practically bouncing in her seat. She's always been good at that. Back when the three of us went places together, we'd tell Serena to use her parking karma, and it always worked. For a second, I let myself wonder whether that spot would've been there if she hadn't been with us. Maybe not. And that makes me miss her, even though she's just a couple feet away.

"Thanks for the ride. I have to get my stuff to the gym lockers before homeroom," Serena calls out as she runs toward the school building, her giant cheerleading gear bag bouncing against her leg.

Jay locks the car doors and starts walking.

"Hold up," I say. "You're going too fast." My legs are tingling and holding me back today. Usually it means rain, but today, I'm sure it's because Reed is here, making all my scars hurt. Inside and out.

I follow Jay to his locker. After he opens it, he turns to me and looks me in the eye.

"I'm really sorry," he says. And because I know he's continuing our conversation about us from the car, my stomach drops like I'm on a roller coaster because I don't know what he's going to say.

"I was avoiding you, and I know that was totally immature," he says. "Of course I'm not done. I'm just dumb."

We both smile at his silly pun.

"So," I say. "You do still want this?"

He bends down so his mouth is close to my ear, and then, his breath warm, he says, "If by this, you mean you, then yeah."

My breath catches in my throat and my body gets warm all over.

"Holy shit," I say.

"I know," he says. The second bell rings. He stands up straight and closes his locker. "See you later."

He walks away toward the science labs, sticking close to the wall.

I give myself a few seconds to breathe, get my books, and head to class.

THIRTY-EIGHT

It's amazing the clarity that comes with psychotic jealousy.
—Rupert Everett (actor)

Jay's not at his locker after the last bell, so I go to look for him in the bio lab. He's there, towering above Mr. Billings, who's sitting at his desk at the front of the classroom. I wait outside the door.

"I'm going against my own rule here. This is the first perfect score I've ever given," Mr. Billings says.

"It's a stupid rule," Jay says. I hold back a snort. "The no perfect scores thing. I mean, you should want your students to get perfect scores. That would mean you're doing a good job teaching the material. Right?"

Mr. Billings sighs. "Right," he says. He closes his laptop and puts it under his arm. "See you tomorrow."

Mr. Billings walks past me and nods.

Jay shoves things in his backpack.

"Perfect score, huh?" I ask.

Jay startles and then smirks.

"You finally worked up the courage to fight that test grade, I see," I say.

"No courage needed. He's been out the last couple of weeks. New baby. I told you that score was bullshit. And I was right."

"Or maybe he's just exhausted from changing diapers all night and he just wants *this* overgrown baby to stop crying."

"Wah, wah, wah," he says, sticks his tongue out at me, and throws his backpack over his shoulder.

At our lockers, Jay pulls out some books and grabs a couple of earplugs out of a side pocket of his backpack.

"Listen," I say. "Is this lacrosse game thing really necessary? I was thinking maybe we should do something just the two of us. We can, you know, hang out."

He groans softly. "I promised Kyle I'd be there. But if you don't want to go, it's okay. I can meet up with you after."

He says the words, but his eyes say otherwise.

I pile about thirty pounds of textbooks into my messenger bag.

"Come on, let's go to the damn lacrosse field," I say, slinging the bag over my head, which makes my shoulder sag about three inches.

"Here, I'll take that," he says.

"Chivalry is dead, He-man."

"Suit yourself," he says.

We push through the heavy red doors to the outside. People are in constant motion, moving around like ants—toward the bus line, the parking lot, the arts center, the gym, the sports fields.

I feel Jay's unease next to me, so I wait for him to get his bearings.

It isn't raining, but the sky is overcast and the air feels thick and wet.

"This weather sucks for my hair," I say. "Come on."

I pull my hair back into a loose ponytail with the band I keep on my wrist. I grab Jay's elbow and pull him along. He's moving too slowly. I just want to get to the game and get it over with so we can make out.

"Your legs hurt? You want some Advil?" Jay asks. I must be limping a little.

"I'm fine. It's just the weather," I say. "What's with all the thoughtfulness? It's bizarre."

When we get to the lacrosse field, we go directly to the bleachers to find a seat. I lead the way, and Jay follows close behind. I know he's staying focused on me so he won't get overwhelmed. There aren't that many people at the game yet—maybe forty, a few more—but it's enough to make Jay's jaw clench and unclench. We sit down and put our bags down on either side of us.

I put my hand on Jay's leg and lean into his ear, catching a whiff of the shaving cream that still lingers from this morning.

"You good?" I ask.

He nods, looking out onto the field.

"What number is Kyle?" I ask.

"Eleven."

I hear Serena's familiar laugh. She's jumping up and down on the sidelines with the other cheerleaders. They're all wearing their black-and-gold cheer uniforms. She does a perfect cartwheel, her long brown legs windmilling through the air. She claps, smiles, touches her hair. I turn to Jay and realize that he's staring at her, a slight smile playing on his lips.

I punch his leg, right at the meat of his quadriceps. He yelps.

"What was that for?"

"You're staring at her," I say.

"Who?"

As if on cue, Serena lets out a loud "No way!" to the other girls, like she's just heard the best gossip in the world.

"Forget it," I say.

The game is about to start.

"Look," I say. "Kyle's starting."

Kyle stands in ready position, looking like some strange masked, padded animal with a stick. And then, after the two guys in the middle do their little stick-crossing thing, the whistle blows and the ball is up for grabs. I watch Kyle as he runs back and forth, holding up his stick, waiting for someone to throw it to him.

Kyle gets the ball and starts running down the field, cradling the ball in his stick.

Jay and I both jump up. "Go! Go, Kyle!" we shout.

Kyle passes the ball to another player, who scores. Everyone cheers. Kyle pumps his fist at us. Jay gives him a thumb's up.

When we sit down, an overwhelming sense of happiness washes over me. I feel so good all of a sudden, with the excitement of Kyle getting the ball and Jay next to me. I take Jay's hand and interlace my fingers in his. He tightens our grip. Serena turns to us and waves, acknowledging Kyle's assist.

Jay pulls his hand away from mine and waves back. And I don't like how quickly he let go of me.

"Oh my god, you totally want her," I say, even though I know it's not true. I can't help myself.

"No, I do not," he says.

I groan.

"I know," I say. "I just can't stand how weird and possessive I feel right now."

"Well," Jay says, looking straight ahead. "How do you think *I* feel? Sawyer Baskin is looking at you."

I scan the players and find Sawyer by the bench with his helmet off, and yes, he does seem to be looking at me. He smiles and waves, then turns back to the game.

"That was weird," I say.

"Does he think you're a thing now that you went to a party with him?"

"No, there's no thing. And, not that it matters, but he's still with Lindsay."

"Do you like him?"

"No!" I punch his arm lightly. "I like you. Obviously."

Jay keeps his eyes on the field, but I see a little smile starting.

"It's too bad we're not the only people in the world," he says. "Then we wouldn't have to get jealous of anyone else."

"But then we'd have no one to talk about. We'd be bored."

He laughs.

Kyle gets the ball again, runs with it for several yards, and then passes it to a teammate. I don't know much, but it seems like he's doing pretty well. And as much as I'm happy for him, I don't want to be here anymore.

"Have I watched enough of this Neanderthal game to satisfy Kyle, you think?" Jay asks, as if he read my mind.

"Yup," I say. "Let's go."

THIRTY-NINE

It felt like a whip came from behind me, curled over me,
and cracked against my forehead.
Life paused, and the world was orange.
—Jessica Roth (lightning-strike survivor)

Jay and I walk back to the parking lot in silence, but it feels normal. The new version of us can still just walk and I don't feel the pressure to talk or hold his hand or anything. The difference is that I feel this extra warmth and giddiness in my chest.

Clouds have moved in and covered the sun completely, so it's starting to feel like it's night instead of four-thirty. The sky is heavy with rain, like a bulging bag of water, and just when it gets too heavy, a seam will burst and out it will all spill.

Jay looks up.

I pull out my phone to check for thunderstorms, but my weather app is loading too slowly.

"That came in quickly," Jay says. "They must have called the game. People are leaving."

A crowd moves slowly and casually down the path to the parking lot. No one seems to be in a rush. I don't see any of the players—most likely they've gone into the locker room to change.

My phone buzzes.

MOM: I'm letting Reed stay for the meeting. I can't turn my back on him right now. He needs us. I know this is hard for you, so if you want to stay at Jay's, I understand.

I stare in disbelief.

"Hey," Jay says. "Everything okay?"

I shake my head no.

"My mom," I say. "She'll never—"

Suddenly, there's a crack of thunder so loud, Jay and I both jump a little. My heart races, and I feel that twisting pressure in my lower belly. It's so familiar, so comforting, in a way. My body reacts to that sound, to the heaviness of the sky as if it's a starting gun in the race of my life. My mind knows I'm done trying, but my body doesn't. My body wants to go for it.

"Rach," Jay says. "Come on. Let's get in the car."

He looks back toward school.

"Hold on," he says. "I see Serena. She may need a ride. Meet you in the car."

He gives me his keys. I nod and clutch them tightly.

The sky lights up for a second, but I don't see the bolt. I wait. One-one-thousand. CRASH. It's so close. Right here. There's no way to know which direction the storm is heading, so the next one could be right here or a mile the other way.

Maybe if I hadn't gotten the text from Mom, I could stop myself. But the text brought me right back to the heart of everything. To the real reason I'd chased lightning for so long. *She'll never choose me* was what I'd been about to say. I know she loves me. I've never doubted that. But the lightning-strike survivors are more important. They need her more. She'll never choose me over them.

Jay has caught up to Serena and now they're walking together.

The sky lights up again and then thunder crashes almost immediately. I'm still staring at Jay and Serena, who start running, along with everyone else, toward the parking lot, trying to beat the rain that's coming down in fat drops. No one seems concerned about the proximity of the lightning. Maybe they don't realize how close it is. But I do.

Please, please, I think, *please come this way. I need you.*

I drop my bag in the back seat of Jay's car, take off my boots and socks, throw them in too, and feel the cold wet asphalt on my feet. I scan the parking lot, settle on an electric pole that juts out from the edge, close to the road. It's slightly raised, and it's the best spot I can find.

Jay has his jacket lifted over his head and is jogging toward the car. Serena's still next to him, holding her arms above her head as if that can shield the rain, but she has no jacket. Her tight little cheerleading sweater is going to get soaked.

They're almost at the car. Once they get here, I'll lose my chance. I run toward the electric pole, my bare feet slapping in the newly formed puddles.

"Rachel!" Jay yells, and at the same time, Serena shouts, "Rachel, what are you doing?"

But they know what I'm doing.

"Rachel!" Serena's voice is closer, but the rain is coming down so hard, I barely hear it. Just as I reach the pole and touch my hand to it, I feel someone grab my other arm, and the sky lights up like it's on fire and the crash of thunder is deafening like an explosion and then—nothing.

When I open my eyes, I can barely see. Rain comes down in sheets. I'm lying on the ground, on the hard, gravelly asphalt of the parking lot. My head hurts. Was I struck? I don't feel different other than the pounding on the top of my head, but that feels more like I slammed my head on something. I reach up and move some soaking hair out of my face. I slowly move each arm and leg and wiggle my fingers and toes to make sure everything's functioning. I stare straight ahead and, through the pounding rain, I see . . . Jay kissing Serena. No, that can't be right. He wouldn't be doing that. Not after everything.

I realize what's happening as soon as Jay moves his mouth away from Serena's and puts two fingers on her neck—he's checking her pulse. Serena has been struck. And she must have stopped breathing because Jay is giving her CPR. I lie there, still, watching. Jay puts his mouth on hers again and a second later, I see her chest heave. Jay pulls away and looks at her face, saying her name over and over. I can't tell whether her eyes are open but she's definitely breathing.

"They're on their way," a girl's voice shouts. And then, through the sound of the rain pounding on the ground next to me, I hear sirens coming toward us.

Serena has to be okay. I would never forgive myself if she's not. This is my fault. Am I okay? Why isn't Jay here with me now? I'm suddenly so tired. I close my eyes.

I feel hands on my head, on my arm, on my stomach, my legs.

"Rach."

I open my eyes. Jay is crouched down beside me.

His face is streaming with water.

"Hi," I say, because I can't think of anything else to say.

I look over to the spot where he'd been with Serena but it's empty now.

"Serena?" I ask.

"They're getting her in the ambulance. She's awake. She'll be okay," he says.

"Because of you," I say. "If you hadn't been here—God, I'm so stupid."

I hear voices close to my ear and someone's touching my head. Jay holds my hand with both of his.

"You hit your head," he says.

"Was I struck?" I ask.

"I don't think so. Serena was. I saw it. I think the force knocked her into you and you hit your head on the pole. But they'll check to make sure at the hospital."

He looks over his shoulder at the ambulances.

The rain has let up and it's just drizzling now, so everyone has stopped shouting.

"You're gonna ride with these guys. It's Joe and Yolanda. They'll take good care of you. I need to go with Serena so I can tell them what happened. We need to watch her breathing and heart rate," he says quietly.

I close my eyes. I don't want him to leave me, but I can't say that because I know he wouldn't stay. He kisses me quickly on my wet cheek.

"I'll see you at the hospital. I'll see you in a few minutes."

I keep my eyes closed as the techs say "One-two-three" and lift me onto a stretcher. I keep my eyes closed and listen as Jay's footsteps run to the other ambulance. I keep my eyes closed as I hear the doors on Serena's ambulance slam and it pulls away. I keep my eyes closed as a female tech's voice says, "Okay, Rachel, we're going to lift you into the ambulance now. Just relax, but try not to sleep. Squeeze my hand if you start to get sleepy, okay? You're going to be fine."

The ambulance ride is bumpy and my head hurts, but I'm much more awake now. Or "alert," as the techs referred to me. I can hear the driver radioing the hospital.

"Girl, seventeen, contusion to the head. Looks like a fall or similar trauma. Abrasions. Possible victim of electrical shock from lightning strike." He goes on to talk about pulse and pain level.

I'm sure I haven't been struck. I'd felt no jolt, no electrical type of pain, only the bump on my head and yes, now I feel some scratches on my hands and elbows from landing on the pavement. But no lightning. Serena had gotten the lightning. Serena got what I'd wanted. I try to block out the image of Jay with his mouth on hers, but it's imprinted on my brain. I try to focus on the point—Serena was struck, she could have died. And it was because of me and my stupidity. Chasing lightning.

FORTY

Love begins by taking care of the closest ones—the ones at home.
—Mother Teresa (missionary)

After a gazillion tests and answering the same questions over and over, they bring me back to the ER room where I started out. Mom's waiting for me in the hallway outside the door. She's wearing her standard bank outfit—slim navy knee-length skirt, white blouse, tailored jacket, and sensible heels. It always takes me by surprise—Mom in that outfit. She looks like a professional, like *a* mom, but not *my* mom, Naomi Ferguson, lightning-strike survivor, knower of soul mates.

"Hi, Mom," I say quietly.

"Oh, sweetie," she whispers.

The nurse pushes my bed into its place, then draws a curtain across the room that separates it into two halves—mine and some other future unfortunate person. Mom pulls a plastic chair up next to my bed and takes my hand.

"You okay?" she asks.

"I think so. The doctor has to read the test results."

"What happened?"

She's looking so hard into my eyes, it's like she's trying to pull out my memory and watch it like a video. I blink. Her stare is too much.

"It was a freak thunderstorm," I say. "We were at the lacrosse game. They called the game but the storm came so fast, the lightning hit when we were all in the parking lot."

Mom could never know that I chased the lightning.

"And Serena was struck?" Mom asks.

I nod.

"Were you?"

I shake my head back and forth on the pillow slowly.

"I don't think so," I say. "They're doing more tests—EKG and stuff—to be sure. But I don't think so."

Mom's eyes soften and she exhales loudly. She keeps one hand on mine, raises her other to her heart.

Her voice cracks when she speaks. "Oh my god, if you'd been struck, Rachel . . ." Now she chokes back a sob. "I would never want you to go through that."

She leans over so her forehead touches my wrist. Then she kisses the back of my hand.

"Mom? Will Serena be okay?"

"I don't know," she says. "Even if she leaves the hospital just fine, we won't know if she's really okay. Not for a long time."

I know what Mom means. The after-symptoms show up later, sometimes even years later. But I don't like the way she said "we." Like she'll be monitoring Serena's health herself. And suddenly, I realize that she will be. Serena is a strike survivor now. Just like Sue and Ron. Just like Reed. Just like Mom.

I turn my head to the side as a tear slides down my cheek.

"Oh, sweetie," Mom says. "She'll be okay—the group and I will be there for her. We'll make sure she's okay."

There's no way Mom can know how torn I feel hearing that—relieved that Serena will be cared for, and crazy-ugly jealous that she'll get Mom and the group, and everything I've wanted.

I close my eyes.

"You rest, sweetheart. I'll go find Serena's mom, and then I'll be back."

She squeezes my hand and leaves just as the nurse is coming in to check my blood pressure.

I must have fallen asleep. When I open my eyes, I see Jay standing with his back to me, looking out the window.

"Hi," I say, but it comes out as a whisper. I clear my throat.

He turns around. He looks tired, his eyes red, his shoulders sloped. He looks older than he is, like an adult with the weight of the world on his shoulders.

"Hey," he says. His voice is gruff. "How do you feel?"

"Okay. Big bump on my head. Have you seen Serena? Is she okay?"

He nods.

"Her proponin is mildly elevated, so they want to watch her overnight to make sure it's going down. It's really just a precaution. She has a burn mark on her shoulder. But her pain isn't too bad, and she's awake and talking and everything."

"I guess that's good, right? Are you okay?"

He grunts, which I take to mean yes but no. He seems cold, mad at me maybe.

"I'm sorry," I say. "It's my fault."

Now his eyebrows rise and his gaze meets mine briefly, then flicks back down to the floor.

"How is it your fault? Lightning struck in the parking lot of our school just as everyone was going to their cars. Did you make that happen?"

Does he not know that I ran for the electric pole, and Serena came after me and got struck instead of me? Did he see what I'd done?

"I thought you were kissing her," I blurt out.

He looks up. "Huh?"

"I was so out of it, for a few seconds I thought you were kissing Serena. Then I realized what was happening. And then I got weird and jealous anyway because you went to her first."

He wrinkles up his nose like he smells something bad.

"You got jealous that I went to Serena first? To resuscitate her?"

"I know. I was so out of it. I shouldn't have told you that. It was a stupid-crazy thought."

"Yeah," he says. "It was. I did what I was supposed to do. I assessed the situation as quickly as possible, and I went to the patient with the most urgent need. If I'd gone to you first, Serena might have died."

"I know," I say. "I didn't mean it. I'm sorry. You saved her life."

He nods, not with pride or with anything really. Just a slow nod.

"Did anyone else get hurt?" I ask.

He shakes his head. "No. A few people thought they'd been struck because the crash was so loud it knocked them down, and some had burst eardrums, but they weren't struck."

His voice cracks on the last word. He bends over and puts his head in his hands. Something is wrong. Something more than Serena and me in the hospital. He sniffles.

"Jay? What is it?"

I sit up, but the movement sends a shooting pain down the back of my skull.

"Uuuuh," I groan, and immediately lie back.

Jay lifts his head. "What are you doing? Don't move."

"Come here then," I whisper, the pain starting to subside.

He walks over and sits in the chair Mom had been sitting in.

I reach out and touch his face. It's damp.

"Are you crying?" I ask. I've never seen Jay cry.

"They're calling me a hero," he says.

"That's why you're upset?"

He sighs, exasperated. Shakes his head.

"They don't know me."

"Who?" I ask. Even though Jay doesn't hang out that much, everyone at school knows him. They've known him forever.

"People from school. Parents. Reporters. They're outside. Newspaper and TV."

"What?"

"People don't get struck by lightning very often, Rach. A cheerleader was struck at a high school lacrosse game. She stopped breathing and was resuscitated by a high school junior EMT-in-training who happened to be at the game. It's a story. And . . ."

"And what?"

"And I'm K.O."

"Ugh. Okay. Then this absolves you of that. No more K.O."

"People are talking about it," he says. "About what happened before. About what happened today. I'm sure the K.O. thing will be a part of this story, too."

I nod and hold tight to his hand.

"We'll deal with it," I say. "We'll ignore it. Whatever we have to do."

Just then the door opens and Mom comes in.

"Is Serena okay?" I ask.

She nods and sits in the chair Jay has just vacated for her. He stays by the door, his back to us. I can tell he's trying to give us privacy without having to go out there where there might be reporters.

"I'm sorry I let Reed stay this weekend," she says. "It was very insensitive of me."

She hesitates, then continues. "But he's here and . . . now I'm glad because his experience is helpful and—"

Jay clears his throat. Mom and I both look at him. His fists are clenched at his sides, his shoulders stiff.

"I guess I'll go see how Serena is," he says.

"Oh, um," Mom says. "Reed's in with her now."

My stomach turns over and I feel like I might throw up. I lean forward and start retching.

Jay grabs a bedpan from the sink and rushes over to me while Mom holds back my hair. I don't throw anything up, though.

Mom looks at me, concerned.

I stare blankly, picturing Reed at the side of Serena's bed. Serena never even liked Reed, but now they share something so big, it's bigger than anything. Reed can be her lightning mentor like a sponsor in AA. I almost laugh. It's kind of like that. And my whole life, my wish to be struck by lightning might as well have been, "If I could just be an alcoholic, then everything would be okay."

Mom touches the back of her hand to my forehead.

"I'm fine," I say. I scooch down so I'm lying flat on my back.

"I can't send him away now. And if Serena's feeling up to it tomorrow or the next day, she can come to the meeting and meet some of the other survivors."

I turn onto my side, my back to her.

"Serena needs us now," Mom says, and I hear the curiosity in her voice. "I know that things between you haven't been great, but can you put those feelings aside and remember that she used to be your best friend?"

Mom doesn't understand. She thinks I'm still mad at Serena.

I nod, then whisper, "I want to take a nap."

She touches my hair and then I hear her knees crack, one, then the other. I hear the door open and close. I can feel Jay still in the room.

"You can leave, too," I say, my voice muffled by my pillow.

"I want to stay with you," he says.

I try to hold it in, I try so badly, but I can't anymore. The sobs come on like convulsions, a seizure. I can't control them. I cry so hard and it feels so awful and so good. I know Jay is still standing there, probably not knowing what to do. I want him to come sit with me, but I'm also okay with him just being here, standing, being near me while he lets me release it all.

Finally, after what feels like forever, the crying subsides and I take a few shaky deep breaths. And then I breathe quietly through my mouth, my nose now too stuffy to let any air through.

"Should I come over there?" Jay asks quietly.

"Yeah." I sit up slowly and reach for a tissue. Wipe my eyes and nose. He stares at my face as he stands next to me.

"Not so pretty, huh?" I ask. I'm sure that my eyes are puffy and my nose is probably bright red.

He shrugs.

I hit him in the arm.

"Ow," he says.

He pushes the chair away with his foot and sits on my bed. Then he reaches over, slides his arm under my back, and pulls me into his chest. I close my eyes and press my face against his soft flannel shirt, still damp from the rain, and I feel his heart beat against my cheek. I breathe in his Jay smell—soap, shaving cream, and boy, plus a hint of hospital. He holds me tight, one hand spread across my upper back, one holding the back of my head.

"When they discharge you, I'm taking you to my house," he whispers into my hair. "You don't need to go back there until they're gone."

I nod into his shirt, feeling the tears sting again.

"I wanted to be moved into the garage by now," I whimper. In a few short hours, my house will become theirs—Mom's and the group's. And now Serena's too. But not mine.

"I know," he says. And he doesn't try to make it better by saying "It'll be ready for the next meeting," and he doesn't try to fix it or come up with a plan, and man, I love him for that. I feel his lips on the top of my head, and the hand on my back moves in circles, and I am really, really thankful for him.

FORTY-ONE

Everyone has a side to them that's kind of unexplained and feels misunderstood.
–Kirk Hammett (musician)

After Mom signs my discharge papers and I'm cleared to go, she seems torn.

"I just need to—give me just a few minutes to—" she says, her eyes darting back and forth between Jay and me. I know she feels like she should take me home and take care of me, but I also know she really wants to stay and "advocate" for Serena. That's what she does.

Jay says he'll take me back to his house and Mom doesn't waste a second thanking him. She kisses me and then disappears.

Jay turns his back while I change out of the hospital gown and into my clothes, which are still a bit damp from the rain, even though Mom had spread them out on the window ledge by the heating vent to dry.

I'm so tired, but I need to see Serena before we leave. Jay leads me to her room. An aide is there, changing the sheets on the bed.

"You just missed her," the aide says. "They moved her up to four."

"That's an observation floor," Jay explains to me. "That's where they'll keep her overnight."

That's probably where Mom rushed off to. I nod and then wince at how the motion shoots pain to the bump on my head.

"If they just moved her," Jay continues, "she probably won't be able to see you right now. The old team of doctors and nurses has to brief the new team and it can get hectic. Let's just get back to Wellfleet. Kyle had one of his friend's drive my car and leave it here for me, so we can go now. We can come back tomorrow morning if she's still here."

I wonder whether Jay's afraid that reporters will be waiting for him outside Serena's door. I know I'm afraid Reed will be there. And seeing Serena like this would be—I don't know—weird. I want to apologize. Things may be bad between us right now, but I want to be at her side. I'm just not sure if she feels the same way.

On our way to Jay's car in the parking lot, he swivels his head around a lot, looking for reporters probably. But there's no one there.

"I guess they got bored of you," I say.

"I hope so."

We get to his car, and he clicks the doors unlocked.

When I get in, I grunt because the hard seat alerts me to an ache on my butt. I must have fallen hard on it and didn't feel it as much when I was lying down.

"You okay?" Jay asks.

"Mmmm," I say, because if I speak, I'll start to cry again. This fresh pain brings me right back to when I was recovering from falling down Reed's stairs. The constant throbbing that was a reminder every second of every day of what had happened, of how stupid I'd been, how hard I'd fallen for someone who'd never really felt the same way. A tear trickles down my cheek. Jay reaches over and touches it, then holds his finger out to show me the drop.

He leans over, though he doesn't have to lean far since he takes up most of the car anyway. He presses his lips against the spot on my cheek, rests his nose on my cheekbone. I sigh.

"You've cried more in the last couple of weeks than in the three years I've known you," he says as he pulls away from me. "Did you know that emotional tears have more protein than basal and reflex tears?"

I shake my head no, but I'm smiling now. "I have no idea what you're even talking about."

He smiles, then starts the car.

I put my head against the window, which is cool against my skin. I close my eyes and listen to the hum of the engine, Jay's breathing, the cars rushing by on Route 6.

When I open my eyes, we're parked in front of Jay's house, and I'm covered with a heavy, scratchy, wool blanket.

I sit up slowly and wipe my mouth.

"What time is it?" I ask.

"You've been asleep for an hour," Jay says. "I thought about carrying you inside but I didn't want to wake you up."

I sit up straighter, stretch my legs, move my neck slowly from side to side. I still hurt, but sleep was good for me.

"Let's go inside," he says. "No one's home."

I'm starving. It only takes us a few minutes to polish off the leftover lasagna Jay pulled out of the refrigerator. We don't heat it up or bother with plates; we just eat it right out of the pan. Jay searches through cupboards and the refrigerator for something else.

"Soup?" he asks.

"Sure."

He pours a can of chicken noodle into a pot and we wait for it to heat up.

"I can't believe Serena could've died. I can't think about that," I say. "You were really incredible."

He shrugs.

"You weren't even on duty. You didn't have anyone to tell you what to do, like in training. You're really good at this. I'm glad it's your thing."

"Did I ever tell you that I was really into guns when I was eleven?" he asks suddenly.

I shake my head, trusting Jay that his conversational one-eighty has a purpose.

"I was into the actual guns themselves, not like violence and shooting people. I watched thousands of videos and I knew everything—how they're made, all the parts, factories, what makes each gun different, all of the technical stuff that goes along with it. I imagined that one day, I'd design guns or something. Because it was what I liked, the thing that I thought about and wanted to spend all my free time on."

I'm not sure why Jay is telling me this. I hate guns, as a rule, but as Jay talks about the way he viewed them, I realize he could just as easily have been talking about any kind of machine.

"And then the K.O. thing happened. And then a couple weeks after the K.O. thing, there was a mass shooting at a school in Providence. A twenty-year-old guy who'd gone there for middle school went in for some reunion thing and shot and killed nineteen people before he killed himself."

"Jesus," I say. "I remember when that happened."

"Do you remember all the profiles and stuff about him in the news afterward?"

I shake my head.

"He was obsessed with guns. And he had Asperger's."

My stomach plunges. I can't say anything.

"You can imagine how things here went after that," he continues. "My mom didn't tell me to or anything, but I decided to stop thinking about guns. Which was really hard. I mean, I was like an expert and I had to give it up.

"I kind of forced myself to become interested in cars. And then, more specifically in emergency vehicles and lights. I learned about the patterns of lights for each kind of emergency vehicle, how they were used. I learned about the police cars, ambulances, tow trucks, everything. And then I clicked on a video thinking it would be about a certain kind of fire truck lighting, but it turned out to be a video of EMTs rescuing three kids from a frozen lake. Everyone was smiling and cheering for them because they'd rescued those kids.

"And that's when I realized I wanted to do that. I shifted to videos about emergency medicine, EMS training. I wanted to see smiles instead of the fear I saw whenever I walked into a room. Wherever I went, people saw that guy. The Providence shooter. And I needed to change that."

"And it worked?" I ask.

"For the most part," he says.

"It's weird that I never knew how you got into being an EMT. I'm glad you found it," I say.

Jay leans his back on the counter next to the stove, facing me.

"Can I ask you something?" he says.

I nod.

"Why did you do it? I mean, why now? I thought you said you were done with that. And I thought—I just thought you were done."

I stare at the ceiling, searching for something.

"I guess 'I don't know' isn't good enough?" I say, my voice cracking on the last word.

He shakes his head no.

"Part of it is habit, I know that," I say. "I hear thunder and I get this adrenaline rush. Probably like a drug addict who's about to get their fix."

"Right," he says, but it sounds more like "Uh-huh, go on, because that's kind of bullshit."

I look at him and his eyes are sad. Hurt. And then I realize that he thinks I was chasing lightning trying to find my soul mate, even though he and I are just starting to become something else.

"Oh," I say. "It wasn't about the soul mate stuff. I—that's not it at all. After everything with Reed, I think I realized it was never really about that. It's always been about my mom. I've been thinking about this lately, trying to remember how it started—why I wanted to in the first place."

Jay turns off the stove burner and ladles soup into two bowls. He brings them over to the counter and I breathe in the salty white swirls of steam that rise from mine.

"When I was little, my mom and I lived in this tiny apartment in Detroit and we didn't have anyone else—no family or anything—but I loved it. It was like the two of us were best friends making our way through the world. And then, after she found the lightning-strike survivors group and started getting involved, there were always people around. At first, I kind of loved that, too—I'd never had grandparents or aunts and uncles or cousins. These people were like our giant extended family. And I was their little mascot. But one day I realized that the life we'd had—Mom and me making our way together—just us—was over. I would never be enough for her anymore."

I blow on my soup to cool it off.

"Why?" Jay asks. "What happened?"

"I was in third grade. My mom was with Sue in the kitchen, and I wanted to show them this drawing I'd done in school. I don't remember what it was, but I'd worked really hard on it and I was really excited to show Mom. They were having a pretty intense conversation about Sue's husband and I knew that I wasn't supposed to interrupt, so I stood outside the kitchen, waiting for an opening to come in. And then I heard my mom say something like 'There's no way he can understand what you're going through. I know for me, it's impossible to be close with anyone who hasn't experienced what I have—being struck or knowing my soul mate. Basically, if it weren't for all of you, I'd feel completely alone.' They held hands across the table then, and since they weren't talking anymore, I burst into the room to show them my picture. They *ooh*-ed and *aah*-ed over it as usual. But I remember it felt like Mom was just phoning it in, and it all felt different, like something had irreversibly changed, and I knew it had to do with what I'd overheard."

I ate a few spoonfuls of soup and even though it was still a little too hot, it tasted so good. Like comfort and health. Jay stayed quiet, ready to listen.

"From then on, I knew that, deep down, she didn't feel like I could relate to her since I hadn't been struck by lightning. It's why I wanted to get struck by lightning. Because

I wanted to understand my mom. I mean, I knew she loved me, but it was obvious we couldn't be our team of two if my not getting struck prevented her from being close to me. So, I guess that's how it all started. But I lost track along the way and turned it into soul mate stuff, or whatever."

Jay's bowl is empty, but he still holds his spoon. He takes both of our bowls and puts them in the sink.

"I can see that logic," he says. "I mean, from a little kid's point of view. But she probably wasn't talking about you—she meant like friends, boyfriends, whatever."

I consider that. Maybe. Maybe I'd just been a kid and had done a bad job reading between the lines. Who knew? I shrug. Suddenly I'm so tired from talking and listening. I yawn.

"Do you want to lie down?" he asks.

"Yeah, I think I want to take a shower first, if that's okay. And then, I'm sure I could fall asleep."

And to prove it, I yawn again.

FORTY-TWO

Excuse me while I kiss the sky.
–Jimi Hendrix (musician)

Upstairs, Jay moves quickly ahead of me.

He grabs two towels from the hall closet, then goes into his room. Clothes spill out of open drawers in his dresser. He digs into one of the drawers, pulls out a folded gray T-shirt, and hands it, along with the towels, to me.

"Here's a shirt if you want something clean to wear," he says. "My pants won't fit you, though."

"Thanks." I carry the towels and the shirt to the bathroom that Jay and Kyle share. There's only men's shampoo and soap—no conditioner—but I wash my hair anyway and scrub my body, wanting to wash away the rain, the parking lot, the hospital, the guilt, and everything with Mom.

After I dry off, I put on Jay's T-shirt. It's soft and hangs to the middle of my thighs. I drape my clothes over the shower-curtain rod. Everything is pretty dry but I don't want to put any of it back on now that I feel so clean. I find a brush under the sink and run it through my hair, working through the tangles. I use my finger to rub toothpaste on my teeth.

When I go back into Jay's room, he's not there. I slide into his bed and pull the comforter up to my chin.

A minute later, Jay comes in. His hair is wet, and he's wearing a clean white T-shirt and sweat pants, no socks.

"You showered, too?" I ask.

"Yeah, in my mom's bathroom. I felt hospital-y."

He starts moving around his room, picking stuff up from the floor, closing drawers.

"Aren't you going to lie down with me?" I ask.

"Do you want me to?"

"Yes," I say.

He drops the stuff he's holding on the dresser and then stretches out next to me, pulling the covers over himself, too.

I move close to him, put my arms around him, lay my head on his chest. His arms slide around my back and he pulls me in tighter. His breath is warm in my damp hair. I want to sleep like this, to take a long nap, but I also feel the familiar stirring in my nerve endings, which means I want him to touch me everywhere, not just on my back. And the fact that I'm not wearing underwear, and he doesn't know that, makes me feel really sexy.

We have the whole house to ourselves. His mom and her boyfriend, Gabe, are out of town, and Kyle isn't home. It feels very grown-up.

I tilt my face up and kiss underneath his chin, loving the sandpapery feeling on my lips. I kiss his jaw, light kisses up the right side, back down, up the left side. His breathing gets heavier, and I can feel his body heat up.

He sighs. Then he softly kisses my forehead, my cheek, my lips.

"Rach," he says. "I don't believe in soul mates."

"I know," I whisper.

Something in me shifts then. I take a breath.

"I'm not sure I believe in soul mates either," I say. "Or at least that there's only one for each person."

That feels right.

I press my mouth against his and I feel his body react.

I tug Jay so he's on top of me. He's so big—his shoulders, his back, his arms. He braces himself over me, leaning his weight on his elbows. This is the first time we've kissed while lying down. It's the first time that I'm not on top of him, leading. He looks at me, and right then I really know what a smoldering look is.

"God, it's crazy how much I want you," he says.

The lower half of my body melts.

He rolls onto his back, puts his hands on his forehead, groans.

"What?" I ask.

"I can't believe I just said that to you."

"It was hot," I say. "I liked it."

"I just felt it so much, but then I heard myself say it and it sounded so fake."

"It's not fake if the feeling is real," I say.

"I don't want to hurt you," he says. "Your head, and you have bruises and scrapes and stuff."

I reach my hand around to the back of his neck to try to pull him back over me. "Come *here*."

"I don't have a condom," he blurts out.

"What? Oh, I—" I'm sure my face turns bright red. "I didn't think—I haven't before, and I don't—I didn't think we'd—"

He looks at me, surprised. "You didn't have sex with him?"

"No, I've never had sex."

"Okay, that's good," he says. "I mean, obviously it's fine if you did, but I only meant it's good because I thought if you did, you'd expect it and you know I have no idea what I'm—"

"You can stop talking now," I say.

Finally, he moves back above me. Kisses me hesitantly. I pull his hips down against mine and I can feel him through his pants, and he must know that I can feel him.

Then he kisses me the way I want. Deep. The kind of kiss you get lost in, where you fit together so perfectly, you're not sure how it's even possible it's really happening.

I pull his shirt off and slide my hands all over his warm skin. Then I lift my shirt up and over my head, and he whispers, "Oh my god," when he sees that I'm not wearing a bra. The lower half of my body is covered by the comforter, so he doesn't know that I have nothing on underneath it. At least, not yet.

I laugh because it's kind of funny to think about the two of us doing this—friends, doing what we're doing. He doesn't laugh, though. He stares, touches, his hands a little shaky. He studies me like a textbook—a racy textbook.

Then he props himself up on one elbow, watching his hand as it moves over my chest slowly.

"What are you thinking?" I whisper.

"I'm trying not to," he says, his fingers circling. It tickles and feels so good. "But it's hard not to. There's a lot of stuff racing around in there."

"Like what?"

"You don't want to know."

"It's bad?" I ask.

"No, not bad. Just . . . a lot."

"Do you want to stop?" I ask. "We don't have to do anything more."

"I don't want to stop," he says firmly. "I want to try to be here, in this moment. I want to do more. If you do, I mean."

"You want to know what I'm thinking?" I ask.

He nods. My heart pounds.

"That I'd like to touch you under here," I say, placing my hand gently on the waistband of his sweatpants.

His eyes are huge as I lift the waistband and slide my hand inside his underwear, and then hold him in my hand.

"Holy fuck," he says, catching his breath. "This is . . ."

I watch his expression. He looks different. Older.

He exhales, takes my wrist, pulls my hand out of his pants.

"Sorry," he whispers. "I think we want this to go on a little longer and that would definitely end it. If you know what I mean."

I giggle a little.

And then we kiss more, and the bare skin of his chest feels so warm against mine.

"This is what you want?" he asks.

"What do you mean?"

"I mean," he says. "What should I do next?"

"Oh. Um . . . you could . . . you know, touch me. Here." I take his hand and put it underneath the comforter onto my stomach, and then I move it a bit farther down but not all the way, just so he knows what I mean. "But you don't have to."

"You're not wearing underwear," he says.

"I left all my clothes in the bathroom," I say.

"Wow. Okay," he says. "But I want you to tell me if I'm doing it right."

I nod.

When he first touches me, I think about how I haven't shaved in a while, but I know that Jay probably doesn't notice or care. He moves his fingers, exploring a little awkwardly, not really in the right places but, even though I said I would, I don't want to tell him that. I imagine what it's like for him doing this. He knows so much about anatomy from EMS training and now, here he is, up close.

And then he finds the right place and I go still.

"Is this your—"

"Yes," I whisper. "Yes, that's it. You can keep doing what you're doing. Just keep doing *that*."

His face is almost too intense, so I close my eyes and I focus on just feeling. He keeps doing it until I know I'm getting there and I tell him again to keep doing exactly what he's doing, not to stop, and thankfully he listens because suddenly, I'm there and I let go and it rushes through me, and I feel every nerve in my entire body, and I make a sound I've never heard myself make.

This never happened with Reed.

I keep my eyes closed while my breathing goes back to normal.

When I open my eyes, Jay smiles like he just got the extra credit question on an exam.

I take a few relaxed breaths, and then I kiss his neck, enjoying the soft skin and his soapy scent.

I want to make Jay feel as good as he just made me feel.

I put my hand on him over his pants.

"Can I do this now?" I ask.

He nods.

I slide my hand down his pants, under his underwear. When I put my hand around him, he closes his eyes and groans. I've done this with Reed, but with Jay it feels brand new. His skin is soft and warm as I move my hand up and down.

His eyes are closed but his face is tense, like he's concentrating. I watch him as his breathing speeds up. His neck reddens. His stomach muscles tense. And then he gets there.

I pull my hand away as his breathing slows down.

"Um, I'll be right back," he says, jumping out of bed. He doesn't look at me as he heads to the hallway. I hear the bathroom door close and then the sink running. While he's gone, I find the gray T-shirt on the floor and put it back on.

When he gets back, he lies on his back and I'm on my side, my arm across his chest. He puts his hand on my arm and squeezes, and it makes everything feel so real.

"I didn't think I'd be able to turn my brain off," he says.

"Me neither," I say. "I never thought I'd be able to . . . you know."

"But you did, right?"

I nod. "And actually . . . that was the first time I was able to with someone other than myself."

He leans back and looks at me.

"Oh my god," I say. "I can't believe I just admitted that."

I bury my face in his chest, suddenly shy that I've told him this thing that's so private.

"What? That you masturbate?" he asks.

I squeak. I might die.

He laughs.

"So, what I think you're saying," he says, "is that it was pretty good?"

"Jay, oh my god, seriously? You want a gold sticker, too?"

He smiles wide.

"I want the gold sticker," he says.

"Created a monster," I mumble under my breath, as I sling my leg over his, and snuggle my face into the area just below his armpit.

We wake up, and it feels like it should be morning, but when I check my phone, I see that it's only ten o'clock at night. And I have a few texts.

MOM: How are you feeling? Are you at home or Jay's?

SAWYER: I heard what happened. Are you okay?

MOM: Serena's doing well. I should be home soon.

REED: I hope you're okay.

Jay stretches his arms over his head. He gets up and checks his phone, too.

I respond to Mom that I'm at Jay's and will be home soon, too, to Sawyer that I'm okay, and I skip over Reed's.

"How are we?" I ask Jay. "Are we good? Not weird?"

"Not too weird," he says. "You?"

"Good. I'm good. But I should go home. My mom said she'd be home soon."

"What about the meeting? You don't want to stay here?"

I shrug. "I feel like I should be home, you know?"

He nods, maybe a little disappointed. "If it's bad, you can just come back. I'll pick you up any time."

I stand up and put my arms around his waist and squeeze.

FORTY-THREE

The ache for home lives in all of us, the safe place where we can go as we are and not be questioned.
–Maya Angelou (poet)

Although there are three cars in our driveway, Reed's van isn't here, and the relief I feel is indescribable. Jay's talking as we pull up to my house—something about a ride that he was on the week before. I suspect he's on a post-hook-up high because he doesn't seem to care that I'm only half-listening and he doesn't acknowledge that Reed's van is gone. His excitement makes me smile. And despite my aching head, and my odd mix of guilt and jealousy over Serena getting struck, I feel pretty amazing, too.

Jay finally stops talking and notices the cars.

"Are you sure you want to stay here tonight?"

"I feel like I should be home," I say.

He turns off the ignition and reaches for his door handle.

"No, it's okay," I say. "You don't have to come in."

I know he doesn't want to have to talk to all these people any more than I do. Less, really.

I lean over the gearshift and kiss him on the cheek. "I'll be okay."

He smiles.

I run my fingers through my hair before opening the front door. Through the glass, I see the reflection of the TV in the living room, colors flashing. Jay starts his car, so I turn and wave to him as he drives off.

As soon as I slide open the door, I hear voices and the sounds of scurrying.

"She's here!"

"Pause the movie, hold on."

"Rachel, is that you?"

All at once, Sue, Ron, and Angela surround me, hug me, touch my hair, my face.

"Oh, honey," Sue says. "We were so worried. Let's see that bump on your head."

I bend my head down so she can see.

"God was looking out for you," Ron says. "You didn't get struck. A miracle."

I nod.

"Are you hungry?" Sue asks.

"We're watching *Die Hard 3*. You wanna watch with us?" Angela says.

"Oh, thanks. I'm so tired, I'm just going to get some sleep, I think."

I start toward my room and I hear them giggling and whispering. They're so sweet, but so weird.

When I open my bedroom door, it's . . . empty.

"What?" I say. "Where's my stuff? What's going on?"

Sue's smile sparkles and everyone seems to have this excited energy.

"Let's see," she says, putting her finger on her lip in a mock-thinking pose. "Where could your stuff be? Hmmm.

It couldn't have just up and walked away, right? Let's look around, see if we can find it."

She follows me back to the front hall where the others are standing in front of the door to the garage, smiling and giggling softly.

Everyone moves away as I approach. I put my hand on the doorknob.

"What's going on, you guys?" I say, my smile widening. "Am I being punk'd or something?"

"Go ahead," Ron says. "Open it."

So I do.

And then I gasp, covering my mouth with my hands.

They finished the room. The smell of fresh paint wafts out—the walls and ceiling have all been painted. The area rug I'd asked the Thrift Shop to hold for me for a few days until I could get some cash is in the center of the room. My bed is against the far wall, all made up, with my dresser and night-stands. Light green drapes hang on either side of the sliding door to the tiny side deck, puddling elegantly on the floor. And over in the corner, next to my dresser, a matching drape hangs from the ceiling. Still speechless, I go over and pull it to the side. Behind it is a clothing rack with all the clothes from my closet, and on the floor below is a handmade shoe rack with my shoes on it.

"You guys," I choke out, then clear my throat. "You did this today?"

Sue nods, her eyes wet.

"You did the hard part, Rachel. We just finished it up for you."

"Oh my god," I say, sliding the curtain back and forth, pointing to the shoe rack, the painted ceilings. "This must've been so much work."

"A labor of love," Ron says, coming toward me and hugging me. "Your mom worked on it, too. The curtains and the rug were all her doing." I breathe in his stale, smoky smell and squeeze him back.

"I don't even know what to say," I say. "Thank you. I love it."

As though someone has given them a cue, everyone leaves the room and the door closes behind them.

I sit on my bed and look around at the new room. My room.

A few minutes later, there's a soft knock on the door, and then Mom walks in. She seems tired. Older. But still beautiful. She looks around the room.

"I left before they'd completely finished, but it came out perfectly, didn't it?"

She sits on the bed next to me.

"Thank you so much for this."

"I knew how important it was for you to have your own space. When I told everyone about it, they just sprang into action. I pretty much had nothing to do with it. Ron ran the whole thing. He was in his element today, that's for sure. Bossing everyone around like a foreman. It was like he was twenty years younger."

"Wow," I say. "I can't believe they did this."

I sit next to her and she pushes my hair behind my ear.

"It made them so happy to do it. They love you so much; they'd do anything for you."

I nod. I want to tell Mom I know that, but I've always felt like their mascot instead of one of them. I'd come so close to being one of them today. And I feel relief that I didn't. I'm happy that they love me regardless, even if I am just their mascot.

She stands and kisses me on the top of my head, to the side of my bump.

I know I need to talk to her about the letters—about Carson, Rafe—I need to understand what happened and how it all fit together. But I'm so exhausted, I can't even think anymore.

"I have so many questions, Mom," I say. "But I'm so tired."

"I know. Tomorrow. But now, you need some rest," she says. "I love you."

"I love you, too," I say as she closes the door behind her. Everyone's out there in the living room, watching a movie, laughing, drinking, but it's quiet in my new room.

I take a few pictures and send them to Jay with a bunch of exclamation points.

I put on pajamas, get into my bed, which has been made with fresh sheets, and snuggle in.

FORTY-FOUR

A quarrel between friends, when made up,
adds a new tie to friendship.
–Francis de Sales (saint)

I wake up the next morning and everything is green. I didn't close the drapes last night, and the garage—my room—faces east, so the sun lights up the entire room. My first thought is that I have a terrible hangover—the worst I've ever had—because my head feels like it's being squeezed in a vice over and over. And then I remember the lightning. My head. I touch the bump. It's tender but it feels a little smaller. I prop myself up and survey my new room. It looks amazing. And cozy. I feel a fresh bubbling up of emotion when I think of them working on the room all day yesterday while I was at school, at the lacrosse game, at the hospital.

I check my phone. There's a text from Sawyer saying that he's glad I'm okay, that he was worried. It's nice, but I don't like the feeling that I'm not sure exactly what he wants from me. Sometimes it's just better not to hang out with someone you hooked up with in the past. Especially when hooking up with him ruined your friendship with your best friend. It's not worth it.

There's also a text from Jay asking if I slept okay. I answer him that I feel pretty good, considering.

I start a text to Serena. Erase it. Start again.

> **ME**: Hi. Are you still at the hospital? I'm sorry for everything. Can I come see you there?

I get up, ignoring the pulsing in the back of my head. They must have moved my dresser without taking anything out because my clothes are exactly where they're supposed to be. And I love pulling back the curtain covering the coat rack to grab a clean pair of jeans. I feel great when I open the door to the main house, like a good night of sleep has healed me physically and emotionally.

I expect the group to be meeting in the back room, but it's quiet in the house. I peek out the front door on my way to the bathroom and notice fewer cars in the driveway. Maybe they all went out for lunch. Once in the bathroom, I undress while I wait for the shower to warm up. I'm happy not to have to worry about any group members needing to use the bathroom. I let the hot water pound on my shoulders. After drying off, I put my clothes on and head to the kitchen to make tea.

I hear Mom's voice in the back room. She and Serena are sitting on the couch, facing each other. Mom is holding Serena's hands in her own, looking at her intensely. Just then, the loud voices of Sue and Ron and the others pour in from the front door.

Of course. Serena got out of the hospital and came right here for the meeting. How convenient. Suddenly, all the good feelings I have for the group, for Serena, for everyone, even myself, drain right out and I'm left with a lonely, empty hole in my chest.

It must be all over my face because Mom looks at me sympathetically like I'm going to cry, which I guess, I am. And Serena just looks, I don't know, sad or something. As the group comes near, I move out of the way of the door and put on my fake smile for them because they deserve only my gratitude at this point.

"Hey guys," I say. "Yes, I slept great, thank you so much." And "you're the best, everything is perfect." I let the words come out of my upturned mouth as I back away, needing to get away from all this, seeing Serena embraced as one of them. I know it's irrational at this point—I *know* this. But I can't help it. By the time I get to the front door, I feel sweat trickling down my back. I slide open the door, welcoming the cool air, and I walk as quickly as I can to our beach stairs, even though the fast pace exacerbates my headache. The tide is coming in but there's enough of a strip of beach to walk on, and if it comes up any higher, I can always just hide out on the stairs.

I'm halfway down when I hear Serena.

"Rachel!" The wind is blowing off the water, so the sound gets muffled.

I stand still as she makes her way slowly down the stairs. She walks as if her body is made of glass. Carefully, slowly. Fearfully. I suddenly feel awful for running away, for not asking her how she is, on top of everything being my fault in the first place.

When she's a few steps above me, she sits down, so I sit, too.

"Can we talk?" she asks.

I nod. "I texted you," I say.

"My phone got zapped. My mom's out getting me a new one."

"Oh. Well, are you okay? The doctors said you're okay? I mean, do you feel okay?"

She nods and I look down at my hands.

"I'm sorry," I say. "It's my fault you got struck, and I'm so, so sorry."

Serena looks up at the sky.

"My mom will help you," I say. "The group, everyone. They're really great. You should go back to the house. They're probably starting soon."

Serena shakes her head and looks at me like I'm nuts.

"I'm not going to their meeting," she says.

"Why not?" Did Mom say something to her? Was she not letting her in? I start to push myself up with my hands. I have to talk to Mom.

"I don't want to," Serena says. "I don't want to be in the group. I'm fine. And even if I end up not being fine, I don't want to be in the group."

I must look as confused as I feel.

"Look," she says. "I know how you feel about your mom and that group. And I know that if I joined that group, you would never want to be friends with me again."

What she says is probably true, but she wants to be friends with *me* again?

"Maybe it's too late," she says. "I don't know."

I clear my throat, not sure if my voice will work.

"I don't understand," I say. "You want nothing to do with me."

"I'll just lay this all out on the table and you can do with it whatever you want. Okay? I know I owe you an explanation for everything from the past couple of weeks."

"Seventeen days, but who's counting," I say, trying to smile. She sighs and leans her head back, avoiding my eyes.

"I just couldn't stand you anymore," she says.

Like a knife to my gut.

"That didn't come out right. I'm so bad at this serious stuff."

She always has been. She turns any serious conversation into a joke as soon as humanly possible.

"What I mean is, I couldn't stand the soul mate stuff anymore. Before Reed, you were obsessed with it but it was like, this thing we could kind of joke about and egg each other on with guys and stuff. But then with Reed, you got all intense and he wasn't even that nice to you. And you weren't seeing that because you were so convinced that he was your soul mate, and especially since he'd been struck, he like, gave you an in with all that stuff, too."

My mouth opens to defend myself somehow, but she puts her hand up to stop me.

"Let me just finish," she says. "So, after you fell and he left town, I felt so bad for you because it was just so awful, but on the other hand, and maybe this is horrible, but I was relieved that he was gone. And I felt like I stuck with you afterward, tried to help you, make you feel better, but it was like, I couldn't do anything for you. And then when we went to that party and you were with Sawyer, you smiled for the first time since Reed left. And when I kept thinking about that, I got so pissed off that after all that time I stuck by you and the second some cute guy flirts with you, you were all happy and it was like you didn't need me at all."

I close my eyes, imagining how she felt that night. She's right, too. The night I hung out with Sawyer was the first time I'd felt any better at all since Reed had left. Realizing that makes me feel so weak, and I hate myself for it.

"The more I thought about it," she continues, "the more hurt I was. I mean, I was your best friend. I loved you and I was right there. But you were totally fine walking away from me to see if some random guy might be 'the one.' What is that even? Why does a soul mate have to be that? Why can't it be a best friend? I don't know. I just kept going around and around with that in my head. I was like, *I* am her fucking soul mate. Me. I am her *best* friend. Her connection with me is deeper than anyone's. Definitely deeper than with that jerk Reed. And Sawyer's nice, but there's absolutely no way she's got any real connection with him."

She continues, "I'm not making sense. I'm exhausted. I guess the thing I wanted to say was that I didn't ditch you to be with Lindsay and those girls, and I didn't judge you for hooking up with Sawyer—everyone knew that they were broken up, including her, and you did nothing wrong. I just couldn't stand that you'd chosen Sawyer over me."

"But," I say. "I didn't. I—"

"You did," she says. "Maybe not consciously, but when you came back from wherever you'd gone with him and you were smiling, I knew you had. Or maybe not Sawyer, but guys. Just, guys in general. Having a guy—a potential soul mate—was more important to you than having me, your best friend, who was already your soul mate, in a way."

I swipe at my tears.

"You're right," I say. "You're my best friend. We *are* soul mates."

"And Jay?" she asks.

I shake my head. "I was like that with Reed, and I didn't think I was with Sawyer, but maybe I was. But with Jay, it's different—"

Her face changes then, like she's disappointed.

"No, I mean, not different like 'oh, he's the one.' I mean, you know. It's Jay. Like, we have no idea what we're doing. And we talk about it. Which makes this whole thing super awkward but also not. We're not really figuring out what we are yet, just kind of exploring."

Serena smiles a little.

"Exploring, huh? So, how *deep* has that exploration gone?"

I smack her knee lightly and blush.

"I will be getting that out of you, so don't even try."

We both laugh and it's like there'd been a craggy mountain between us and the laughter blew it up with TNT and now there's just some rubble and debris left—a few bigger rocks scattered around, too, but nothing we can't break up with a pickaxe over time.

"Hey," I say. "I'm sorry about everything. I'm sorry I was such an asshole. And I'm sorry it's my fault you got struck by lightning."

"It'll be okay. At least if I have to have some sort of label, now I'm 'the girl who got struck by lightning' and not just 'the black girl.'"

"Oh," I say. "I didn't think that was—I forget sometimes."

She stares me down.

"You forget that I'm black?"

I feel my face flush with heat.

"Kind of," I say. I can feel that what I'm saying is all wrong and insensitive but I try to explain anyway. "I mean, you're so gorgeous and everyone's all over you, and—I didn't think it really mattered that much."

"It matters," she says. "People don't forget I'm black because I wear short skirts and hang out with pretty white girls. There's no such thing as colorblind. Every single time you look at me, I'm black. That never changes. It's not something you can forget."

"I know," I say.

"I love who I am," she says, her voice softer now. "But it matters."

"I love who you are, too. I'm so sorry. I'm sorry about everything. I love you and I just missed you so much."

I'm practically sobbing now, and I reach for her hand. She lets me take it, threads my fingers through hers.

"I should've just talked to you about it," she says. "I'm sorry I checked out."

"I get it," I say. "I'm a lot of work. But I think I'm getting better."

I pull our clasped hands to my face, wiping my tears with the back of my hand, and I look at the water.

"So," I say. "What have I missed over the last seventeen days?"

She looks at me and smiles. "Tim Erickson."

"So, it's a thing then?"

She nods. "I think it's a thing."

"That's good."

"Yeah. And my dad. He called this morning. He's coming down tonight."

I squeeze her hand.

"What about you?" she asks. "What else have I missed?"

Suddenly, I can't believe that Serena doesn't know about the letters.

"I read some letters between my mom and my father," I say. "Well, my mom says he was my father, anyway, but now I don't know for sure."

I tell Serena about the letters—the lightning, Carson's final letter, the abortion, and about Rafe.

Afterward, she just stares out at the bay.

"Wow," she says. "And you and your Mom haven't talked about it?"

"Not really. We were about to and then everything happened."

"You need to talk to her," she says.

"Yeah," I say. "I will. As soon as everyone leaves."

Her face brightens a little. "Speaking of which, you moved into the garage? Can I see?"

I smile and stand, pulling her up with me. We walk back to the house, arms linked, just like old times.

FORTY-FIVE

In search of my mother's garden, I found my own.
—Alice Walker (writer)

I tiptoe by the back room to the kitchen, find a box of Froot Loops, and bring it back to my new room. Serena and I sit on my bed, eating them dry from the box. We try to catch each other up on every detail of the last few weeks. I tell her more about the letters and Jay, she tells me more about hooking up with Erickson—how she kissed him on a stupid dare at a party and then she kept thinking about him, and she got more attracted to him and, yeah, he's kind of a stoner, but he's smart and funny and she likes hanging out with him.

She shows me the marks on her shoulder where the lightning exited her body. They're red and puffy now but they told her that they'd fade mostly, though she'd have to get periodic scans to check on bone, muscle and scar tissue, maybe for the rest of her life. Even though she says she feels fine, I notice the purplish tint underneath her eyes and the way her voice starts to slow down.

"Hey," I say. "You should get some rest. Didn't they tell you to stay in bed today or anything?"

She nods. "Yeah. But my mom is driving me nuts, all over me. She only let me come here because she was going out to get me a phone and she didn't want to leave me home alone."

"Do you want to take a nap here? The meeting will break up for the afternoon soon, so it'll be quiet."

"Yeah," she says. "Okay. But promise me you'll talk to your mom about everything. You really need to." She pushes the covers down and slips in underneath like she used to when she slept over all the time. It's nice seeing her here again, on "her side" of my bed in my new room. It seems right.

She falls asleep almost immediately. I can tell by her steady breathing.

I have a text from Jay checking on me, letting me know he'll be home if I need him. I know he probably wants to come over, but Serena's right. I need to talk to Mom.

I text Jay about making up with Serena and tell him that when she wakes up, if she's up for it, maybe we'll go over there.

> **JAY**: It's good you two are working it out. Text me later—I can pick you guys up.

I leave Serena sleeping and go to the kitchen. The meeting has broken up and there aren't any cars in the driveway. Sometimes after the afternoon meeting, they stick around and sit on the deck smoking, drinking, telling the same stories I've heard a thousand times. The one time I actually really hoped that they'd stay so I could talk to Mom, and she isn't here.

I gather up a few glasses from the back room and bring them to the sink. The dishwasher has finished its cycle, so I empty it. I should call Mom and tell her I want to talk, but I'm stalling. And then a car pulls in and the ignition turns off. Mom's car—I can tell by the little pinging noises it makes when the car door opens.

Mom comes in a few seconds later. I look behind her but she's alone.

"Oh good," she says. "You're here."

She drops her bag and keys on the kitchen table and pulls me into a hug. I flinch for just a second, but then I realize I want this hug. I put my arms around her, too, and rest my head on her shoulder. She's a couple of inches taller than me, and very thin, but her arms around me are strong and her shoulder is solid.

"Mom?" I ask, my voice muffled by her shirt. "Will you tell me more about my father now? Please?"

Mom pulls back and holds my face in her hands. Looks into my eyes.

"Yes," she says. She nods, up and down. "I'll tell you everything."

She grabs two bottles of water from the refrigerator and strides out to the deck. I follow. We sit in the two good chairs—the ones with no rips or uneven legs. We don't bother opening the umbrella since the sun's peeking in and out of clouds.

Mom breathes in deeply, lets the air out slowly, and then takes a huge swig of water.

"It smells like spring," she says. "I came here every summer for my whole life, but until we moved here when I was eighteen, I never knew what spring on the Cape smelled like. Spring smells even better than summer. I'd never known what I was missing."

I breathe in the smell, too—salt water, marsh, and a hint of new leaves fighting their way out despite the unpredictability of the temperature now.

"God, Rachel. I've been trying to see things the way you must see them." She winces like the pain is physical. "I'm sorry I've kept him such a secret from you. It's just, how things ended, it was so painful. And now. I didn't know until I found that letter the other day that he'd gone to the clinic. We'd fought that morning and I've always felt so guilty that he was killed that night before we had a chance to apologize to each other. But now I know how much pain he was in that day. And that box . . . his mom probably didn't find it until after I'd already left, so it's just been sitting in this garage all these years."

She clears her throat.

"I always thought that I had no control, that this thing—whatever it is—was in charge of everything and would make it all right in the end. I didn't know how much Carson was suffering. I was doing it to him and using my ability—using my vision of him as my soul mate—as an excuse so I wouldn't have to make any difficult decisions. Not intentionally, though. But it ruined him, and us, it ruined my relationship with my father." She pauses. "And with Rafe."

She looks at me—her eyes so much like mine.

"It's him, then?" I ask. "Rafe is my father?"

FORTY-SIX

Grief is the price we pay for love.
—Queen Elizabeth II (queen)

Mom shakes her head no.

"Carson was your father," Mom says.

"But I don't understand," I say. "You had an abortion and then he died that night."

"No," she says. "I didn't have it."

I stare out at the bay and watch the slow, lazy flight of a gull.

"So," I say. "Once you were at the clinic, you changed your mind? You decided you wanted to have a baby?"

Mom looks down at her hands in her lap and stays quiet.

"Mom?"

"I never wanted you to know this," she says. "You are the best thing that's ever happened to me. I need you to understand that."

My heart is pounding now.

"Just tell me, Mom."

"I was so young. And so confused. I didn't even have a real job—I was helping my father at his office, but he was basically giving me an allowance. And when I found out I was pregnant, my father said he wouldn't support me and a baby. My father was a tough man, Rachel. He never really understood how damaged I was after the lightning strike. He never actually said it, but I think he always thought I was weak, faking it all, that I was always one half-step away from messing up my life. And then when I wasn't even married and I got pregnant, it was like I had proved him right. Carson wanted me to go with him to Detroit, to get married, have the baby, but I wasn't ready to do that life. I didn't know what I wanted."

She's silent. And she still hasn't answered my question.

"I didn't change my mind at first," she says quietly. "The doctor was just about to start when the clinic received a bomb threat. They evacuated everyone."

My heart beats into my throat. I'm alive because of a bomb threat?

"That night, we found out about Carson. That he'd been killed."

I know about this part. On his way to Detroit, an SUV driving on the wrong side of the highway had plowed into Carson's little VW. Both Carson and the driver, whose blood-alcohol level was through the roof, had been killed instantly.

Mom narrows her eyes at me, like she's studying. Like she's waiting for me to ask the next question. But I don't say anything. I want to hear the next part first.

"I was in shock," Mom says. "We all were. Carson was—he was perfection. Strong, handsome, smart, good-hearted, the best friend anyone could ask for. He was like, like a god almost, like it didn't make sense he could die at all. We couldn't believe he was gone.

"After the funeral, I was so angry," she continued. "I didn't understand how I could have fallen in love with Rafe when I was supposed to be with Carson. When Carson was away at college, Rafe and I spent a lot of time together. I fell in love with him. We never had a physical relationship—neither of us could do that to Carson—but the thing between us was bigger than that. It was Rafe who I found the scallop shell with, right before I was supposed to move to Detroit with Carson, before I found out I was pregnant. We knew that we'd never be able to fit the halves together again, but we wanted to hold on to us somehow."

Mom cleared her throat.

"I wanted to blame the lightning for everything," she continued. "But I could only blame myself. If I'd just gone with Carson like I was supposed to, maybe he would've been alive. So after Carson died, I couldn't stay with Rafe. He wanted to be there with me however I chose—he wanted to raise you with me, but also would have taken me back to the clinic. He never pressured me to choose. But I was such a wreck. My dad was right. I was flighty and I couldn't make a decision whether I wanted scrambled eggs or over-easy, let alone whether to keep a baby. My father told me I was too self-involved to raise a child. He was a single father practically my whole life, and he said I didn't have what it took to do it."

Mom's eyes are wet. She swipes at them with the back of her hand.

"I waited for a sign." She shakes her head back and forth. "For my ability to tell me what to do. Now that Carson was gone, what was my future? The soul mate the lightning had shown me was dead. What now?

"And that's when I realized that maybe what I'd seen even from the beginning—Carson as my soul mate—was really you. You were my soul mate, and because I needed to love Carson in order to have you, the lightning showed me him. I know you must think that sounds crazy. And it probably is. But at the time, that was my big epiphany. So, I just took off. I left everyone—my father, friends, Rafe. I barely said good-bye. I moved to the apartment Carson had rented for us in Detroit. I started a new life on my own and waited for you to arrive. And when you did, it really was the best day of my life. And I knew I'd made the right decision."

She takes my hand in hers and squeezes.

I swipe at the tears streaming down my face with my free hand. "I'm your soul mate?"

Mom nods. "You're everything."

She releases my hand, leans forward and pulls my head onto her shoulder, strokes my hair.

I stay like that for a while, my eyes closed, my heart full.

I have more questions, though. Reluctantly, I pull my head off her shoulder to look at her.

"But what about your father? Didn't he want to see me? I was his granddaughter."

Mom nods. "He did see you. Once."

My eyes widen.

"I wouldn't answer his calls. He'd leave messages on my answering machine, still talking at me like I was a little girl who needed to grow up. But I was already grown—the second you were born, I grew up. And then one day, he just showed up at my door. You were about nine months old. Against my better judgment, I told him he could stay two nights."

Mom smiles.

"He was actually very sweet with you. He'd lay you down on the couch and put his hands out, and you'd kick at him with your chunky little legs. He loved that. Said you'd be a little soccer player. But after only one night, we were fighting. He didn't trust me to take care of you well enough. He wanted me to move back home. But I couldn't. I told him to leave, and he did. I sent him pictures of you every few months. But we could never let go of our anger. I missed them all so much—my dad, Rafe, everyone. But I felt like they were better off without me. All I did was cause them pain."

"I'm sorry, Mom."

She nods. "I'm the one who's sorry. I should've figured out a way for you to know him."

"What about Carson's parents? They're my grandparents? Where are they?"

Mom shook her head. "They were much older when they had Carson. They died within months of each other, only a few years after Carson. I don't think they ever recovered from his death.

"I'm so sorry, Rachel. I made so many mistakes, but I've never lied to you. Carson was your father. He was a wonderful person, and it breaks my heart that he never got to love you the way I know he would have. But I need you to know that everything I do, it's for you. You are my real soul mate."

I pull my hand away.

"I believe you," I say. "But it hasn't felt that way since you started the group. It's always seemed like everything you do is for them."

I realize how whiny that sounds, but I don't care anymore. If we're getting everything out, she should know how little she's made me feel like her soul mate. I don't care if I make her mad.

But she's not mad. She just nods.

"I understand that, but it never felt that way to me. I didn't have anyone but you, and I wanted to give you so much more than that. When I realized that they looked to me for help, I felt like I could finally help heal pain instead of cause it. I guess I thought that I was giving you this alternative family—they all love you so much, and as far as I was concerned, I thought you could never have too much love and attention. I didn't have much of that growing up."

"But I only wanted it from you," I say, my voice cracking. Damn. "But it's okay," I add quickly after clearing my throat. "I'm okay. They do love me, and I love them, too. I just thought that you would never be able to connect with me really since I hadn't been struck by lightning."

"What?"

"When I was little, you were talking to Sue once and I overheard. You said you couldn't connect with anyone who hadn't been struck or knew their soul mate. And since I was never struck, and you wouldn't tell me my soul mate, I thought . . . you know."

Mom gasps.

"Oh, Jesus." She half-laughs. "I don't remember saying that, but I do remember feeling that way. About romantic prospects. Sue was always trying to get me to go out on dates, find a man, a father for you. So that's probably what we were talking about. Not you. Never you. Oh, Rachel." She kneels in front of me, puts her hands on either side of my face. "You are everything to me. Everything. I'm so sorry that I've done such a shit job of showing you."

She pulls my head down so my forehead rests against hers.

"I'm going to cut the meeting a bit short, get our house back to ourselves," she whispers.

"No, it's okay," I say. "I'm okay."

"They love you, honey. You know that, right?"

I nod. "Yeah. I do. I love them, too. And I sort of get now why you didn't tell me that much about my father. I know you feel guilty about what happened to him. But I still really want to know more about him."

"I'll tell you everything. I will, I promise. I'll give you all my memories of him. And anything I still have that was his is yours."

We stand up and she holds onto my hands.

"Mom?"

"Yes?" She lets go of one of my hands and pushes some hair behind my ear.

"I think you should talk to Rafe. He still has the other half of the shell. I saw it."

Mom's body goes rigid.

I pull the necklace she'd given me over my head.

"Here's your half back," I say. "Maybe it's not too late for another chance."

Mom takes the shell, puts her arm around me, and looks out at the water.

I can sense that she needs to be alone with those thoughts now.

"I'm going to see if Serena's awake. We might go to Jay's," I say.

Mom hugs me and I go back to my room to check on Serena.

FORTY-SEVEN

Things are never quite as scary when you've got a best friend.
—Bill Watterson (cartoonist)

When I open the door to my new room, I find Serena fixing her hair in the mirror that Ron and the others had hung above my dresser. I have no idea where they found it, but it's perfect. The frame is pale green with dark green ivy painted all the way around. The mirror has some spots on it, making it appear vintage or antique, which only makes it better.

"Hey," I say, and Serena flinches a little. "Sorry, I didn't mean to scare you."

"I'm just a little jumpy, I guess. Your mom said sudden noises and stuff. Probably you too—everyone who was there," she says, leaning forward to swipe a finger under her eyes. "Yeah, this is permanent, not makeup."

"You look good," I say. "You just need more rest. You hungry?"

She shakes her head no. "And I can't sleep anymore, so don't try to make me."

I hold up my hands. "Hey, I'm not your mother."

"And thank god for that," she says. "I can't go back home to her hovering. Can I hang here?"

"Jay asked if we want to go there. He said he's got some yard work to do, but afterward we can get pizza or something. Is that okay with you?"

She rolls her eyes. "Third wheel?"

"It's not like that," I say. "He wants to see you. He's worried. It'll be the three of us. Like before. No couple-y stuff. I promise."

She nods. "Okay."

She continues to fiddle with her hair while I search under the bed for the boots I'd kicked off last night.

Normally, I'd wear them without socks, but it's chillier than it was yesterday, so I grab a pair of socks from my dresser. As I put them on, I notice a blackish-brown spot the size of a button on the sole of my left foot. Ew. I try to remember whether I'd been outside barefoot in the last day and had stepped in dog shit or something. And then I remember that yesterday I'd been barefoot running through the school parking lot in the rain, hoping to get struck by lightning. It feels like ages ago.

I sit on the edge of the bathtub, scrubbing my foot with a rough washcloth, making the water hotter and hotter. But nothing will get the smudge out.

Is it a burn? Had the lightning spread through the puddles on the ground to my foot? Is it possible I was struck and no one knew it? Maybe it's just a stubborn stain from hot tar or something. Maybe it's nothing. I suspect it's something, though. At this point, would I want anyone to know, even if it is something? I want everything that I have now. I don't even want that anymore.

Serena drives, even though she promised her mom she wouldn't go farther than my house.

"I feel fine," she says. "My mom's acting like I'm suddenly stupid and can't drive or—wait, what's that sign mean again?" She points at a stop sign ahead.

"What?" My eyebrows fly up.

"Ha!" She says slapping my leg and slowing to a stop. "Got you."

"Jesus, why?"

"'Cause it's funny to get a rise out of you."

"Whatever. Just drive."

My phone buzzes. A number I don't recognize.

Hey. It's Tim. Serena's mom said she's with you but she doesn't have her phone. I just wanted to see how she is. Maybe you can ask her to call me?

"Interesting," I say.

Serena glances at me. "What?"

"It's from Erickson. Wants you to call him. He's worried about you. I think he looooooooves you."

"Shut up." She stares ahead for a second and the side of her mouth turns up. "Read me what he wrote."

So I do.

An hour later, Serena and I are sprawled out on the hammock, rocking gently, watching Jay clip hedges. Dark spots have started to show through the back of his T-shirt, and I want to go over to him, reach my arms as far as they'll go around his waist, and inhale the sweat between his shoulder blades. Until that moment, it has never occurred to me that I'd want to smell someone's sweat. I feel like a cavewoman or something. But I promised Serena none of that while she's around, so I hold it in, and the deprivation makes me want him even more.

I'd given Serena my phone to call Erickson and she's in full-on flirt mode, laughing at everything he says, playing with a loose string on the hammock. She makes plans to call him later when she gets her new phone, then hands mine back to me.

We rock and watch Jay.

He finishes the hedges and is now picking up the clippings and dropping them into a black garbage bag. He squats down to reach some branches that had fallen underneath the hedge.

"I never really appreciated Jay's butt until now," Serena says. "He has a very nice butt."

I sit up. "What? No! Stop looking." I clap my hand over her eyes. But I look. His jeans do hug his butt nicely. And as he leans over farther, his shirt rises an inch and I admire that small strip of smooth, sweaty skin peeking out above his jeans.

Serena pries my fingers off and leans her head on my shoulder.

When Jay's done, he stands in front of us, drinking a bottle of water. We ogle him some more but he doesn't seem to notice.

Serena and I scooch over to make room for him. He sits carefully next to me, making the hammock sink a couple of inches and lifting Serena up a bit higher in the air on my other side. She giggles. Jay stretches his legs out and starts rocking slowly, so Serena and I lift our legs up, letting him do the work.

I take his hand in one of mine, and Serena's in the other, and pull so our hands are all together resting on my stomach. For a second, I feel this strange déjà vu sensation, like we've all been here before. I love this moment. The three of us. All the questions that have been swirling in my head for so long finally answered. Knowing Mom and I will be okay. Knowing that what I've been chasing isn't really real—what's real is this. My friends, Mom, the survivors—my family.

The sky is gray, not even a hint of blue anywhere. I realize that I haven't even checked the weather today.

A distant rumble sounds from so far away, it's almost inaudible. But I feel it.

“Let’s go inside,” I say.

We get up, still holding hands, and walk toward the side door.

“Maybe we should just get the pizza delivered?” Serena says, and there’s a little shakiness in her voice.

“Everyone want pepperoni?” Jay asks.

“I want plain,” I say.

“Right,” Jay says, squeezing my hand. “And then you’ll just steal my pepperoni.”

He opens the screen door for us.

The sky lights up for a second. And, for the first time for as long as I can remember, I don’t count to see how close the lightning is.

Acknowledgments

Thank you for helping me bring *Soulstruck* into the world:

My agent and friend, Linda Epstein, and the Emerald City Literary Agency team.

My editor, Nicole Frail, and the Sky Pony/Skyhorse team, including Alison Weiss, Emily Shields, Emma Dubin, and Kate Gartner for the most gorgeous cover.

My critique partners: my daily work-wife Marcy Beller Paul, Jennifer Shulman, Kendall Kulper, Laura Hughes, Kristin Brandt, Karen Haas, Orla Collins.

My Online Sandbox agent-siblings, Pneuma Creative, Fall 15ers, Fearless 15ers, Sky Pony pub-mates, and many other author friends.

Bloggers, reviewers, booksellers, librarians, and readers of young adult books.

Lightning Strike & Electrical Shock Survivors International, Inc., for their *Life After Shock* books, which provided stories of life-changing suffering, bravery, and community. Jessica Roth, for her story and her huge heart. J.R. Rudzki, for his patience with my never-ending questions. Any mistakes I've made regarding lightning, including strikes, trauma, medical treatment, survivors, and post-trauma are solely my own.

My people: Amy, Lisa, Claudia, Mara, and the rest of the SFS girls.

My post-April 29, 2016 team: see above, plus Dan, Steven, Ari, Ari, Justin, Jeff, Stacey, Kenny, Katie, Nick, Casey, O.J., Bonnie, J.P., Dannielle, Laura, Ron, April, Stacey, Rick, Steve, Kristen, Leigh, Matt, Julie, Jovana, Joe, Godwin, and everyone else who helped us through.

My extended family: Norene and Larry Green, Suzie and David Cohen, the Lewands, Pedersens, Offenbergers, Hersches, Duchanos, Winnicks, Pyners.

My parents, Ellen and Norman Sinel.

And finally, my world: Andy, Nathan, Zach, and Justin Cohen.